Download your free e-book copy of
"Mabel the Mafioso Dwarf"
today!

Purchase the print edition and receive the eBook free, in the format you want: ePub, MOBI, or PDF.

Go to www.bitlit.com to find out how.

Mabel
the mafioso
Dwarf

For my brother and sister-in-law
Darrell and Cheryl

Acknowledgements

To my family. My parents Jake and Barb, my brother Darrell, my sister-in-law Cheryl, your support means the world to me. My nieces Katarina and Angelica, and my nephew Thomas. You have motivated my writing and this book in too many ways to count.

Neyve and Ryan, my teen beta readers, who once again proved to be invaluable first readers.

Members of my writing group, Evan Braun and Bev Geddes for your support and friendship.

My editor, Samantha Beiko. You did an amazing job! Thank you so much for all your hard work on this book, making it the best it can be.

My cover artist, Jordy Lakiere, who so beautifully gives Mabel life in images.

E. C. Ambrose, who gave me a swift kick in the pants when I needed it most. All my writing friends who through retreats and conversations over wings and pizza, have encouraged me to keep going, to keep growing, and to never give up.

Garth Nix, who kindly took time to talk with me at the World Fantasy Convention in 2014. Without that talk, this book was likely to have never seen the light of day.

And last, but not least, Gerald Brandt, Adria Laycraft, and Robert J. Sawyer. Thank you. You've done more for me than you will ever know.

To be honest with others necessitates honesty with yourself.

—Dr. Thaddeus
"Living Your Authentic Life"

CHAPTER 1

WHEN WE entered the cosmopolitan city of Leitham, I had only one thing on my mind: adventure. Real adventure, not just imaginary ones. The adventure of getting my shredded right shoulder fixed and starting a new life for myself. The adventure of seeing all of the possibilities now open to me.

Technically, the adventure had started the moment Da and my brothers disowned me and I agreed to move here with Mam.

The four weeks on the road from Gilliam to Leitham had not been the adventure I'd imagined it should have been, considering two of our traveling companions were the wizard Radier, and my friend Aramis, the greatest elven adventurer in history. I didn't really expect we'd encounter dragons or other dangers, but I'd hoped for something to give some excitement to the endless hours on the road. The only thing we stopped for was sleep.

The trip wasn't entirely uneventful. I was traveling with my mam. I would call getting to know her a bit of an adventure, a big part of building my new life. Da had exiled her when I was a dwarfling, and let me grow up believing she was dead. I'd learned she was alive and soon after that, I met her while acting in a movie being recorded in Gilliam. The total of seven weeks we'd had together was not nearly enough time to share everything about our lives. I thanked the gods that wasn't the only time I'd have with her. It was just the start.

Finally my mam was going to be a part of my life.

The long road trip also gave me time to get to know Aramis a bit better. Radier had been his cart-mate for most of the trip, so my conversations with Aramis had been short and usually only when we stopped for the night or before we started out in the morning. A few days before we arrived in Leitham, Radier left our traveling caravan without a word. When he did, Aramis joined Mam and me and traveled the rest of the way with us.

Now, as the four- and five-storey buildings rose up around us, crowding each other and the road, my heart fluttered, and I swore my eyes nearly popped out of my head. I'd always known my home city of Gilliam was small and conservative. But compared to Leitham, Gilliam was nothing more than a quaint little town.

This city held everything for me: Mam, healing, and most important, a new life.

The road was lined with tall buildings and stretched for miles. I felt like I was in a deep and endless tunnel. I kept looking up, hoping to see the sun and sky. My neck cramped and my wounded shoulder hurt more. Carts passed our caravan, cutting in front of us and out again. I gasped. I'd been on a crowded road before, in Mitchum, but there had just been dwarves there. There weren't only dwarves driving the carts here. There were almost no dwarves here, at least not in this part of the city. Elves, pixies, and a handful of trolls surrounded us on the road and on the walkways beside us—deadly beings I'd been warned about in childhood stories were walking around freely, like they weren't dangerous.

I gagged and covered my nose with my sleeve as the stench hit me. I was sure it wasn't just from all the horses and ponies. Mam, who sat beside me, driving our cart, appeared not to notice.

"Well, what do you think of your new city?" Mam asked.

There was too much to take in to have a moment to formulate a thought, much less an opinion. I pinned my right arm against my chest with my left, still trying to block the smell. Holding it this way reduced the constant agony a little. "It's um, not like Gilliam at all, is it?"

"At first glance, no, it isn't," Mam said. "But when you get to know the city, you'll find they have a lot in common. You will love it."

Aramis put an arm around my shoulders. When we first met, he would touch me and his elven magic had done some marginal healing of my injury, but his powers were limited and had stopped working not long after we left Gilliam. Even though he could no longer heal me, Aramis was the only one who could touch me and not hurt me. Simply not hurting more than I already did was amazing. It almost provided me some actual relief of my existing pain.

"Frerin is right," he said. "You are going to love it here."

Mam steered our cart off the main road onto one side street and then another. The buildings pressed in on us. There were so many streets branching off in every direction. How did anyone find where they needed to go?

More importantly, how was I supposed to find Aramis's father? Radier had promised he would take me to see him, but he'd left us so suddenly that I never got a chance to make any definite arrangements. I could have asked Aramis, but there was something between him and his father. From what I understood, Aramis never talked to him. I had a strong suspicion that, if I asked for Aramis's help, he wouldn't do it. I had to trust that Radier knew how to find me, and that he hadn't forgotten his promise.

A few of the other members of our caravan left

us, veering off onto various side roads. I wondered if I'd ever see them again. The entire movie crew, including the actors, had traveled together from Gilliam. They'd become like a family to me and now this family felt like it, too, was falling apart, just like mine had back in Gilliam.

Mam was the only family I had left. Well, her and Sevrin.

The Sevrin.

Sevrin being a part of my family could be an adventure in itself, I hoped. He was a legend among Dwarves for his heroics as a warrior, explorer, and dragon slayer. His adventures with Aramis and Radier were epic.

Mam told me how Aramis, being their mutual friend, had introduced them soon after she'd arrived in Leitham. They'd become close friends instantly. A few years ago, they acknowledged their friendship had grown into something bigger. It was then that they moved in together. She wouldn't call him a life-mate—she still wore the golden ring in her beard that Da had given her, and she maintained her promise never to remove it—so she called Sevrin her life-partner.

That Sevrin accepted Mam's loyalty to her mating vows and still loved her, made me love him. As far as I was concerned, Mam had no reason to remain loyal to Da, not after the way he had treated her all these years.

Mam maneuvered deftly through the crowded

streets, swerving around other carts as easily as everyone else. Finally the traffic diminished, and the buildings were pushed back from the street and from each other. The sky was still next to impossible to see thanks to the giant elm and birch trees now lining the road.

We turned into what appeared to be another business district. The trees shrank in size and number. The buildings were not as tall as before and I couldn't tell what was a business and what was a home. Here, at least, there were more dwarves. A lot more.

The toy shops carried dwarf-made toys for all species. How many had come from the toy workshop in Gilliam? It was kind of exciting to think that some of the toys I'd made when I'd worked in the toy workshop might have been sold here. It would have been so much fun if we'd been shown where our toys ended up. Of course, we understood that what we made was traded elsewhere. When we sat in that workshop day after day, making things for other species, things that had nothing to do with stone or gems, it had been nothing more than busy work until we were old enough to mine. Had we been able to see our toys in the hands of children, maybe it would have given some of us a bit more enthusiasm for the job.

The blacksmith shop windows displayed decorative ironwork fencing and furniture, and so many items I'd never seen before. We passed stores selling every kind of sporting equipment imaginable: bows and arrows, battle axes, uniforms, and boulders of all shapes and sizes. My shoulder twitched and I whimpered when I saw some beautiful throwing axes.

At last Mam pulled into a bit of a clearing. Several large white-washed windowless buildings stood before us, protected by a great steel fence with a guarded gate.

"Almost home," Mam said as she stopped outside the gate. "Just a quick stop."

"What is this place?" I asked.

"Studio City," Mam said. "This is where I usually work, and where movies are finished in editing and production."

"Of which I need to get started on," Aramis said, hopping off our cart and stretching. At twice the height of dwarves, it must have been an incredibly cramped trip for him this last week.

"Aren't you tired?" I asked. We'd been traveling for four weeks, and maybe Mam and Aramis were used to it, but this last part of the trip through Leitham was the longest and most exhausting of all.

"I am already behind," Aramis said with a smile, flashing his gorgeous deep dimples.

"You are not," Mam said. "We're back a day ahead of schedule."

"All right, then. I feel like I am behind. There is so much to do."

Who would have ever thought an immortal elf could be so impatient and eager to get so much done in a day?

"Make sure you leave the editing room every few days," Mam said.

"I shall try," he said. "Tell Sevrin I have pierced the big one with the tip of my arrow. He can come by and pay me my winnings any time."

Mam laughed. "I don't dare get in the middle of your wagering, but I will pass on the message."

I had no idea what they were talking about, and that was perfectly okay. I was witnessing true evidence of the legendary friendship between Aramis and Sevrin!

"I will see you all later," he said. "Welcome to Leitham, Mabel."

Mam snapped the reigns and we were moving again. "Next stop, home."

We left Aramis behind. After a few silent minutes, I finally had an opinion about Leitham I could share. "I'm stunned."

Mam smiled. "I was, too, the first time I set foot in Leitham. Still am, sometimes, considering how much it's grown since then."

The road tilted up in a gentle incline. It was only then that I noticed the mountains like a dark blue shadow in the distance, and the edges of the foothills rising around us. The houses here were more spread out here. In Gilliam, the homes on the mountains were crowded together in the owner's efforts to be as close to the mountain as possible since they couldn't be under it. Just like in Gilliam, the houses here were made of stone. Unlike the houses in Gilliam, they had all kinds of wood and iron ornamentation gracing the outer walls. The biggest house in Gilliam could have easily fit within the walls of the smallest house in Leitham, with plenty of room to spare.

Mam stopped the cart outside one of these massive houses, enclosed by a stone fence and an open iron gate, like arms outstretched, welcoming us home. Mam pulled in. Oak and pine trees in her garden lined the driveway and held me in awe. As a dwarf, it went against every natural instinct to like the trees. Thanks to meeting Aramis, and a panic attack during the regional Dwarf Games qualifying competition, I'd developed an appreciation, and almost an affection for trees, including their smells and the birds that inhabited them. These trees were taller than Mam's house, shading the drive. Their arching branches created a spectacular tunnel of green dappled with golden sunlight, leading directly to the house.

Mam's house was huge. She'd said she had no other family, that Sevrin was the only one that lived with her. The sheer size of the building made it hard for me to believe, except I knew she had only been honest with me from the start. There was so much room in Leitham, and so many large homes. Crowding families into homes was a Gilliam way of thinking. I had no reason to believe they did the same here.

The front door opened and I gasped as Sevrin, *the* Sevrin, stepped out, arms outstretched. "Frerin. Welcome home. And you must be Mabel. I am so happy to finally meet you." Sevrin helped me down and hugged me. "Frerin has done nothing but talk about you since the day we met."

Sevrin hugged me! "It's… it's nice to meet you, too."

He then helped Mam down, embracing her and kissing her. Mam pulled away from him pretty quick, glancing in my direction, like she was embarrassed by the display of affection in front of me. She had no need, as I was grinning at them. She smiled and relaxed into Sevrin's embrace. When she passed on Aramis's message, Sevrin only grunted.

"You two go on in," Sevrin said. "I've got a fire going and the kettle on for some tea. I'll bring in your things."

I stared up at Mam's three-storey house. There was no wood or ironwork to decorate the outside, other than the shutters and the doors, though even those were plain compared to some I'd seen. Still, the place was majestic, the sun glinting off the spotless windows made of the clearest glass ever.

Mam and I walked inside while Sevrin unpacked for us, making several trips from the cart to the house.

The inside was more spectacular than the outside, so open and spacious, all stone, and yet blessedly cozy. In the living room, a fire crackled in a large fireplace and water boiled in the kettle. "I'll take you to your room after some tea," she said.

We sat on the armchairs in front of the fire. Mam smiled. "I am so happy you're here. It has long been a dream of mine that I would have my family in my home with me, especially you."

I had spent so many years growing up wishing Mam was alive, living with me. I'd dreamed about telling her my problems, asking for help, but mostly spending time with her, laughing, going out, doing mother-daughter things. My dream had come true. Mam was alive, and I was here, living with her. We'd spent plenty of time together while we'd been traveling, but there had been enough distraction and time apart to keep it all from sinking in. Now that we were here, inside her house, it became all so real.

Mam had built a life for herself. A pretty phenomenal one by the looks of it. And yet there, over the mantle, was a portrait of my family. All of us. Da, my brothers, and me as an infant in Mam's arms.

I got up and looked closer. It was weird to see all my brothers without beards, although Frankie looked like his might have been starting. Everyone was so young. I scrunched my nose at my scrawny, bald, infant self. "Ugh. I didn't really look like that, did I?"

"You did," Mam said with a smile. "I'll never forget those beautiful tiny hands of yours. How you would grasp one of my fingers so tight it would go numb."

Mam looked so happy in the portrait, and I heard so much sadness in her voice now. "If Da had asked you to stay in Gilliam, said everything was forgiven, to please come home, would you have?"

Mam was quiet for a few moments. "Your da's

forgiveness isn't really forgiveness. You saw that when he told you that if you quit the movie all would be forgiven. You knew that you would forever be an outcast in his eyes. I would love to live in the same city as my family. They would never have to acknowledge my existence, as long as I could see them and know for myself that they are all right. He didn't ask, and I can't be there. I am so happy to have you with me, Mabel. I have had a family-sized hole in my heart since I was exiled from Gilliam. Having you here is helping to fill it."

It must have been so hard for her, coming to this strange city, having her dwarflings torn away from her, never knowing if she would ever see them again. "Do you ever get lonely?"

Mam looked down, pensive, and I thought for a moment she was going to avoid the question entirely. "Yes," she said at last. "I have been lonely. Lonely for my family in Gilliam. I have plenty of friends which helped allay the loneliness. I'd forgotten how much I missed all of you until I returned to Gilliam. The ache of loneliness for my family had become so much a part of my life it was just always there."

"And Sevrin?"

Mam attended to the boiling water. "He helps. I love him, though I was fine without him, and I would be again if it doesn't work out. I've learned to live on my own, and it isn't so bad."

That was the first time I'd heard anyone say that. Hearing it from a female dwarf was a double shock.

She'd seemed remarkably independent to me before, but this solidified it. I believed she might understand my need to discover new things and who I was, without having constant pressure to have a life-mate. It was one of the reasons I had to leave Gilliam. "You should tell Emma that. She'd never believe it's possible."

Mam poured the tea into three mugs. "That's the first time you've mentioned Emma since we left Gilliam. What happened between you two? You used to be inseparable."

I stirred milk and sugar into my tea. Emma wanted a mate and would do anything to get one, removing anyone she thought was standing in her way, including me. I was a female and by our nature, and the fact there were few female dwarves, every one of us was a potential threat. Except I was never a threat to her and her mating prospects. It didn't stop her from trying to poison me by giving me an ancient painkiller potion that ended up making my shoulder injury much worse than it would have been otherwise. "We came of age, and she changed. Or maybe I didn't grow up."

Mam put a loving hand on my knee. "I'm sorry, pet."

I shrugged with my good shoulder. "It was probably bound to happen."

"It doesn't have to be that way, Mabel, not here."

"This is some magical city then," I said. I desperately wanted to believe what Mam said, that Leitham could deliver its promises to me, of healing and a place where I belonged. "Maybe I need to do some exploring."

"I'll go with you, if you'd like," Sevrin said, joining us. He squeezed Mam's shoulder and pulled up a chair beside her. "I've put your things in your room, second floor, third door on the left, when you're ready to go up."

We drank our tea in silence for a while. It was really nice not to have the noise of other travelers milling about. Sevrin took care of the silence soon enough. In minutes he was lying back in his chair, feet up on a settle, snoring.

Mam shook her head. "You'd think he'd been the one traveling for weeks." She took the drooping mug out of his hand and set it aside. "Come on, Mabel, I'll show you around."

After a quick tour of the main floor, I followed her up the stairs. I couldn't wait to get my shoulder healed so that the real adventure of building a life for myself, the way Mam had, could begin. "Do you know how I can get in touch with Radier?" I asked.

"I don't, but Aramis should. Why?"

"Didn't he tell you?"

"Tell me what?"

"Radier was going to talk to Aramis's father about healing my shoulder. I'd hoped we'd have made some arrangements before we parted, but he disappeared so quickly I never got a chance to talk with him, that's all."

"I see. Does Aramis know about Radier's promise?" Mam asked.

"I think so," I said. I hadn't heard them talking about it, but then I hadn't been around them most of the time we were on the road. It was possible Radier hadn't told Aramis. There had been some kind of falling out between Aramis and his father. He'd suggested as much to me in Gilliam, though he'd never gone into specifics. "Is it going to be a problem if I see his father?"

"I'm sure it won't be, not if Radier thinks it's okay."

"Do you know what the tension between Aramis and his father is?" I asked.

Mam shook her head. "I just know they have been estranged for decades. Aramis has never spoken of it."

I rubbed at my beardless chin. Six weeks since I shaved off my beard and not even a hint of stubble had grown back. I'd done it because Aramis had asked me to. I'd been happy to do it, and I'd probably do it again if he asked, but I'd expected it to have grown at least a few inches by now. I still felt naked without my beard.

"What exactly did Radier tell you?" Mam asked.

"He just said that he knew someone who could heal my shoulder, that it would be no trouble and done quickly, and that it was Aramis's father."

Mam opened up the third door on the left. My room. My bags were placed neatly at the foot of a bed big enough to fit five of me across and so high I almost had to jump to get on it.

"Is that why you came with me?" she asked.

How could she ask that? She witnessed Da disown me and my brothers turning their backs on me. I had nowhere to go… . Oh. I hadn't said that I was happy to be here. She thought I didn't want to be here, with her. "Initially. But I wouldn't have come if you weren't here. I just feel like my injury is holding me back. As soon as it is fixed, I can start to live again."

Mam hugged me and kissed the top of my head.

I cherished her warmth and love. "I'm glad you came back and rescued me."

I CRADLED my jewel-encrusted throwing axe in my lap. I'd decided to spend my first full day in Leitham unpacking and setting up my room to make this house feel like it was home. I'd stopped unpacking when I pulled it out of the bag. My brother, and axe-throwing coach, Mikey, had given the axe to me when I'd started competing and working toward going to the Dwarf Games. It was a beautiful gift that was now a painful reminder of how quickly my once close relationship with my brothers had turned sour. Except for Max. If it hadn't been for Max rescuing my axes before Da burned all my things, I wouldn't have it now. I was grateful to Max for saving my belongings. As painful as it was to be reminded of all I'd lost, I was grateful to have the axe in my hands.

I'd loved axe-throwing. I had never experienced anything like the purity of being alone in the arena focusing on the target and the exhilaration of a perfect throw until I'd competed, and I likely never would again. Practicing, as exhausting as it could be, was bliss.

I wiped away a tear and set the axe aside.

I'd lined half the walls of my room with the throwing axes my fellow competitors and miners in Gilliam had given me in tribute. A few months later and I'd lost everyone's respect and Da had me exiled. The axes still meant the world to me, but they couldn't help. They were only a reminder of what I was, what I had lost, and what I might never be again.

I didn't know if I wanted to be an axe thrower. I'd loved it, but there had been a lot of pressure that went along with it. I'd like to try, someday, to work toward getting back into axe-throwing. But I didn't know if I belonged in that world any more, or if I wanted to.

I looked away from the axe and up at the remaining blank walls. I decided to leave them that way for now. I was in Leitham, in my mam's home. I was here to start a new life. I had unknown opportunities ahead of me. I would fill those walls with whatever represented what I decided to become. Maybe it was acting, maybe it was something else to do with movies, but gods only knew what might be out there for me to discover.

I couldn't begin to think about how to fill the remaining walls until I had some answers about my shoulder. How long would it take to fix it? Would I be able to have full mobility ever again? What if I couldn't? What kind of restrictions would I have to live with? Were the doctors here any better than Dr. Flint back home? If Aramis's father wasn't around to heal me, I hoped to the gods of all things dwarven that the doctors here could do the job. Dr. Flint could have fixed me, but it would have taken six months to a year. I hoped the doctors here would be able to fix me faster.

Not that I didn't have the time to heal. I would have back home too, if I'd been allowed to stay.

It might take a while and I might not be able to do much at first, but I would find a way to work and figure out what I really wanted. I might even find some kind of employment that I loved.

I left my room and ran into Mam on the stairs. "Mabel, I was just coming to see you," she said.

Before I could ask about dwarven doctors, she said, "Radier is here. He said Aramis's father will see you this afternoon."

My jaw dropped. After all this time of waffling between hope and utter despair, believing it would never happen, I could be fixed within a few hours!

"He's waiting for us downstairs." Mam continued.

"Us?" I asked. "You're coming with me?"

Mam smiled and put a hand over mine on the banister. "Of course I am. You're my daughter. I want to make sure everything goes well for you."

Back home, my brothers had been the same way when it was time for me to see Dr. Flint about my injury. Back then, I wasn't too keen on having anyone else with me. Now, I couldn't be more grateful. "Thank you. I just… do I need to change my tunic or trousers?"

"Your clothes are fine," she said. "You've been crying, love. What's wrong?"

I rubbed at my eyes. "Just unpacking, thinking of home. Let me just splash some cold water on my face and I'll be ready to go."

In the washroom, I pumped a bit of water into the ceramic basin and washed my face. I grinned as I let the water drain and toweled off.

My second day in Leitham, and already I was going to see Aramis's father. I'd hoped, but I hadn't expected this to happen so quickly.

I rushed down the stairs, ending up a little breathless at the door where Mam waited. "Where's Radier?" I asked.

"Outside. I wanted a few minutes alone with you. Are you sure you want to do this? Before you answer, Mabel, I want you to know that you don't have to. There are some excellent doctors here who can help you. I understand your desire for a quick fix, I do. But you have a home here, now. You can take as long as you want to get better and to figure out what you want to do. This is a risk. I know Aramis did some magic on your shoulder in Gilliam, and it helped a lot. You have to understand, there is no evidence of what effect elven magic has on dwarves in the long-term. Maybe it's fine. It might not be. This may be an answer to healing your shoulder. Certainly it will be the fastest option. But it isn't the only one. Having said that, if you really believe this is your best option, I support you."

She raised some good points, and I appreciated knowing I had her support no matter what, even if it took years for me to get better. Still, just thinking that it might take a year or more if I went to a regular doctor felt like a dark cloud had settled over me. It didn't just weigh me down, it made everything bleak. I thought about the next day, waking up still in this pain, and all I could see was darkness. Maybe seeing Aramis's father was a risk, but it was my best option. "It can't hurt to go talk to him, see what he can do. If he can't help me, or if the elven magic is too great a risk, we can always say thanks but no thanks, right?"

Mam smiled. "Absolutely. Let's go get your shoulder looked at."

We stepped outside. Radier stood by his cart. It was good to see him again. It had felt like forever.

Radier helped us into his cart and we were off. Both Mam and I dangled our feet from the bench in the front. It was awkward for me, but Mam seemed fairly comfortable with it, calmly chatting with Radier, letting her body move in synchronicity with the cart. I couldn't relax. Instead, I held on for dear life, clutching the edge of the seat with my one good arm every time we hit a bump, praying I wouldn't bounce off the seat and into the road.

We headed east out of the city, past a couple of small farms that reeked of hogs, and into a thick forest near the foothills.

"Here we are." Radier pulled up at the edge of a dense section of the forest. "We have to go the rest of the way on foot. It isn't too far."

We descended from the cart and were instantly greeted by two elven soldiers, their arrows pointed at us, primed and ready to be released at the slightest erroneous twitch.

They bowed their heads to Radier then stepped back a couple of feet to let us pass, though they did not turn away their arrows. Who exactly was Aramis's father that he needed guards? He was Lord of the Elves, yes, but I wouldn't have thought he would be threatened in his position.

Radier cleared his throat and marched on ahead. I followed, wary of the guards behind us, and no doubt the countless others in the trees watching, prepared against any attack or suspicious movement. It was like a scene right out of one of the movies I had watched and imagined myself re-creating during my axe-throwing competitions. Although my imaginings had been about Aramis, saving him and winning his love, not about me getting anything healed or fixed.

My Aramis. My friend.

What would he think of me right now? Did he know I was going to see his father? Would I lose his friendship over this? Would I still have come if Aramis had asked me not to?

I was over-thinking this. Aramis probably didn't know, and even if he did, he probably didn't care. He may be estranged from his father, but he knew how important getting back to full health was for me. He would never be upset with me for this.

We came upon a large tangle of trees, their thick roots and branches intertwining. Radier paused at an opening among the roots and tapped his staff against one of them. We waited several minutes. Radier was about to tap his staff again when an elf who looked nearly identical to Aramis, the only real difference being his silver hair compared to Aramis's blond, came to the opening.

"Radier." The elf smiled and embraced the wizard. "Come in, come in."

Mam gasped and grabbed my arm, shoving me behind her. "Aleric!"

She knew him?

"Aubrey, actually," he said with a smirk. "Hello, Millie," he said. "It is good to see you again. This must be your daughter, Mabel." He extended a hand.

How did he know me?

Mam backed off, pushing me with her. I felt her trembling through her grip on my arm. "Stay away from me and my family," she snarled.

"Come now, Millie. I have traveled a long way,

at Radier's request, to help your daughter. Are you so unforgiving that you will keep your daughter injured because of a small incident years ago?"

Oh no. Oh no! This was him!

"Mabel," Mam said in a low voice. "We will find you the best doctor there is in Leitham, or anywhere else. But you will not have anything to do with Aubrey."

He was the one who stole everything from my family. It was because of Aubrey that Da exiled Mam.

Radier moved to stand behind Aubrey. Aubrey raised his hand and gave a quick wave. We were surrounded by elves, their arrows aimed at us. We had nowhere to go.

"I came here as a favor to Radier and to you, one which I am happy to bestow because we are old friends, even though this is a great inconvenience to me."

Mam grunted and sneered. "Aleric, Aubrey, whatever you're calling yourself, you have taken enough from my family. You will leave us alone. Let us go. Now."

Aubrey's eyes darkened though the rest of his demeanor remained light, almost amicable. "I do not appreciate my time being wasted. I will give you two choices. You can allow me to do as I was asked to do, what I came here for, which is to heal your daughter's shoulder. No payment will be made now, but Mabel will be in my debt, to be repaid when and how I decide. Or, you can face my wrath, brutal and relentless. What I did to your family in Gilliam is nothing compared to how I will ruin you."

"Do your worst," Mam said without hesitation, her voice low and gruff, menacing.

My heart thumped in my ears, my knees weak. I couldn't imagine anything worse than what he'd done to my family. He'd taken everything, but worse than that, he'd broken my family. I couldn't allow that to happen again, not because of me. "No, Mam," I said.

"Mabel, we have doctors—"

"I know. This isn't about my shoulder. I'm not going to let your life be ruined again." I was a no-body. I had nothing to offer him. There was nothing he could possibly ever want from me.

"Smart girl," Aubrey said.

One of the guards grabbed me away from Mam. Another held her back.

I was terrified, shaking. I kept my eyes on Mam, but the whole time my mind spun, wishing none of this had happened, that Radier had never mentioned Aubrey to me. I reassured myself that he would never ask a favour of me because I had nothing to offer. If I was ever in a position where he could call in my debt, he would have long forgotten about me. I hoped.

Aubrey rubbed his hands together. "I hear you have great potential. I know you will not disappoint me," he said, putting his hands on my injured shoulder. The tingling started right away, the same healing tingling like when Aramis had touched it.

This time it was stronger. Much stronger. Almost unbearable. It was most intense at the muscle tear where my injury had started, and stretched out, up my neck and down to my finger tips.

It ebbed, easing away from the periphery, pulling back to the source of the injury. With one last flare of pain, it was gone, and Aubrey removed his hands.

In shock from everything, I wasn't sure it had worked. I flexed my fingers and it felt great. I raised my arm without a wince or cringe. I was pain free.

Physically.

The guards let Mam go. She rushed to me and embraced me, extracting me from Aubrey as she did so. "Are you all right?" she whispered in my ear.

"Fine. You understand, right?"

"I do, my brave girl." She kissed the side of my head. To Aubrey, she said, "We're done now. We owe you nothing."

"You, no. Mabel, however, does. Payment will be made. Enjoy yourself, for now. I will be in touch."

CHAPTER 2

AUBREY WAVED his hands and Mam and I found ourselves at the edge of the woods, just beyond reach of the guards, Radier's cart in front of us.

"Get in," she said.

"But, it's Radier's—"

"He's a wizard, he doesn't need it."

As horrified as I was about what just happened, and Aubrey's promises, I had to admit, it felt great not to need any help getting into the cart, and being able to hold on with both hands.

Mam snapped the reigns, in full control of the oversized cart and horses.

We were quiet. Mam didn't look at me. Her jaw was set, and her body tense, exactly how I was when I was furious.

"Please don't be angry at me," I begged, my voice trembling. She had every right to be, but I wouldn't be able to stand it, not on my second day living with her, not ever. I couldn't have both parents disown me.

"I'm not," she said curtly.

She had to understand why I'd allowed Aubrey to heal me. She said she did, but I needed to make sure. "He'd done enough to us—"

"Mabel," Mam cut me off. She took a deep breath. When she spoke again, her tone was gentler. "I'm not angry at you. I'm angry at myself. I should have looked into this more, I should have known who Aubrey was. I can't believe I didn't know this."

"Mam—"

"What's done is done. We'll get through this. We'll make sure Aubrey will leave us alone from now on."

"You don't have to have anything to do with this. I'm the one he'll come after, not you. It's up to me to figure out a way out of it. Besides, what could he possibly want from me?"

Mam shook her head. "That's not how this works, sweetheart. Aubrey isn't just a vile thief. Not only is he the Lord of the Elves, which gives him immense power, he is also Lord of the Elven Mafia."

"He's what?" I'd heard the stories of the Elven Mafia when I was young. They were horror stories we told to scare each other, stories about how they destroyed businesses, and anyone who got in their way or refused them. "You knew that Aramis's father was Elven Mafia?"

"No. I knew Aleric was. I learned about it soon after he disappeared from our lives. That made your da even more furious with me."

My heart sank and that dark cloud descended around me again. "This is still better than if I hadn't let him heal me, right? Because he would destroy us if I hadn't. Right?"

"Only time will tell. It all depends on what he decides he wants from you. Listen, love, don't get down on yourself. The choices he gave weren't really choices. Either way, we lose. You did, however, buy us some time to try and figure out a way to protect ourselves, and that can only be a good thing."

"Is it even possible to protect ourselves?" Hope wasn't in the stories I'd heard about the Elven Mafia.

"Maybe. We'll talk to Sevrin when we get home."

I'd only just met him and I was already getting him involved with the Elven Mafia. If I were Sevrin, I'd regret the day Mam mentioned she was bringing me to Leitham. "Is he going to be angry?"

"I doubt it. He won't be happy, but his issue will be with Radier who should have been clear from the start about what he was doing, and maybe with Aramis for not telling us who his father is."

"Sevrin doesn't know?" That seemed odd. He and Aramis had been friends for so long, how was it possible for Sevrin not to know about Aubrey? I could understand him forgetting in his old age, but to not know at all?

"Aramis never talked about his father. As long as they have known each other, he has never known Aramis to see his father, or talk about him, come to think of it. Neither of us have. No. Sevrin will not be angry. I think he'll enjoy the challenge. He's been a bit bored lately."

"A challenge? You mean like this is some adventure to slay a dragon?" That sounded even crazier than the situation itself. It made more sense to me to run from it all, or to brace for a fight, not to look for one and be excited about it.

Mam shrugged like she didn't understand him either, but her grin betrayed something else. Her joy? No. Her pride, in Sevrin. "Exactly like that. I know, it doesn't make sense, but that's Sevrin, a life-long adventurer, and it's one of the things I love about him."

Mam and Sevrin could not be more different than my family in Gilliam.

"Look, I'm not making light of the situation. It is precarious and it is likely we will be ruined in the process. All I'm saying is that we are lucky to have Sevrin on our side. We stand a much better chance with him than without." Mam waved her hand as though she were wiping everything away. "Enough doom and gloom. At least you were able to get your shoulder fixed. Don't let this ruin that moment."

Mam reached out with one arm and embraced me.

I flinched, expecting pain, but it didn't come. I

chuckled, "Sorry, Reflex."

Mam smiled and pulled me a little closer. Instead of protecting my right arm as I had done for so long, I put it around her and returned the hug.

It felt wonderful.

I couldn't wait to give her a proper hug for the first time. Still, Aubrey's threats tainted what I'd wanted to be a purely joyous moment in my life. "Can we still make an appointment with a dwarf doctor? I want to make sure the elven magic isn't going to cause some other kind of damage down the road. I know I was fine with elven magic when Aramis was using it, and before I knew what Aubrey is, I just want to make sure I don't have to worry about his magic causing me some other kind of harm, on top of his threats."

"I agree. In a few days I'll make an appointment for you to see Dr. Thora. We'll talk with Sevrin first, make sure he will have protections in place by then." Mam said as she pulled into the driveway.

"Before we go in, there's something I've been wanting to do since the day I met you," I said.

"What is it, love?"

I reached out and hugged my Mam, with both arms, for the first time. Well, I'd probably done it lots as a dwarfling, but I didn't remember it. Right now I didn't want to let her go.

Mam sniffled and returned my embrace. "Thank you, my darling daughter."

Sevrin opened the front door. "It worked?"

I hopped out of the cart without any help. "It did."

"I'm so happy for you," he said, hugging me.

"Don't be," I said.

"What do you mean?" He let go of me and we entered the house.

Mam and I told him what happened. Sevrin kept a gentle hand on her arm. It was such a simple, loving gesture. There was no warning or rebuke to it, only a reassurance that he was there for us and would protect us.

"Right," he said at last. "I'll talk to a few of my friends. He won't get near us."

It couldn't possibly be that easy.

A WEEK later, I woke up early, ready to find a job, become a productive member of society, and figure out what I was going to do with my life.

I had no idea how to start, but I was looking forward to figuring it out.

Since Mam and I returned from seeing Aubrey, Sevrin had suggested I stay at home, relax, settle in, and allow his friends to set up a protective perimeter. He wasn't particularly pleased about the situation, though I could tell he wasn't upset by it. Mam had started recording a new movie a couple of days earlier, and Sevrin had insisted on taking her to and from Studio City. Last night he'd said protections were in place, but he still wanted to keep us close.

I couldn't stay home any more. In spite of the

size of the house, I needed to get out. I was getting incredibly bored, especially now that I could use both arms.

I heard Mam downstairs and I made a quick decision.

In mid-dress, I poked my head out the door to make sure Sevrin wasn't around before hurrying to the stairs. "Mam," I called down.

She came to the base of the stairs. "Good morning, Mabel. What can I do for you, sweetheart?"

"Can you wait a couple of minutes? I want to come with you." I finished fastening my trousers and tunic as I jogged down the stairs.

"Absolutely! I'm dying to show you off to everyone," she said. "There are shops near the studios. We can have lunch together and dinner if it gets late. Let me just get some extra money for you." Mam went upstairs. I heard her rushing around for maybe a minute before she returned, a new brown leather satchel in hand. "Here," she said, handing it to me. "There's a purse with some money and plenty of room for you to put whatever you pick up or need for the day."

"Sounds great." I followed her out the door. "I was also thinking maybe I could start looking for work."

"Already? Why don't you just enjoy yourself for a while?"

"Mam, I love staying with you, but I can't just live off you indefinitely."

"I'm not suggesting indefinitely, but in case you haven't noticed, I'm kind of rich," she said with a cheeky grin. "I don't need you to contribute to the household. I want you to take your time, figure out what you love to do."

"What are you two talking about?" Sevrin asked as Mam and I stepped up onto the cart.

"Mabel wants to look for work. I'm telling her she should take her time."

"I agree, Mabel. We're protected from Aubrey, but it might be best for you not to do anything to draw his attention for a while."

"Surely whatever limited income I bring in won't interest him," I said.

We left Mam's property and the smell of the city hit me. "Oh," I gasped, covering my nose and mouth as we drove into the wind, into the stench. At Sevrin's chuckles, I lowered my hand. I lived here now, I had to get used to it, just like I got used to the smell of the trees in Gilliam. Of course, I'd learned to like the smell of trees because they reminded me of Aramis's natural aroma and I loved all things Aramis. I couldn't imagine loving anything or anyone who smelled this bad.

"It isn't the income he'll be after," Sevrin said. "It will be the kind of work that you do, very likely, that will be of most interest to him. Take your time, explore your options, explore the city. Let his other interests distract him."

"I'll do my best," I said. It wasn't going to be

easy. It wasn't in my nature not to work. Even with my injury I'd helped extract gems, acted in movies, and carved.

Mam added, "Think of it as me catching up on all those years I wasn't able to take care of you. Let me do it now."

"Mam, you don't need to make anything up to me. It's not your fault you weren't there."

"I want to make it up to you."

I sighed. "I guess."

Mam squeezed me. "Thank you."

A few moments later, Mam said, "I expect it to be a long day today. I have my own dressing room on this project. I'll give you the key and you can use it at any time, especially if you need to rest. If it gets too late, Sevrin can bring you back home whenever you want."

"Thanks, Mam."

"My pleasure." She hugged me again. "I've been talking about you to everyone on set, telling them you're here. They can't wait to meet you."

"Frerin," Sevrin muttered.

Mam rolled her eyes. "I know. I know. I won't push." To me she said, "You only have to do as much as you want, and you only have to meet as many of the crew as you want, or none at all. You don't even have to leave my dressing room if you would prefer."

"Of course I want to meet your coworkers. And I'd love to watch you work," I said.

I straightened my cap and tried to straighten my

tunic. The thought of meeting others suddenly made me nervous. Was I dressed right? Would everyone expect me to look like the other female dwarves in Leitham? What exactly was the look of the other female dwarves?

Watching the crowds as we drove through the business district of Leitham, I saw plenty of dwarves dressed the same way Mam and I were, the kinds of clothes I wore to the mines. There were just as many, if not more, dressed in shiny tunics that hung to their knees with really tight trousers underneath.

Just how many female dwarves were there? By my calculations, it looked like at least half the population was female. Why weren't they mating and having dozens of dwarflings? Were things really that different here?

Maybe I was in the right place after all.

As we got closer to the studios, I noticed even the male dwarves wore nicer tunics and trousers. They didn't wear clunky boots like I did, but shiny boots with thin but hard soles. Mam's boots were like a miner's boots, but looking a little closer, I saw that they had the same thin, hard sole. Sevrin's too.

The only time I'd really cared about my clothes before was when I was finally able to go up a size. Clothes were practical, for warmth against the cold of the stone, to wick away the sweat so we didn't get hypothermia or pneumonia, for protection against the mine dust. I think I needed new clothes, to make me look like I belonged here, not in a mine. "Mam?

I hate to ask, but do you mind if I do some shopping, spend some of the money you gave me, on clothes?"

"Of course not." She looked at me like she noticed my mining and traveling clothes for the first time. "You look fine, but if you want to get yourself something, you should have plenty for whatever you want. If it isn't enough, just come back to my dressing room, I'll leave my purse there for you to get more." She smiled. "You're turning into a city dwarf already."

I hoped so, but really, all I wanted was to blend in.

Sevrin pulled up to the guard-house at the gated entrance of the studio lots. He paused for a moment while the guard opened the gate with a nod and a wave. We passed between two large buildings and immediately came to an open lot filled with carts and horses and every species imaginable walking around. Not just elves and dwarves and sprites or trolls, but griffins, chimeras, centaurs and minotaurs, and all kinds of other… things? Creatures? People I'd never seen before—some tiny as sprites but did not fly so much as float; horses with manes of spikes; something the height of a dwarf but way too thin to be one, with a big bald head and enormous green eyes bulging from its bone-white skin. And oh, good gods, a gigantic, ten-times the height of an elf and twice as long as my home back in Gilliam, green and gold scaled dragon sauntering by at the back of the lot.

"Mam," I said, absently tapping her arm. "Um,

Mam? There's a dragon." My voice trembled almost as much as the rest of me.

"Yes, dear, that's Dakkar."

"I don't really care what his name is," I said. "Shouldn't we run?"

"Dakkar's harmless," Sevrin said. With a sly smile he added, "I made sure of that a long time ago."

I stared after Dakkar, who I noticed now was calmly being led by an elf pulling a long rope as a leash. "What? How? You slew every dragon you encountered." I knew every story of his adventures. I would know if he had let a dragon live.

Sevrin continued out of the lot, down a narrow street barely wide enough for our cart. "Not all. Not most. Only the truly dangerous ones. The others were either tamed or moved to dragon preserves. Dakkar was just a baby when I encountered her and her mother. Dakkar's mother was one of the dangerous ones, had been attacking a nearby dwarven settlement. Her mate had died and she had lost her mind from grief. We tried to settle her, tame her, move her, but she couldn't or wouldn't be. She was going madder by the day. By the time we put her down, it was an act of mercy. Dakkar had shown the same tendencies toward madness and danger but we couldn't justify killing her. It was then that I discovered the gem piercing all dragons' hearts. It's what causes their greed and consequently their tendency toward harming all around them. I was the first to discover the gem. I was also the first to attempt, and be successful, in removing it."

I stared at Sevrin long after he'd stopped at the edge of another lot. The real stories were so much more detailed and interesting than what the tales told us. "Wow. You did that to Dakkar?"

"I did. Calmed her right down. Made her a gentle soul, really."

"Here we are," Mam said.

The lot we were in was void of any other carts. Instead there were flat trees and what was supposed to look like the entrance to a cave. Fronts of homes were stacked against each other, leaning against a building on one side of the lot.

Sevrin helped us both down, not because we needed it, but because that was just his way. "Have yourselves a good day. Send a messenger for me when you're ready to leave." He climbed into the cart, turning it around and leaving, barely missing one of the flat trees as he did so.

I followed Mam into the building beside us—the studio. Three quarters of it was open space with more set props in it, set up ready for recording. Dozens of dwarves, a few elves, and a wizard milled around, preparing for the day's session. On the far right were offices, and the dressing rooms.

Mam's private room was huge, easily the size of the main floor of my home in Gilliam. She had it all to herself. It crossed my mind then that maybe Da no longer believed Mam allowed Aubrey to take everything from us. Da was just jealous because she had so much more now than my family ever would have in Gilliam, their lifetimes of earnings combined.

"Feel free to come back here any time," she said, handing me a key. "If you want to rest, hang the sign on the other side of the door." She motioned to a "Do not disturb" sign hanging on the door handle.

"You're probably going to be a while in hair and make-up, so how about I do some looking around, and come back and join you for lunch?"

"Good idea. Once you're outside, turn right, follow the road past a few smaller buildings, and you'll reach the market square."

"Great. I'll come back in a couple of hours and watch you work then."

"I'll be on set, either inside or out on the lot in front."

"Can't wait to see you in action." Not that I hadn't seen her work before. We'd both been cast in Aramis's movie in Gilliam, but this was different somehow.

"Just be careful," she said. "I'm sure nothing will happen, but please stay in well-populated places."

"I will."

When I left the soundstage, I realized the massiveness of Studio City. I walked toward the market square, past about five different studio buildings and lots.

Unlike Mam's lot, the studios I passed were quiet, almost all were unused, except for one. The doors were open, a cacophony of sound coming from inside. I poked my head in to check it out. A battle scene between centaurs and sprites was being recorded. By the sheer volume of sprites and their battle cries, I thought the sprites were winning. Good for them. It must have been a fantasy movie.

I kept walking and eventually the road broke into a market square. It was like I was in a city within a city. The best part: the smell was normal, livable. More than livable. It was perfect. Sure there were some smells—not every species emits a sweet scent—but there weren't that many of them walking around, and whatever bad odor was here, it was more exotic than offensive.

The square itself was a massive open space covered in slate stones. Restaurants and pubs occupied one side, their tables spilling into cordoned off patios in front.

The odd minotaur, dwarf, or sprite crossed the square. There were no market stands though, only a few board signs advertising sales for all kinds of things from candy and snacks at a grocery store, to fancy clothes in boutiques.

I didn't have a lot of time before I needed to go back to meet Mam for lunch. I was sure I'd explore every one of these stores dozens of times while I lived here, so I decided to head straight to the boutique, intrigued by the fancy clothes they sold. Maybe someday I'd need something from there, like for the premiere of Aramis's movie. I'd heard some of the other actors talking about it while we traveled.

It sounded like it was a huge deal, with really elegant clothes, lots of food, and a big celebration. I'd go to the regular clothing shops that afternoon, though.

The boutique carried clothes for all manner of species. It took a few wrong turns before I found the section for female dwarves. I scanned the few racks of long sparkly tunics, dresses they were called. A sapphire blue dress caught my attention, though I could not imagine wearing it. There were no sleeves, only thin straps, and the material was way too thin. I looked at the price-tag. This flimsy piece of material cost the equivalent of forty diamonds, half a year's salary for top Gilliam miners. I quickly put it back on the rack. I'd be better off going to the regular clothing stores. Maybe they had something nice I could wear. I hoped the other shops in the square were more reasonably priced.

I returned to Mam's studio. She sat at the edge of the lot, talking with another female dwarf who looked to be about my age. Mam laughed at something her friend said. When she saw me, her smile broadened and her eyes lit up.

"Mabel." She jumped out of her chair. "Come, come. Mabel, this is Lillian, my co-star. Lillian, I'd like you to meet my daughter, Mabel."

Lillian smiled, getting up. "It is so nice to meet you," she said, shaking my hand. "Is it true you were a miner?"

I still was a miner, wasn't I? Maybe I wasn't working in a mine but… at that moment, I realized a part of me had assumed I would go back to it. Mining was my vocation. It was how everyone in my family and all of my friends identified ourselves.

"I mean, that is so awesome. Most of us dwarves in Leitham, at least those of us in the movie business, are long removed from our mining roots. Are you staying in Leitham for a while? You'll love it. I can show you around some if you'd like. Show you the fun places to be. You are so going to love it here."

"Oh, okay." I hoped it would be all right for me to have friends. Mam and Sevrin had said it would be, but I didn't want anyone else to be threatened by Aubrey like I had. I had to trust Mam. She wouldn't introduce me to anyone, or allow me to befriend anyone, if she thought it was going to be a problem. "I'd like that."

"Fantastic. Gods you're cute. Are you going to go into acting with Frerin?"

"Um, probably not. It's not really my thing."

"Phew." Lillian exaggerated wiping her brow. "Then I don't have to worry about you being my competition. I'm kidding. It's too bad, actually. We could do some movies together. There are so many male dwarf buddy movies but nothing decent for female dwarves. We could make history. Think about it."

Something about her reminded me of Emma, my former best friend. Both were super friendly, talkative, perfect. I hoped Lillian wasn't as vindictive or mean as Emma had been. "I did a little acting in

Gilliam, but I think I prefer working on props and set design."

"Frerin's told me about your statuary. Perfectly noble profession."

Carving was noble? Imagine that. No one in Gilliam would believe it.

Lillian continued, "It's fantastic having some genuine dwarven art on sets. But think about acting with me. I'm working on a script right now. Can I show it to you when I'm done?"

I didn't know what she expected me to do with her script but I was flattered. "Sure."

"Frerin, Lillian," the director called. "Places."

"Sit here," Mam said. "This is the last scene for the morning, then we'll do lunch, all right?"

"Of course."

"You're fabulous, Mabel," Lillian said. "We're going to be best friends. I can tell."

Mam and Lillian left me and I settled onto Mam's chair. A few of the crew walked by and I introduced myself. They all seemed pleased to meet me. They all knew about me. It was like Mam was showing me off. It was almost like she was now able to prove to everyone that she really did have a daughter, maybe even that she had been capable of having one. I hadn't considered what she must have gone through. It had been hard enough for me listening to Emma talk about the number of dwarflings she wanted to have, and worrying that I would never meet a mate and have any. To have had dwarflings and be made to leave them behind must have been torture. Everyone Mam encountered and told about her family must have, at some point, thought she was making it up, or maybe that something was wrong with her because she wore a golden ring in her beard and yet she appeared not to have any dwarflings or a mate to have dwarflings with.

Mam and Lillian jumped right into the middle of their scene. Lillian intrigued me. Were all female dwarves that friendly? In Gilliam, it was rare to find two female dwarves who were friends. Not impossible, since Emma and I were friends, though coming of age strained and eventually ended it. There just weren't enough female dwarves. You would have thought that being outnumbered by the males the way we were, it wouldn't have been a problem to find a mate. It would shock most to know just how few male dwarves were interested in mating, especially the most desirable males: the miners. Maybe there wasn't competition among the females here. Or maybe Lillian was as competitive as Emma and wanted to pretend to be my friend so she could control the males in my life and take them from me, the way Emma had, or would have, if there had been any males in my life. With Emma around, no males ever looked at me. Maybe that was Lillian's plan. She needed me with her to make her look even better to the males. I'd befriend her because I would like to have a friend, but I'd be careful around her.

No, that was the Gilliam way of thinking. This

was Leitham and Leitham was different. Mam had said so. I'd seen it already. Mam knew what had happened between me and Emma and how I'd felt about it. Mam would have warned me if Lillian was like Emma.

"Okay, sweetheart, are you ready to go?" Mam said, walking off the set.

"I am."

"Great. Usually I'd eat here, from food services, but there's a fabulous eatery in the market square I want to take you to. Did you have a good morning?" she asked as we started walking.

"I did. This place is huge."

"And it has everything you need. Did you buy anything?"

"No. I just started looking. I thought I'd take more time this afternoon."

"Frerin. Frerin!" One of the crewmen called, running up behind us. "Sorry, Mabel. Frerin, you're needed back on set. Dave just announced a shortened lunch break. You don't have time for the market square. Not today."

"But—"

"I'm sorry."

Mam sighed. "I'm sorry, Mabel. We'll have to wait until dinner to eat together."

"That's all right. You have to work."

"Well, you go on and have lunch at the White Rabbit."

Mam returned to the set, and I returned to the

market square. I wasn't particularly hungry yet.

One of the stores I'd seen earlier, The Fancy Frock, sold clothes for dwarves and I wanted to see what they carried. I doubted their prices would be more reasonable than the boutique I'd been in earlier, but I thought it might be fun to look.

I stopped at the window, admiring one of the outfits on display. The knee-length tunic was a shimmery blue with a charcoal grey undertone. The trousers were much tighter than traditional trousers, and they matched the tunic. Both were a thin silk material. The belt was encrusted with diamonds. I didn't think they could possibly be real, but they looked spectacular. The boots with the outfit, and the cap, were both charcoal grey.

I could imagine myself wearing it. The blue was my color, and the grey would look great with my dark hair.

"Mabel?"

I jumped, my heart stopped for a moment at the sight of the tall elf. It took a breath or two before I realized it was Aramis, not Aubrey, who stood next to me.

"Aramis, hi." I cleared my throat. My cheeks burned, embarrassed that I'd thought he was his father, and out of anger for the position he'd put me in.

How could Aramis have kept his father's identity secret from everyone?

"It is great to see you. How have you been?" he

asked.

"Fine. Thanks." I wished I could just disappear.

"Your shoulder. You are not wearing a sling any more. Does that mean…" His face changed, from happy to see me and happy for me, to sadness and what seemed like hurt. "That means Radier took you to him," he muttered. Aramis swore. "I told him not to."

He knew Radier had planned to take me to his father and yet he'd said nothing?

"I am so sorry, Mabel. I thought Radier understood. He left us on our way here and I thought that was the end of it. Not important. I am sorry."

I no longer had any interest in shopping, or in having lunch. Hiding in Mam's dressing room seemed like the best thing to do right now, away from everyone, especially Aramis.

"I am not like him, Mabel."

Maybe not, but I wasn't so sure. I could understand why he wouldn't tell me. We were friends, though not particularly close friends. Sevrin was his best friend. By default, so was Mam, because of her relationship with Sevrin. He had to know what Aubrey had done to my family. Why hadn't he told them?

"I should go," I said, backing away.

He reached for me but stopped short. "Please, let me take you for lunch, we can talk about it."

"I don't think—"

"I should have told you. Give me a chance to

explain."

Why did he care what I thought? "Mam's working right now, but Sevrin should be home, you can talk to them."

"It is you I need to tell. Please. Let me take you for lunch and we can talk."

We would be in public. And he was my friend. He'd given me a chance after Da barged onto the movie set in Gilliam. He'd come to see me later that day. He understood about difficult family relationships. I supposed I should listen to what he had to say. He had already done as much for me. "All right."

We crossed the square to the White Rabbit, distinguishable from all the other masses of tables spilling into the square by the sign of a, well, a white rabbit, over the door. The hostess, a sprite, greeted us right away and sat us at a table inside by the window—Aramis's usual table, according to her. I could see why, and assumed he came here with Sevrin a lot because one of the chairs was elf sized, and the other was elevated for a dwarf to sit on with a foot rest so the legs didn't dangle embarrassingly.

Everything on the menu looked fantastic, but my stomach churned too much for me to want to eat anything.

"What would you like?" he asked.

"I'm not hungry," I said. "Thank you, though."

He paused a moment before waving over our waitress, another sprite. "We will both have the flame grilled skewered coney with rosemary and basil marinade on the garlic mashed potatoes, with a side of seared mushrooms and onions. To drink, we would both like your stout ale. And we would like to begin with the coney dumplings."

He didn't listen to me. Relentless, like his father was going to be.

"Coming right up," the sprite said, taking our menus.

"It is my favorite," Aramis said. "I hope you like it. And whatever you do not eat, you can always take it home."

"Thank you." Like he cared. He was stalling. I looked at him impatiently, willing him to say what he had to say and let me go.

Aramis licked his lips and cleared his throat. "This is very difficult for me. I apologize. This is something I have never told anyone. I should have told you everything the moment you decided to come to Leitham. I should have told Frerin a long time ago that I suspected that my father, if he was not the one, knew of or had some involvement in what happened to your family in Gilliam.

"Radier betrayed all of us by merely suggesting he take you to see my father. He and I had talked about Aubrey endlessly when I first left my clan. Radier knows how much I loathe my father and all he stands for and all he does.

"Sevrin and I have been friends for a long, long time. I have not known Frerin as long, but she is a good friend as well. I would never do anything to bring harm to her. I wanted to reunite her with her family, not bring threats to them. That is why I, in part, chose Gilliam. I knew how much she missed you and your brothers and wanted to see you. I wanted to help. Maybe make some amends for what I suspected my father had been involved in."

"You say you suspected, but you know exactly what he did." I couldn't keep the hurt and accusation out of my voice.

"I knew an elf lord had robbed your family. I had my suspicions. I suppose a part of me truly hoped to be wrong. Not because of any familial loyalty, but because I knew that if I was right, I would be guilty by association. It was not until we left Gilliam that I knew what my father had done. Radier told me, sort of. After we left Gilliam. We were on the road and I told him to leave you alone, that he never should have mentioned my father to you. I made it sound like I knew. Radier never denied it."

My jaw dropped. "If Radier knew all along... why would he have so easily suggested he take me to Aubrey? Why would he do this to me? Why does he hate our family so much?"

"I am afraid I cannot answer that."

Our waitress brought us each a tankard of stout ale. It was perfect timing. I took a large pull on mine.

Aramis left his untouched. He clasped his hands and rested them on the table. "You asked me once if I would tell you about starting over in Leitham."

I remembered. It was in the back garden of the

house Mam rented in Gilliam. Da had disowned me that morning. I'd been terrified Aramis hated me. I was devastated by the coldness of my family. Mam was all I had left. Aramis had come to me and told me how he understood what I was going through.

"I came here because of my father. I refused to be like him so he disowned me. I was more than happy to leave. I would have within a day or two anyway.

"I do not know the full extent of everything my father has done. Or, more accurately, what horrors his orders are responsible for. I do know that what he wanted of me was bad enough. At his very best, he was harsh with our own clan. He rewarded betrayal and punished honorable behavior. He stole from his own, but more than that, he encouraged theft and the destruction of others: elves, dwarves, any creature he and his loyal followers came across."

Our waitress came back with a bowl of dumplings and another of dipping sauce.

Aramis pierced a dumpling with his fork and cut it into pieces. He dipped a tiny piece into the sauce. He ate it, then continued. "I had been long gone by the time he truly organized his operations to maximize his profits from his criminal activities. That was several centuries before he was in Gilliam. That is why I could only suspect him. Given his position, and his preference for giving orders, I could not see him being directly involved. I have had nothing to do with him since I left home, so I could not know with absolute certainty what he had or had not done.

"Sevrin told me what happened to your family. The way he described the elves, it sounded exactly like something my father would condone. I knew that Sevrin wanted information, hoping I might know who it was. I could not say for sure, so I said nothing. I deeply regret that now.

"My inaction goes deeper than not knowing, or even my distaste for my father's business practices. He… he was brutal and controlling. Not just to me. My sister… "

"You have a sister?" I didn't know what to think of this revelation. I was curious about this side of Aramis. I helped myself to a dumpling. It seemed a waste to leave them untouched. My stomach betrayed me when it growled. One or two couldn't hurt. It was so tasty. Just the right amount of salty meat mixed in with the sweet dough. It didn't even need the sauce.

"*Had* a sister. Elves are immortal, but there are ways we can die—in battle, for example. I liked to be reckless in my adventures. It has been mentioned more than a few dozen times that I have flirted with death. For a time, I sought death. I saw it as my only means of escape from my father. Eventually, though, I had found a new life, thanks in large part to Sevrin. I had a way out, and so could Arienne. I went back for my sister. I was too late."

The pain was strong and evident in his eyes as though it had happened just yesterday. My brothers had turned their backs on me, but I couldn't imagine the horror of knowing one of them had died because of something Da had done. I reached across the table and put a hand on Aramis's arm.

"Thank you," he said. "Arienne, she, well, she was wonderful, loving, caring, a free-spirit, a bit of a trickster. He crushed her. I vowed to never have anything to do with him, to forget him. When I left Aubrey, I made him promise that he would stay away from Leitham, from everything west of the Haddam Mountains. We agreed to the territorial split.

"I had been successful in forgetting him, and over time, my father became a shadow. Radier was my one last connection to my father. Radier and I had a long-standing agreement: he was to never, ever mention my father to me or to anyone. I did not want to know about the odd occasion he went to see him.

"I was furious with Radier for suggesting he would take you to see my father. It was a blatant breech of our agreement." Anger laced his words.

Aramis stopped, took a breath, glanced out the window then back at me. When he continued, he was calmer, remorseful. "I am so sorry, Mabel. When your father barged onto the set in Gilliam, when I saw how he was with you, I saw my father and Arienne all over again. I should have protected her and I wanted to protect you. I thought I was doing just that when I told Radier to leave you alone. I cannot apologize enough for how I have failed you.

"I will not let my father harm you."

He covered my hand with his own. I knew now that I could truly trust him. He was more than a friend to me, he was family. "Thank you," I said.

Our waitress and another came over carrying our main dishes.

"It's not all bad," I said with a smile, picking up my utensils. It was going to be nice to use both hands to eat. "Sevrin has talked with some friends. He said they're protecting me, us."

Aramis nodded. "Good. I shall add reinforcements. And I will talk with Sevrin and Frerin."

LILLIAN WAS horrified when I'd returned to the set empty-handed after my lunch with Aramis. She insisted she take me shopping herself because I couldn't continue to walk around in my mining clothes. Mam was hesitant. I knew she was worried about Aubrey. Lillian said it was because Mam probably wanted to take me herself, but Lillian had insisted that while there were times to shop with a mam, this wasn't one of them. To me, Lillian said she loved my mam, but Frerin had no idea about fashion for our generation.

We made a date to shop during her free time the next day.

So there we were, in the same shops in the square of Studio City. I browsed for a little bit but I had no idea what to look for. Most of my clothes, admittedly, had belonged to my brothers before they came to me. Lillian and the sales clerk sized me up and sent me straight to the dressing room. A minute or two later, Lillian reached around the curtain thrusting a handful of outfits at me.

They were colorful: red, purple, teal, blue, and silver. Some were just the one color, others had patterns stitched into them. Some were tunics and regular trousers. Others were long tunics with tight trousers. One or two were dresses. I refused to try those on the moment I saw them. For all the variety, every outfit was made of a thin, shimmery material, just like the costume I wore in Aramis's movie we recorded in Gilliam.

"Put the teal one on and show me." Lillian said.

It was really nice, a longer tunic with diamond patterns stitched into it, with coordinating tight trousers. I loved the color on me and though I wasn't entirely sure I liked the idea of my legs being so exposed, the outfit was surprisingly comfortable.

"How are you doing in there?" Lillian pushed aside the curtain. "Lovely. Wait a second." Lillian pulled up the hem of my tunic and reached for my trousers.

I gasped, stepping back. Lillian simply pushed my hands out of the way and adjusted the waist of the trousers. I could have died of embarrassment.

"Mabel, honey, if you're going to be in movies, you can't be so modest. It isn't uncommon for you to be seen in half-dress, especially in wardrobe. Sometimes even on set."

What kind of movies did Lillian make? "I'm not

going to be in movies."

"Frerin says you have a lot of talent. You must, you're her daughter. There's no reason you can't work behind the scenes and act." Lillian straightened my tunic. "This one is perfect on you. Now do the blue one with lace embellishments."

Lillian gave me a couple of minutes to change before unceremoniously pulling back the curtain again.

"Definitely this one too. With some accessories." She smiled, pleased with her choice of outfit for me.

I looked in the mirror. I did look nice. And I liked the normal trousers that came with it. I wasn't sure about the lace cutouts on the sleeves, but it wouldn't take much to get used to them. "These are lovely, for a premiere, or something. But I need clothes for every day."

"Premiere?" Lillian chuckled. "Oh, honey. You are so cute. This is hardly suitable for a premiere. No, no. This is for every day."

They were comfortable enough, and they were what I saw other dwarves wearing, but they were too impractical. "What am I supposed to do in this? I can't mine or carve, or work in these. I'll get stone dust all over it, if the tools don't catch or tear the material."

"You're not mining anymore, Mabel. When you've figured out what kind of work you're going to do we'll find you some appropriate work clothes for it. If you decide to carve or whatever, you wear your work clothes for work, and then change into these after, just like when I'm on set wearing the clothing designated for my character, my work clothes."

"But I don't go anywhere I might need such fancy clothes."

Lillian crossed her arms and jutted out a hip. "Mabel, you're in Leitham now, and you are the daughter of one of our biggest movie stars. These are not fancy clothes. These are plain clothes. You're the one who wanted to look like you belong. You're not sitting at home now, are you? No. You're in Studio City, walking around in your mining clothes, looking like you've walked off set still in costume. Besides, you won't be staying home much longer. You're going to be invited to all the top parties soon."

Parties? Aubrey's threat echoed in my mind. Sevrin and Aramis had promised protection, and I felt safe enough, but I didn't want to endanger anyone else, and I certainly didn't want to make connections with anyone who would attract Aubrey's attention.

"And it isn't just the parties," she continued. "We're going to go out plenty with our friends."

"Our friends?" I didn't really have any friends. Family and Aramis didn't really count. I supposed I could call Lillian a friend, but she was the only one I knew here.

"Of course. We're going to meet them tonight. Speaking of parties, though, we need to find you some proper party clothes."

"Aren't these good enough for parties?"

"Ha! Hardly. I like the miner look. It works for

you so we don't want to lose it completely. Every female dwarf has a standard accessory, something they never leave home without. For me, it's my earring. It came from my mam's golden ring from my da. She gave a piece of it to all her dwarflings when we left home. Of course she might not have if Da hadn't given her a new one, but still, it's my piece of home. For you, I think we're going to get you some accessories with axes. They'll symbolize your mining background and your axe-throwing prowess. Keep trying on these outfits, and I'm going to go see what kinds of accessories they have."

I tried on several more outfits. Lillian and the clerk had a great eye. Every one of them looked good, fit perfectly, and were comfortable. I also tried on a few pairs of boots, including an incredibly soft black pair, with a slightly pointed toe and lift in the heel.

Lillian insisted I wear the teal outfit with the boots out of the store, and pack my old clothes in a bag. If I wasn't going to burn them, Lillian suggested I at least put them in storage.

She helped me put the dozen tunic and trouser sets on the counter, along with matching caps, and a silver chain with a double-headed axe pendant.

I was stunned at how well I'd done. I'd never had this many clothes that hadn't been worn by one of my brothers before me.

As the sales clerk added up the cost I panicked. Mam had given me enough to pay for all of the clothes, and then some, but it was just too much. The total was more than Patrick, my second-oldest brother, top diamond miner in Gilliam, made in two years. I couldn't spend that much of Mam's income. I couldn't spend that much of anyone's earnings on clothes.

"You know, maybe just this teal outfit for now," I said.

"What? No. Don't listen to her," Lillian instructed the clerk. "Mabel, you need to fit the role of Frerin's daughter. She's proud of you, as she should be. She won't care what you spend or what you look like, but executives will. It will matter if you want to work in the industry. I promise you these clothes will help."

"I don't know."

"She's right," Aramis said.

Aramis? When had he come in? How had I missed seeing him? An elf in a dwarf shop kind of stood out.

Lillian's jaw dropped. She quickly closed her mouth and smiled.

"Hi Mabel," Aramis said.

"Hi." After yesterday's talk, I felt much better about him. We were friends again.

"This one is spectacular," he said. "These will all look great on you. The necklace is a nice touch. You really should get them. Frerin can afford it."

"Are you sure?"

"I am. What you have there in your purse," he pointed at it. "That is nothing to her. That was one day's wage for her on the movie in Gilliam."

Wow. Mam wasn't kidding when she'd said she was rich. "All right, then. I guess all of them it is." It was a rush to spend so much. I couldn't help but giggle.

"Good." Aramis said. "Frerin will be happy. I was actually looking for you. Frerin said I could find you here."

"You were?"

"I have been going over the movie and I would like your opinion of a couple of scenes. Can you come by my office tomorrow?"

Tomorrow I had an appointment with a dwarven doctor to make sure my shoulder was all right. "I'd love to. I can't tomorrow, but the day after I'm free, if that works for you." Aramis wanted my help on the movie!

"Great. Here is the location." He handed me a slip of parchment with an office and building number and a map of Studio City.

"Looking forward to it."

"Me too." He smiled and winked.

After his deep sadness yesterday, it was nice to see him happy. "See you in a couple of days," I said and waved good-bye.

I paid for the clothes and Lillian had to help me carry the packages out of the store.

"Aramis," Lillian said. "You're working with Aramis? Frerin never said. I mean, she mentioned you'd been in his movie with her, but not that you were working with him. I'm impressed. And here I thought *I* would be introducing you to the important executives. I think I should be asking *you* to make the introductions instead."

"Well, sure," I said with a chuckle. "But you've already met the only one I know."

Lillian rolled her eyes. "You're so useless." Then she smiled. "Totally kidding. Let's go get a drink and you can tell me all about mining. It must have been so exciting."

"Mostly it was dusty, but finding the gems was… indescribable," I said.

She was a whirlwind, and so positive about everything. She reminded me of Emma when she was nice, except Lillian was genuine. I really liked her.

CHAPTER 3

"YOU HAVE to wear it." Lillian tied a belt around my waist and fitted one of my competition throwing axes into it. The axe handle dangled against my right hip, a sparkly accessory of sapphires and diamonds embedded in the handle, adding to the already shimmery material of the blue tunic and trouser set with the lace cut-outs. "Like that. Perfect. Wow, it is so beautiful," she stood back admiring her handy-work.

It felt natural to have the weight of the axe on my hip, like I was back in the mines with my pick-axe ready for the sensitive and detailed work of extracting gems. I did like the way it shone and the sapphires matched my outfit, though it seemed too fancy to wear as an accessory to a tavern, especially since

I wasn't planning on getting into an axe-throwing contest tonight. In theory, my shoulder was all better, so I could throw axes if I wanted to. The thing was, I didn't feel confident enough in my shoulder's strength. Who knew what damage the elven magic could cause if I tried to throw an axe?

Still, I liked the idea of having the axe with me. I felt like it embodied who I was. While it was a painful reminder of everything that had happened back home, there were also a lot of fond memories attached to it. I'd won the respect of my brothers and my city with it. I'd almost qualified for the Dwarf Games with it. I'd been most comfortable when I was throwing it. "What if I lose it or someone steals it?"

"Where we're going, no one would dare take anything."

Her tavern. Her friends. An inexplicable panic settled over me. I was usually pretty good at being sociable, but I wasn't anything like the apparently gregarious dwarves in Leitham. Maybe it was a good thing I had the axe with me. It gave me courage. It reminded me of how much I had accomplished with it. "I hope your friends like me."

"Of course they will," Lillian said with a dismissive shake of her head.

"How do you know?"

"Because I like you."

"You hardly know me."

"I could say the same to you." Lillian paused.

"You do like me, don't you?"

This had to be the first time anyone had asked me that. Had others worried if I liked them? I'd never considered it. I was always too worried about what others thought of me. It felt strange to think about it. I can't remember ever not liking someone unless they gave me a very good reason for it, like Emma had. "Of course I do."

"Oh, good." Lillian smiled and then was back to her chatty self. "You had me worried there for a minute. I want us to be friends. I have to say, I was nervous about meeting you at first because Frerin and I are so close. She's been like a surrogate mam to me since I moved to Leitham and we first worked together. I didn't want you to think I was taking over your family. I'm not. I swear it. I would love it if we could be like sisters… or friends, or whatever works for you."

"So you want to be my friend because of Mam?" This was unexpected and disheartening. At least she was up front about it and not vindictive like Emma.

"No, not, that's not what I mean. I'll step away, if that's what you want. Family is family and that comes first. No, I was afraid you wouldn't like me. Then we met and I thought that you were great and sweet and nice, which you would be because you're Frerin's daughter. Just spending the bit of time I've had with you, I really like you. I don't care who your family is. I remember what it was like to be new to Leitham, knowing almost no one. It's only right that I return Frerin's kindness to me. You'll have to trust me. I wouldn't do this if I didn't like you or if I thought my friends would have any reservations about you."

Fair enough. I'd go out with her and her friends. I'd think of this as a real-life adventure, not one I'd day-dreamed up. "I guess I'm just feeling paranoid after Emma's crazy stunts," I said.

"Who's this Emma?"

"My former best friend who did everything possible to make me feel bad about myself, to make others think less of me, and blamed me for everything wrong in her life." I took a deep breath and felt my cheeks flush. I hadn't intended to spew what I thought about Emma, but now that I had, it felt great.

"I'm so sorry, Mabel. So you know, I don't play games with friends. I don't manipulate them either. If you do something that bothers me, I will tell you. Just promise you'll do the same for me."

I smiled. I liked her so much. "I promise."

She grabbed my hand and we walked out of my room, down the stairs and out to her waiting cart. "I'll have her back before dawn," she called back to Sevrin. To me she said, "You have got to tell me more about this Emma. She sounds like a crazy evil character." We turned out of the driveway, heading into the heart of the dwarven neighborhood.

"That she is," I said. "Where do I start?"

"How about at the beginning."

So I did, with how Emma and I been inseparable

practically from birth, and quickly jumped to how that had all changed the day my beard started growing.

"Wow," Lillian said when I was done.

"I know. You're probably wondering what is wrong with me that I stayed friends with her so long. I ask myself that every time I think about her."

"You could, but why waste time beating yourself up about it? I think it shows me how kind and patient and good-natured you are, which makes me like you even more."

I felt warm inside, and relieved and accepted. It felt amazing. "Thank you."

"We are definitely having a character like her in our movie."

"Our movie?"

"You know, the one I told you about when we met."

"No, no, you said nothing about an actual movie, just that we should work together."

"Right. On our movie. I have no idea what it will be about, but we've got our first character. This is so exciting."

Adventure and opportunity. This could be fun. "When are we supposed to make this movie?"

"No idea," Lillian said with a laugh. "I've only been talking about making one since I arrived here, which is what makes it so much fun. I can be as imaginative as I want until I, and now we, hit on the right idea."

It was like when I imagined different stories while throwing axes and once or twice when mining. The difference being Lillian actually imagined movie ideas, and talked about them without fear of reproach. I loved Leitham.

Lillian parked the cart in an almost full lot beside the Dragon's Lair Tavern. "Come on."

She pulled me inside. I closed my eyes for the briefest of moments, breathing in the overwhelming smells of ale and pipe smoke, mingling with the roar of a room crowded with dwarves who were drinking, or already drunk. It was just like The Bearded Prospector back home, only the Lair was bigger, and no one talked about mining. At the table closest to us they were talking about the upcoming Dwarf Games.

I was pleased Lillian had convinced me to wear this outfit. It was very much like what everyone else was wearing.

I was wrong in one way, though. This tavern was nothing like The Bearded Prospector where everyone was a miner, talked about nothing but mining, wearing their work clothes, coated in mine dust.

This might actually be fun. There wasn't any pressure on me, like there had been back in Gilliam, to impress the fellows and find a mate. As far as they all knew, they had to impress me. Well, maybe not, but still, I didn't need to put the pressure on myself. I could just sit back, have some ale, and get to know everyone, see how the social circles worked here. I assumed it was the same as in Gilliam.

That was probably erroneous thinking on my part. Everything else was different, so why would sitting in the tavern with friends be the same?

Because we were dwarves and drinking and socializing in taverns was as much a part of us as the love of axes and gems and stone. Actually, it would be better because we could talk about things other than mining.

"Over there," Lillian said, pointing to a table toward the back of the room. We stopped at the bar and each picked up a pint first. Holding our drinks aloft, we wove through the press of bodies, toward her friends. I caught snippets of conversation, almost all of them about the Dwarf Games. The rest of the conversations, I assumed, were about whatever they did for work.

"Hey everyone," Lillian said. "This is Mabel Goldenaxe. Frerin's daughter." Lillian introduced me. "She's going to help me with my movie idea. Our idea, now."

"Good gods, we're on that already?" One of her friends asked, but he smiled when he said it. Good natured teasing then, I hoped. "Lovely to meet you Mabel. I'm Brent. Here, take my chair." He had a fantastically resonant bass voice. No braids in his beard, but he did have a sparkle in his eye.

"Excuse me," someone from the table next to ours said. "Did I hear right? You're Mabel Goldenaxe? *The* Mabel Goldenaxe?" A male, voice not quite as low as Brent's, but he did have the fullest beard I'd ever seen, and he wore two braids in it.

How did he know who I was? "I am."

"Fantastic to meet you. My cousin competed in the Regional Games in Mitchum, in the Boulder Toss. He watched you compete, impressed by your skills. He and everyone watching were horrified by your injury. What a shame. He said you would have been spectacular, could have even won the Dwarf Games. Here, let me buy you and your friends a round of drinks."

I was known in Leitham! I'd imagined something like this when I was throwing, that somehow Mam, or Aramis would hear about me because of my throwing. Mikey had said it would get me noticed. Now I knew it had. Just not by the fellows in Gilliam like he thought it would. This was so much better! "That's very kind of you, thank you."

"You are a good one to have around," Lillian said with a laugh. "Right, so you met Brent. This is Samantha, but we call her Sam, Chris, Jeff, and Hannah."

I waved at them all, said hello, and sat back, sipped my ale, and observed their interactions. Not one of them wore braids in their incredibly thick beards. Beards looked so much better when they weren't coated in mine dust or semi-wet from the cleansing pool. Not one of Lillian's friends, or any of the tavern patrons, were particularly stout either, which, I had to say, was a relief. It was tough being the thin one in a room full of desirably stout dwarves.

It made me wonder if perhaps stoutness was really only attractive among miners.

Come to think of it, I hadn't seen any stout dwarves in Leitham, except Sevrin, though even he wasn't as stout as some miners in Gilliam. There also didn't appear to be a huge press to find a life-mate and have a golden-ring ceremony. Everyone seemed rather casual about it, like they wanted to have some fun for a while first, like they were waiting until they'd found true love and partnership.

I liked that.

A lot.

"Mabel," Brent said. I loved his voice—it vibrated at my core. "Lillian says you're an artist."

An artist? What's that? "She did?"

"I told him about your carvings," Lillian leaned over, helping me out.

Oh, right, carvings. That was art? How did she know about my carvings?

"She's so good, Aramis used one of her statues in his movie," Lillian said.

Mam must have told her.

"Brilliant," Brent said. "I'd love to see your work sometime. Maybe we could talk about featuring some of your carvings in my gallery."

What was he talking about? "Oh, well, I think I only brought three or four with me."

"No problem. You should come by the gallery some time and bring the carvings with you. Remind me to get you the address before the end of the night."

"Brent owns *the* dwarven art gallery in Leitham," Sam said. "Displays the work of only the best dwarven artisans. Show in his gallery, and you're guaranteed sales and plenty of commissions by the wealthiest residents of the city."

I doubted my carvings were good enough for such a place, but it was kind of Brent to offer to look at my work. "Sure, I'll see what I have."

"What was it like working with Aramis?" Jeff asked. "My brother has acted with him, said it was incredibly tedious. He said Aramis kept asking to re-record each scene, never satisfied with his own performance, always changing things. Sounded like a total nightmare."

"I didn't think so. I mean, yes, he's a perfectionist, but it was his movie, his reputation, so why shouldn't he expect perfection?"

"Be careful of Jeff," Lillian said, quiet enough that only I could hear. "He tries to dig the dirt on everyone in the business, tries to use it to his advantage. He'll use you too, if you let him. Be nice, but don't get personal with him."

"Thanks." That was the kind of warning I should have had about Emma. My friends Jimmy and Phillip might have saved me a lot of trouble if they had said something.

"Speaking of Aramis, sort of," Hannah said, "I heard he sacked Radier and blacklisted him from the industry all together."

"What? Why?" Chris asked.

"No one knows," Hannah said. "Something must have happened on that last movie they recorded in Gilliam. Mabel, you were on the set. Did you see any conflict between them?"

Not on set. They didn't have to know that other part, about Aubrey. "Not true," I said. "Radier wasn't sacked. They got along great on set."

"Then something must have happened after," Hannah said, "because he was supposed to be at the studio today recording the movie I'm in, and he's been replaced. Neither our director nor the producers will talk about it. It's like he's taboo."

"You must know what happened," Jeff said to me.

I did, but they didn't need to know. If I told them, they could be embroiled in the whole mess with Aubrey. I shook my head. "Haven't a clue."

I COULD not get used to the stench of the city. Because I'd been either in Mam's house or in Studio City, I'd been protected from it. Now as we traveled through a neutral business to my first doctor's appointment, it was overwhelming.

There were too many horses in the streets. It was rare to see horses in Gilliam. Back there, the only smell we had to worry about was the odor of the forest, and the animals that lived in it. How could Sevrin stand this? Sitting there, smiling, waving at pedestrians and others on carts, like he was breathing the purest air. Our own horse raised its tail and a putrid gas escaped. I nearly gagged and covered my nose. Sure it had been bad traveling from Gilliam to Leitham, sitting behind the horses, riding through forests. But here, all the smells combined. Dear gods of bodily fluids and sanity. I thought I was going to die.

Sevrin chuckled and patted my knee.

"What?" I glared at him.

"You'll get used to it," he said.

"How would you know? The city grew around you. You probably have no idea how bad it is." I dry heaved. I'd talked too much, let too much of the fumes into my body. No wonder Mam kept her home so isolated. The trees that surrounded it probably helped filter the air.

Sevrin laughed harder. "I haven't lived here that long. It is an acquired taste, that's for sure."

Great. That was a taste I wasn't sure I wanted to acquire. How did the stench not seep into the homes, embed itself in on our clothes, our skin, our hair? Really. If Da wanted to keep me from acting with Aramis, and living with Mam, all he should have done was let me smell this place.

Thankfully we didn't stay in the business district long. We'd barely entered it before we rode out, back into another residential neighborhood, closer to the foothills. There weren't many horses here, and only dwarves walked the streets. A few sprites flitted here and there, but they were hardly worth noticing. The houses here looked a lot more like the homes in Gilliam, like the home I left. Small cottages made of stone, with small front and back gardens, close to the road, close to each other.

The road widened, becoming another business district, smaller and much less crowded than the main one. This was a dwarven business district. The smell was much better here. I let go of my nose. The air was almost fresh compared to where we'd been. The stone had such a sweet and salty scent to it. If I closed my eyes I could have sworn we were inside the mountain. Gods of stone and sky, I almost missed mining.

Sevrin stopped the cart and I hopped down with his help. All the businesses here were in individual buildings, like small shop fronts. Sevrin held the door for me; the sign above it read "Dr. Thora."

I expected a bigger office building, with maybe nice leather chairs in the waiting area, and I don't know what else, but it wasn't this. The waiting room was small and empty. A handful of chairs in a corner, a small table with a few magazines scattered on top of it among the chairs.

"He's the specialist? The best one in Leitham?" I asked. Shouldn't he be in a big fancy office? Perhaps in the centre of the city? With a waiting list a year long?

"She is."

The receptionist looked up from the magazine

she was reading, *DwarfStyle*, its glossy cover featuring a fabulously stout female dwarf in a sparkly red dress. The receptionist was wearing a nice green shiny tunic with embroidered embellishments on the collar and cuffs. Even her cap had some embroidery on it. Lillian had been right. I was glad she convinced me to buy these clothes. The receptionist put down the magazine next to a book opened to a page with a diagram of a dwarf's insides. "You caught me on a study break," she said with a smile.

"Hiya Stacie."

"Hello Sevrin. And you must be Mabel," Stacie said, smiling. "Come on in,"

I followed her into one of the two offices off the waiting room. It didn't look any different than my doctor's back in Gilliam, except maybe the tools of needles and knives and other metal things were newer, or maybe just shinier.

Stacie motioned for me to sit in the chair next to the desk. "I'm going to do a preliminary exam before the doctor comes."

"Okay."

"An axe-throwing injury." She smiled. "I used to throw axes, only at the tavern though, and I was terrible at it. I heard you made it to the finals at the Black Mountain Regional Competition. Congratulations."

"Thanks." I felt like a fraud accepting her praise. It was a great accomplishment, yes, but usually regional finalists were only known in their region. It seemed my injury had made me more popular than my throwing might ever have. Maybe I should thank Emma for the poison that made my injury so much worse. "How did you know?"

"Frerin told me, when she set up the appointment for you." Stacie opened up a file folder on the desk and looked over the parchments inside. "What we don't have, is any detail on the kind of treatment you've received."

"Oh, well, mostly rest, some small exercises to keep my shoulder mobile. I did get some healing from an elf—" At that, Stacie cringed. "That's why I'm here. I want to make sure no other damage was done by it."

"Got it." Stacie wrote quite a bit. I wished I could read upside down to know what she said. "Now, what about this ancient pain-killer you were taking? Can you tell me what it was called, or what was in it?"

"No. I don't remember any of that. My doctor, Dr. Flint, back in Gilliam, may be able to get you that information. A friend of mine gave it to me. It was an old family recipe. All I know is that it was poison. Dr. Flint said it weakened my muscles, my bones, everything, that's how my shoulder ended up shredded and I was too numb to notice."

Stacie was quiet for a few moments. I guess my bitterness had come out. "Sorry," I muttered.

"It's quite all right, Mabel. You've been through a rough time."

At least she was nice about it all. "Thanks."

"Have you taken any pain medication today?"

"No. Don't need it."

"Elven magic. Right. Stretch your arm out, straight in front, palm down."

I did.

She picked up a quill, dipped it in ink and scratched something on the parchment. "Can you lift your arm out to the side?"

I did.

Stacie scratched a bit more on the parchment. "Good. Full range of motion. What about before the elven magic?"

"Pain, all the time. I couldn't move it at all. I had to hold it like this," I clutched my arm to my chest.

"Was that the most comfortable position for your arm?"

"Yes."

"Did you feel pain in that position?"

"Yes. It was a dull ache though, not the sharp stabbing of dozens of spears all over my shoulder, running up and down my arm and back and body. That's what I felt when I tried to move it, or if someone touched it, or when I got jostled, or accidentally knocked it against the edge of a cart."

Stacie nodded as she wrote down everything I said. "So it hurt all the time, for every reason."

"Pretty much," I said with a half smile.

"And now nothing."

"Right."

"Well, then, let's hope it really is that way." She

put down the quill. "Sit tight, Mabel. Dr. Thora will be with you in a few minutes."

"I'm right here," Dr. Thora said, entering the office. "Hello, Mabel."

"Hello." She was awfully young to be a doctor; her beard didn't have a single strand of gray in it yet. At least she wore a proper tunic and trousers.

"I've finished the preliminary for you," Stacie said, vacating the chair.

"Thank you." Dr. Thora sat and reviewed what Stacie had written. "Well done, Stacie."

The receptionist smiled and left the room.

"She's in training to be a doctor herself," Dr. Thora said.

That would explain the book on dwarven anatomy. I didn't know what it took, but I had liked Stacie's demeanor and the time she took with me to write everything down. If that was anything to go on, she would make a good doctor.

"Well now," Dr. Thora said. "Let's see what we can do about this shoulder of yours." She put a hand on my shoulder and gently massaged it, feeling the scar tissue and the extent of the injury and determining my mobility. She frowned and focused her examination on one specific spot. I couldn't quite remember, but it felt like she pressed the exact same spot Aubrey had touched when he healed me.

My breath hitched. "What is it?" I asked.

"I'm not sure," she said, still massaging it, moving my arm in gentle circles. "It feels like there's something there. I'm not sure if it is damage that occurred after the original injury, scar tissue, or what." She examined it a bit longer. "It feels foreign. Elven, or a trigger for elven magic. It appears to be dormant. I don't know how long the dormancy should last, or what or who might set it off."

So that's how Aubrey would guarantee I would do whatever he asked of me. I'd be fine as long as I paid my debt to him, whenever he might come to collect.

Dr. Thora wrote something down then said, "It might never happen, but I don't want to take that chance. I highly recommend we try to get rid of it before it does damage."

"If you do remove it, does that mean whatever healing has happened will be reversed?" I was calm. Curious. "It's okay if it does, honestly." And I meant it.

Dr. Thora was quiet for a moment. "I don't know. I'm going to have to consult some colleagues on what to do. If I find out anything sooner, I'll send you a message to come right away, otherwise I will see you in two weeks. By then I should have some idea if I can help you. I won't lie, Mabel. This may be beyond any of our capabilities."

"Great. Sure. What about other damage? Has the magic done anything else to me, or is it just the trigger?"

"I didn't feel anything specific but there are some tests I'd like to do. Let me just pluck a few of your hairs for analysis, to determine the effects of the magic. I should also be able to determine the extent of the poisoning from the old medicine."

"Go ahead." If she could figure out all of that, then things were more advanced here than in Gilliam.

Dr. Thora picked up a pair of tweezers, plucked a few strands of hair, put them in a jar, and set it aside.

"I'll have more extensive results for you in a few weeks, once I've completed the analysis of your hairs, combined with my findings."

"Thanks, so much, Dr. Thora."

"You're welcome. I hope I'll have good news when I next see you. Set up an appointment with Stacie before you go."

"Will do."

I hoped she could find a way to remove the elven magic in my shoulder. I would welcome the pain back if it meant I would be free of Aubrey. Surely, once his healing had been reversed and his services were no longer necessary, he couldn't ruin me, or my mam.

CHAPTER 4

I WANDERED around the outskirts of Studio City looking for Aramis's office. I had the directions in my hand but nothing looked like it was supposed to or had the right name or number, until I'd read it a handful of times.

I stopped. All the buildings at this end of Studio City looked identical with their white walls and red doors. I re-read the instructions Aramis gave me, and looked at the door in front of me and the one next to it. The numbers went up. I'd gone too far. I turned around and walked back, studying the numbers more closely until I found the one that was Aramis's studio. I'd finally found it.

I knocked on the door and poked my head into his office. Aramis sat at a table, a small screen in front of him with the wizard's crystal projecting the movie on it in miniature. Three other crystals lay on the table. He looked up from the screen and smiled.

"Come in," he said. "Have a seat."

I climbed onto the stool next to him, keen to watch and learn.

"I am just finishing up some editing and then we will get started," he said.

"No problem." I watched him work, his deft and delicate hands tapping one crystal then switching it with another, then another, as images flashed on the screen, starting, stopping, reversing, speeding forward. Watching the process fascinated me. I wondered if any dwarves did this work or if only the gentle and slender hands of elves could work the crystals this way. I'd love to try it sometime.

He removed the wizard's crystal from its holder, shook it and replaced it between the two tines of the golden fork. "I have watched this so many times, I have no idea what is going on. I need your fresh set of eyes to watch the whole thing and point out inconsistencies, or where there are odd shadows, basically whatever needs to be fixed."

"Really? I get to watch it before it gets released? Wow." I loved all this behind the scenes business. I would never have been able to do anything like this in Gilliam. I loved that Aramis trusted me to have opinions on how to fix or change something. That kind of thing wasn't tolerated in most miners. Even my brother Frankie, when doing his job exploring abandoned stopes, had faced criticism for questioning the general opinion that those abandoned mine stopes had no more gems to produce. Frankie had proven his critics wrong on several occasions, but it didn't stop the older miners from disapproving of him for not listening to them.

"Do not get too excited," Aramis said with a smile. "It is still a mess, there is a lot of work needed, but I cannot see what that work is anymore. I have snacks for us, some almonds and dried meat." He pulled out a couple of bowls with the snacks and a couple of pints of ale, and set them in front of us. "Tell me as soon as you notice something, all right?"

"Absolutely." I wouldn't let him down.

Aramis tapped the tines of the fork which vibrated against the crystal, projecting the image onto the screen. I picked up a fistful of almonds and stopped with them half-way to my mouth. It was so strange to see Gilliam there in front of me; the city, the view of moving in toward the mine entrance, using the same path I'd walked for so long, the same path Da and my brothers still walked. All of it was so real. Like I was there still. Like I should have been there. Like I was spying on Gilliam. I almost expected to see my brothers pass through the image on their way into the mines. I jumped when my friend Jimmy did just that.

"Are you all right?" Aramis asked.

"Yes. I think so." I popped a few almonds into my mouth, concentrating on their woody nuttiness.

I was watching a movie, not real life. Except it

had been my life for so long. The scenes inside the mine were spectacular. Aramis had truly captured their beauty, maybe even made them more stunning than they were. The crystal stalactites and stalagmites gleamed. The smooth yet craggy rock, the caverns and endless intertwining tunnels sparkled with the veins of gems being excavated.

Dear gods of diamonds and coal. What was wrong with me? I should want to be there, mining and discovering gems. I should want to feel the smooth wood of the axe's handle in my hand and the reverberations as the iron axe-head hit the stone. I should long to chip at the stone and feel the elation at finding a new vein of gems, extracting that first gem and feeling its glorious weight as my mining mates admired it.

I didn't. I didn't miss the smell of the cold stone or the grit of the mine dust in my beard. I was relieved not to be in that world any more.

I watched the scene in which I worked with Emma and Jimmy. Jimmy had stayed close to me, asking if he could work with me. I'd thought that was all he'd wanted. Looking back, watching him on screen, it was obvious by the way he looked at me that he liked me. I was glad I hadn't seen his interest in me. If I had known, if I'd reciprocated, I would have stayed in Gilliam, living a boring and unhappy life.

My big scene came on. Me, alone with Aramis, acting as brother and sister. I looked stiff as any cave stone. I was wide-eyed, in awe of Aramis, shocked that Mam was there—I had met her for the first time only that morning—and amazed at everything going on around me. I could see how hard I tried to get my lines right so that Aramis wouldn't sack me and replace me with Emma.

"Ugh. Can we re-record these scenes?" I asked.

"What? Why?"

"Look at me! I'm stiff, and awkward!"

"You were just fine for your first role," Aramis said.

"Well, thanks for your kindness, even if it isn't true. Wait. You need to change this scene, we re-did it after I shaved my beard."

"Right. Thanks." He looked around and picked up another crystal.

"Hopefully I did better in that version."

"You are too hard on yourself, Mabel. You should be proud. You took a great risk being in my movie. You had just met your mother It was a lot to handle your first day on set. You should have seen my first efforts, or Frerin's. You would never stop laughing."

"I doubt it, but I would love to see those early movies."

Aramis smiled. "Then it is a good thing those crystals were destroyed."

"Aww, no!" Though I hadn't given it much thought in a long time, it was a secret ambition of mine to find the first recordings ever made and watch them. "Please tell me that some of the early recordings still exist."

"They do. Archived. But I will never tell you where, as you are far too eager to laugh at me," he said with a smile.

"Fine. I'll just have to find them myself."

"Good luck," he said.

Feeling emboldened, I asked, "Can you show me how to change out the scenes? Just tell me what you're doing as you're doing it?"

He glanced at the crystals then at me. "You want to learn how to make and edit movies?"

"Since the day I saw my first one. I don't know if dwarves have the dexterity for it, but I'd love to try."

"Sure. I shall walk you through this change. After we have watched the movie, I can get you to try it out on some cut scenes."

This day just got better and better.

KNOWING THAT Sevrin and Aramis had friends protecting me and Mam, I felt safe enough to explore the amazing city of Leitham. I asked Sevrin if he could drop me off in the dwarven business district.

After we left Mam at Studio City, he took me into town. "Is there anything in particular you're looking for?" he asked.

I shook my head. "No, not really. I just want to find out what all is available in Leitham. It is so much bigger than Gilliam, I'm bound to discover something new and exciting."

Sevrin smiled. "You remind me so much of Frerin when she first arrived."

He pulled up to a store near Dr. Thora's office. "Have fun," he said. "When you're ready to go home, there is a taxi stand a few blocks down the road. Do you need some extra money?"

"I'm fine, thanks," I said, patting the purse Mam had given me. I still had loads of gems in it, even after my shopping spree with Lillian.

I hopped out of the cart and waved good-bye to Sevrin. I looked around, soaking in the atmosphere of the bustling street. I decided to just saunter, browsing the shops if I saw something interesting in their windows, but mostly just see what there was to see.

It didn't take long before I found a display window with all kinds of carvings made of both stone and wood. "River's Edge Art Gallery" the sign said. That was an odd name, since it wasn't anywhere near a river. Lillian had talked about art galleries. Brent owned one but I couldn't remember if they had even said what it was called. I decided to go in, to see what it was and to know what Brent and Lillian were talking about.

It was incredible. There were paintings on the walls, statues and stone carvings everywhere.

"Mabel?" Brent asked, walking around a larger-than-life statue of, well, some dwarf; I didn't know who it was supposed to be.

"Brent?" I bumped into the statue. I grabbed it, limiting the wobble. "Is this your gallery?"

"It is. It's great to see you." His warm smile lit up his eyes.

"You too."

"What brings you by?" he asked.

I fidgeted with my cap, nearly bumping the statue a second time. "Just exploring the city, saw the display, and thought I'd stop in."

"I'm so glad you did. Let me give you a tour."

"I'd love that, thanks," I said. "If it isn't a problem."

"It's never a problem, especially not for a friend," he said with a warm smile.

I'd liked what I'd seen in the gallery's window and those works paled in comparison to the spectacular craftsmanship on display inside. I felt my mood lift just being surrounded by such beauty. It was comfortable here. Brent created this space. We both appreciated the beauty. This could be a good friendship.

"Let's start over here," Brent said, taking me to the back wall.

Hanging on the walls were some amazing sketches and paintings of dwarves, mines, and historical battle scenes, each with impressive detail of fine lines and excellent highlighting. My work was downright pedestrian compared to these.

I looked closer at the cards next to some of the carvings that were similar in size to the ones I usually made. My jaw dropped. They were going for a handful of diamonds. Could I get that kind of income from my carvings? "Maybe I should have charged Aramis for the use of my carvings on his set," I muttered.

"What? He didn't pay you?"

"Of course not. I was making them while I was watching them record. It wasn't like he bought my carvings. I still have them." They were in one of my bags in the corner of my closet. I hadn't unpacked them because it felt odd to display carvings in Mam's home. She didn't have any others around her place. In Gilliam, if anyone bothered to carve, it was a hobby, a way to practice your stonework skills for mining. At best, the carvings might be put out in the back garden to frighten the forest creatures away from the vegetables. Usually, the stone work was admired then tossed out.

"Doesn't matter," Brent said. "He should have at least paid you for the usage. You didn't bring any of your work with you now, did you?"

"I'm afraid not. I didn't think I'd be here today. I just stopped in on a whim."

"You have them at your house?"

"Yes, a few."

"Sidney," Brent called out. "Look after the gallery for me. I'm going out for a bit."

"No problem." Another dwarf came out from the back.

"Let's go," Brent said. "I want to see your work."

"Right now?"

"No time like the present," he said with a smile.

I followed him around to the back of the gallery to his cart. In minutes we were on our way back home.

"Can I ask why you chose to name your gallery River's Edge?" I asked.

"Of course. It's sort of named for the town I grew up in, Gypsum. It is a small settlement largely alongside a river. That's the elaborate reason. The more practical explanation is that before I moved the gallery to the current location, I started out with a cozy space on the bank of Leitham River. I'd already build a reputation there, so it seemed impractical to change it when I moved."

"Makes sense," I said. "I'll be honest. I don't think I've ever heard of dwarves deliberately settling next to a river. Where is Gypsum?"

Brent pulled onto Mam's driveway. "The other side of the Haddam Mountains. We guarded the river pass into the mountain range."

Dwarves did that? I was learning so much being here. I wished my brothers and friends in Gilliam had the same opportunity.

I left Brent in the living room and went to my room. I dug out the bag from the back corner of my closet and opened it up for the first time since leaving Gilliam. I didn't have to search too hard; my carvings of Aramis, Antinae, and Radier were right there on top. And one I'd worked on the first few days of traveling, a carving of Sevrin. I'd forgotten about that one. I considered leaving it behind, but maybe Brent would want to see one of my works in progress.

As I tossed the bag back into the closet, a book fell out. *Living your Authentic Life* by Dr. Thaddeus. I stared at the cover for a moment and wondered what Dr. Thaddeus might have to say about my situation. Reading him had helped me say no to Jimmy's proposal, and to move to Leitham.

I set the book on my bed. I would read it later. Dr. Thaddeus could help me decide what to do with my life, help me figure out what I really wanted. Perhaps I could use one of his tools to help me get out of this nightmare I found myself in with Aubrey.

I hugged the carvings next to my body, being as careful as I could with them, and took them down to Brent, who was standing in the living room.

He took the carvings from me. He held them as lovingly as any dwarf I'd ever known. He didn't say anything for the longest time, picking them up one by one, turning them over, smelling them, running his fingers along each etched line, tapping them with the pads of his fingers. He spent the most time with the work in progress, just looking, studying it. Then he started all over again.

No one had ever judged my work so closely, not since I did my masterwork anyway. Everyone had said how amazing that was, a life-size dwarf warrior. Compared to what I'd seen at the gallery, it was garish. Though, I thought I'd improved some since then. The longer Brent looked at my work, the more nervous I became. He was clearly an expert on art, on carvings. I was sure he must think they were horrid. At least he did a good job of keeping his face neutral so I didn't know how bad he thought they were.

After what felt like hours later, he finally stopped picking up the carvings. He arranged them on the table and stood back and looked at them. "Incredible," he said.

Was that good or bad?

"You have an amazing talent. You need an agent."

"Excuse me?"

"An agent. Someone to manage your business dealings and contracts, so you don't get taken advantage of again."

"I wasn't taken advantage of."

"You were. Look, Aramis is a nice bloke. I'm sure he wasn't thinking, but he should have paid you. Your carvings enhanced his movie so he should pay for it. He paid everyone else, no doubt. I want to show you in my gallery, but I have a policy not to accept any work not represented by an agent, that way it's fair for everyone. I'm sure your work will bring in a lot of gems, and many more commissions. You need someone to look after your business interests, make sure you get what you're worth."

I wasn't entirely sure I wanted to carve for a career. I'd had such a great time learning how to edit films from Aramis though I was clumsy at it. It was going to take a long time to get it right. Then again, I loved to carve. I always had, but it was never the kind of activity I could have considered a career, until now. I was intrigued. "How do I get one of these agents?"

Brent smiled. "I work in the industry. I know them all. I'll recommend you to a few of the best ones if you like."

"Oh, that would be great, thanks." I never could have imagined this spectacular adventure.

"Wrap these up in soft leather and put them in a bag, have them ready to go. I'll contact some of the agents this afternoon and arrange for some meetings," Brent said at the door. "Do you want to come back to the gallery with me?"

This was far more excitement than I was used to having in one day. "No, thanks. I think I'm done for the day. Thank you so much, though, for the tour of the gallery, the lift home, and for looking at my carvings."

"My pleasure. I'll see you at the Lair soon. If we aren't going to see agents before then."

"Definitely." I closed the door and leaned against it. Two career possibilities. Both in areas I loved. How was I going to choose?

Dr. Thaddeus had to help me.

CHAPTER 5

FULL OF encouragement after studying Dr. Thaddeus, I slung my bag of carvings over my shoulder as I hurried down the stairs to meet Brent for my first meeting with an agent.

He stood by the front door chatting with Sevrin. For a moment I thought about Da and wondered how he would have treated Brent; if he would have grilled him. Of course he would have. Da had treated every male dwarf I encountered as the one who would be my life-mate. If it was only a question of wealth, Da might have liked him. Except that Brent wasn't a miner, and mating with a miner was more important than anything else to Da. I doubted Da would have tolerated *friendship* with a non-miner.

Sevrin wasn't Da. He and Brent seemed to be

having an amicable enough conversation. I relaxed.

Sevrin had no real investment in me mating. Another good thing about Leitham.

"Here she is," Sevrin said. "It was good meeting you, Brent."

"You too, sir."

"Good luck today." Sevrin patted Brent's shoulder and gave me a hug.

"Ready to go?" Brent asked.

I was sure I grinned like an idiot. An agent was actually interested in my art. I could really earn a living carving and I would still be respectable.

Wouldn't that be something?

Dr. Thaddeus had said that it was worth exploring all options when considering a new career path. He said to try everything, to find out what I really liked, but to be honest with myself. If anything felt wrong or any part of it wasn't enjoyable, I should make note of it and try something new.

This was an opportunity of a life-time, and so far everything about it felt right.

Brent helped me into his cart. He then hopped in beside me and took up the reins.

"What will happen at the meeting?" I asked. I was excited, but I was still nervous. This was all so new to me.

"Olin will have a look at your work and decide if he wants to represent you. He'd be a fool not to, but he is the top agent. It will depend on his client load. Though, frankly, any agent can make room for another client if they really want to sign them. I can't make any guarantees that he'll sign you or anything. I'm hopeful because he's so anxious to see you. On the other hand, you might want to meet with the other agents before you accept any offer, see which ones you like, if you want to work with them."

"Is that possible? That more than one will want to represent me?"

"Without a doubt."

I liked Brent's confidence in me and my work. And he knew the business. I, on the other hand, had no idea how things worked. "Of the agents you've arranged to meet with me, which do you think is the best, and why?"

"That's a tough one. They are all very good. They do very well by their clients though they do have different styles. It's really a matter of taste and personality."

Brent drove us through the residential streets, like he was avoiding the business districts, where the smell was the worst. I appreciated that, but it did feel like we were taking the long way to the dwarven business district. Maybe his nose was sensitive to the stench too.

"The agent we're going to see now, Olin, is probably the biggest, most well known agent. He has a lot of clients, so it is difficult to get him to represent you, because all artists send him their work. His client list is long, some of them are quite famous, but he does have a number that don't earn as much as they would like. If you do well for him, he'll do well by you. He will give you a lot of personal attention to make sure you're looked after, and that you earn as much as possible. His newer clients, and those who aren't the big earners, are assigned to his junior agents. This isn't a bad thing. Junior agents are eager to make a name for themselves. They will do everything they can for you, though they aren't as well known. Chances are, if Olin signs you, you'll be with one of his junior agents, but I don't think you will be for long."

"That seems kind of rude," I said. "Taking over the client after they've started earning. That's like taking credit for the junior agent's work."

"Perhaps, but that is the way the business works, and the junior agents know it. They still share in the commissions received from that client, which often increases their own income when that client is taken over by Olin, so they don't mind."

"So it's like when one of a team of miners discovers a vein or bed of gems. They share a percentage of the gems extracted."

Brent shrugged. "Sure, I guess."

Right. He wasn't a miner. Probably had never been inside a mine. What a pity. For someone with such appreciation for beauty, he really should see the craftsmanship of the mines. Gilliam's entrance cavern alone was a splendid place of beauty that always left everyone awestruck the first time they saw it, and every time after that.

I kind of missed that part of living in Gilliam, walking into the mine every day, and enjoying the cleansing pool and the sparkle of the stalactites and stalagmites, a reward for my hard work at the end of a long day.

"The other agents," Brent continued. "There are two others I'm going to take you to see over the next couple of days. They aren't quite as big names in the industry as Olin is, and their client lists are smaller. Olin and his juniors don't have any specialties; they represent all artists, which sometimes makes things a bit chaotic. Though they provide a lot of personal attention, they maybe aren't as focused on particular markets as they should be. The other two agents, Fion and Varv, both focus on dwarven artists, particularly carvers and gem workers. They will take good care of you as well. Though they may not initially earn you as much as you would under Olin, they know the carving and gemstone markets like no one else, and they'll find you the right places to exhibit and sell your work.

They all sounded great. How was I supposed to decide which one to go with? Ha! Listen to me, assuming they'd all want to sign me on. Just like Emma had assumed all the fellows wanted her.

There was no guarantee any of the agents would want me as a client. I'd be lucky if one of them showed any real interest in my work. Surely compared to all the other art they must see, mine would pale in comparison. I had no real training. I was a miner from Gilliam.

Then again, Aramis was right. I was being too hard on myself. Brent was busy and important in this industry. He wouldn't waste his time if he didn't think I had potential. Not even for a friend.

He pulled up outside a stone cottage at the eastern edge of the city, on the slope of the foothills. "Here we are."

"He works out of here?"

"No. His office is actually in the central Leitham business district. His father died yesterday and this morning was the funeral procession. He's here cleaning up his father's home."

"And he's willing to meet me today?"

"He insisted on it."

Brent helped me down, and I clutched my bag of carvings close to my chest. I followed Brent up the short walk to the front door. Olin must be really dedicated to his work, if he wanted to meet me today of all days, and at his father's home.

Olin, the thinnest male dwarf I'd ever seen, almost as thin as I was, answered the door. He didn't have a thick beard either. It was long, well trimmed and neat, not unkempt and over-grown like most dwarf beards. It was just starting to turn silver, with streaks of light brown fading to white and silver running through it.

"Brent. Good to see you lad. Thanks for coming. And you must be Mabel. Come in, come in. I apologize for not meeting you in my office. This mess, unfortunately, couldn't wait." He stepped over a stack of ceramic dishware in the centre of the floor, one of many piles of household items. "My father was a bit of a hoarder, and it needs to get sorted. I've been after him for years to take care of it. But as always, he left it to me." He pushed some clothes off a couch for us to sit on. Brent found himself a corner on a chair beside the fireplace, not far from me, but far enough to not really be a part of the discussion. "So, Mabel, Brent tells me you're a fantastic talent from Gilliam."

"Thanks." Was that the right thing to say? I had to relax. Dr. Thaddeus stressed the importance of being yourself. He said it was far more important to be liked for who you are than to be liked by everyone. If Olin was going to sign me, I wanted it to be because he liked me and my work for what we were, not for what he thought we were.

Olin smiled. "I understand you've just moved to Leitham."

"Yes, almost three weeks now."

"And what brings you to our fair city?"

My da kicked me out of my own city? I had no choice? "My mam, Frerin, she lives here, so I came to spend some time with her, and find out if there were other opportunities for me besides mining. Like carving." Good answer. Right? *Should I mention the movie editing? Stop. Be myself.*

"I understand you had one of your pieces used in a movie coming out soon."

"Yes. I was working on the movie with Aramis and Mam, I did a bit of acting, but mostly I helped Radier with the recording of the scenes. When things were slow on set, I did some carving, and Aramis liked it and even used one of them. He said it added to the dwarven atmosphere of the set."

"Do you have that piece with you?"

"I do." I finally relaxed my hold on my bag, set it on the floor and pulled out one of the carvings.

Olin took it from me and examined it much the same way Brent had, turning it over, tracing the etched lines. "What kind of career as an artist do you see for yourself?"

"I—" I looked to Brent for help, but he stayed silent. *Be myself.* "I'm sorry, I don't understand."

"Where would you like to see your carvings displayed? Are you interested in showing only in galleries, in parks, in personal homes, or on movie sets."

"Oh, well, I guess when I came here, I'd thought only of movie sets, but I don't know. I didn't know the other things existed, especially the art gallery thing, or, showing in homes, really. That isn't done in Gilliam, that I know of."

Olin looked at the other two carvings I had, studying them for a little while. "Well, Mabel, I like what I see, I think you have a lot of potential and can have a great career as an artist. Thank you very much for stopping by. I'll get back to you in a few days."

That was it?

Brent and I stood. "Thank you very much for agreeing to see me, and my work," I said. Had I offended him?

"You did great, in there," Brent said, as we drove away. "He was very impressed with you and your work."

What interview was he watching? We just got kicked out with no contract. "You think so?"

"He said he'd get back to you in a few days. That is a very good sign. Agents never sign on the first meeting. They have to discuss the client with the other agents in their office, even Olin."

"Yeah, but, doesn't that mean he's already made up his mind that he won't represent me?"

"I don't think so, not the way he was looking at your work. He may have made up his mind to take you on, not turn you down. He's probably only deciding which junior agent will be the best for you, or if he'll work with you himself. Which, by the way, would be unprecedented. He hasn't represented a client at the beginning of their career since he started taking on junior agents."

Brent seemed very sure of himself. I supposed I should listen to him, he knew the business better than anyone, from the other side. He knew the agents, probably had known them for years.

We stopped outside the Dragon's Lair Tavern. "Time to celebrate with some ale."

"Sounds good." I hadn't realized how thirsty I was.

We sat down and Brent ordered two pints of stout ale.

"Thank you so much for taking all this time for me. I really appreciate it."

We raised our glasses and Brent said, "Here's to a profitable and happy future for both of us."

"DO YOU have any questions before we begin?" Aramis asked as I climbed onto the stool beside him.

Like the last time I was here, a small screen was set up in front of us, as were the projection fork and a few wizard's crystals. I couldn't contain my excitement. "So many questions," I said. "Can only wizards record? How do you get the sound on the crystal? How do you copy them for distribution?"

Aramis chuckled, the sound of birdsong. "We will get to all of that. To answer your first question, no, not only wizards can record. In the early days, of course, we thought only they could, but eventually a few of us learned the spell and how to make the crystals vibrate just right. If it were only up to the wizards of this world to record, there would be no movie industry, simply because there are too few of them around, and fewer still interested in making movies."

"What about dwarves." I held up my hands, rough and calloused. For the briefest moment, I thought I saw some stone-dust under my nails, still from the mines. "Our hands are thicker than an elf's or a wizard's. We're used to working with stone and wielding heavy weapons. Are we really able to record and manipulate the wizard's crystal?"

"I have no idea. You are the first one I have met to show any interest in it. The dwarves I know in the business are usually only interested in acting and building sets. I imagine dwarven dexterity with stonework might make you an excellent movie maker and editor. You already know how to be gentle with stone and gems. I am a bit concerned with the calluses, but we may be able to find something that can help soften them if they become a problem."

"As long as it isn't some kind of poison," I said, laughing. Aramis looked aghast. "Sorry, that was a terrible joke."

"Oh," he said after a moment. "I get it. Like the medicine Emma gave you."

"Right." I cleared my throat. "Anyway. I've read loads on making movies, but start from the beginning. Teach me everything."

Aramis started with some of the early history of the wizard's crystal; the methods used to replicate the early recording process. There was sound in the first recording ever done, but that had been by accident and Radier hadn't known what he'd done to record anything in the first place. Turned out he'd stubbed his toe and knocked his staff against a stone causing the crystal to vibrate. He'd sworn in elvish, which ended up being the spell needed to add the sound.

The early efforts were disasters, often resulting in nothing more than shattered crystals. Once the right combination of spell and vibration was determined, adding sound was next. Several trials later, Radier and Aramis had it figured out. "We still use many of the same techniques as we used back then. There have been attempts at modification but they either do not work as well as the original ones, or they do not work at all," Aramis said.

"The first key to capturing a great recording is knowing how to set the crystal in the fork," Aramis continued "On first appearances, the crystal looks perfectly smooth and oval shaped. On closer inspection, you will notice that there is a definitive top and bottom. Go ahead, pick up the crystal and see if you can spot what I am talking about."

I tentatively picked up the crystal. "I'm terrified of crushing it or scratching it. If I hold it too loosely, though, I'll drop it."

"It is not easy to break," Aramis said. "It is magic that shatters them, not dropping them or holding them too tightly."

I turned the crystal over in my hands, feeling its smoothness, flipping it over and over, until I saw a pin-prick of an indentation on one end. "That's the bottom," I said, pointing to it."

"Exactly. The crystals are held in place by a needle-thin spindle on the wizard's staff. We have replicated that on the recording and projection fork." Aramis handed me one to look at.

The last time I'd been in here, I had seen him using the fork with the crystals, and I'd done some work tapping the crystals. This was the first time I'd really had a chance to study one. I had to squint, but I could see the spindle in the center, where the two tines divided. It wasn't very high. "It's tiny. How does it keep the crystal in place?"

"There is just enough stability. We do not want it to have too much or it would stop the vibrations from having any effect on the crystal." Aramis had me put the crystal on the fork, which I managed to do on my third try. "Very good. Now, do you want to learn how to edit or how to record?"

I hesitated for half a second. I had come here only to learn how to edit but… "Both."

Aramis smiled. "Very good." He pointed out the front and the back of the crystal. "To record the visual only, take this metal rod and tap the tines here."

He turned the crystal so that it was facing us. I picked up a small metal rod, the size and thickness of a quill, and tapped the tines where Aramis had shown. The tines and the crystal were soon vibrating. "Now make some faces or gestures," Aramis said.

I did the only thing I knew how to do. I pretended to throw an axe. The motion felt incredibly awkward. I decided I wouldn't do that again for a long time.

"Good. Now stop the vibrations by holding the rod against the tines."

I did so.

Aramis turned the crystal around to face the

screen. "Take the crystal out, shake it three times, put it back, and tap the other tine."

I did, and my recording started showing on the screen. I squealed with delight. "I did that. I did it! It's that easy?"

"Recording with the right knowledge and equipment, yes, it is that easy."

"How do I get the sound?"

"That is much harder. We discovered that to add sound we needed a specific spell, an elvish curse, actually. For sound alone, it does not need to vibrate, but if we want the two together, the crystal needs to be tapped just right and the spell said at the same time, in a certain cadence, and your breath on the crystal to seal the spell."

"So why, in Gilliam, did Radier keep muttering the spell?" I asked.

"Old habits are hard to break. It was the way we first thought it had to be done. We have discovered otherwise since then. Obviously in the first recording he had not been uttering the spell the entire time. I think he feels more secure knowing the spell will keep the sound in the recording. Either way is fine. I prefer not to have to mutter the spell over and over."

We spent the rest of the lesson with me trying to get the crystal to record sound alone. We decided to stop for the day after an hour of me trying. I was getting closer to saying the spell right, but I would need a lot more practice, and Aramis had other things to do.

"Here." Aramis handed me a couple of wizard's crystals and a recording fork. "Keep trying at home. Come back maybe next week and show me what you were able to do. I will help with any difficulties. Once that is sorted, we can move on to the editing process."

Of everything I had learned from Dr. Thaddeus about being myself and recognizing where my true passions lay, I was pretty sure I'd found it. Making movies.

I NEEDED a break from practicing with the wizard's crystal, and my meeting with Brent and Fion wasn't for another day. I decided to go for a walk, to get to know the neighborhood. I knew Studio City and the business district better than where I lived. Dr. Thaddeus said that in order to feel truly comfortable and at home somewhere, I had to take the time to get to know it. I hadn't done that with the neighborhood and it was time I did.

I also missed walking. In Gilliam, I'd walked everywhere. Here the only walking I'd done was from the door to the cart and back. If being so sedentary had helped me grow stout maybe I wouldn't mind, but I wasn't gaining any weight so there seemed no point to it. It would have been nice to tell Da that, since he'd argued I shouldn't throw axes because it was preventing me from gaining weight. It kind of felt good to prove him wrong. And not just about gaining or not gaining weight; in Leitham, stoutness wasn't necessary to be considered attractive or a sign of dwarfling-bearing prowess. And if that was the case here, it might be the case elsewhere.

I took the leather satchel Mam had given me and a set of keys for the house and gate. It was a beautiful day, hardly a cloud in the sky. It wasn't too hot or too cold. The trees offered enough shade but didn't block the sun entirely. A high stone wall ran along both sides of the road, and every few steps, there was a stone carving inset in an alcove of the wall. Each statue depicted something different; a dwarf, a battle from our history, or scenes from every-day dwarven life.

I was enjoying one of these carvings of a young family playing mage-stones, when a particularly strong scent of oak tree overwhelmed me. Aramis? I smiled and turned around to see Aubrey standing behind me. I took a step back, right into the wall.

"Hello, Mabel," Aubrey said, sneering. He was relaxed, casual, like it was entirely normal for him to be in a dwarven neighborhood out for a walk, chatting with anyone he encountered. "I am so pleased I ran into you."

I trembled. He was too close and I was too short. I couldn't escape his reach.

"I see so much of Millie... I beg your pardon, Frerin, in you," he continued. "She was so sweet. So young and eager to make a difference."

Which you preyed on.

"She was a bit rude to me, after I had done so much for you. Rather ungrateful, really." Aubrey took a half-step closer. I couldn't back up any farther, but I tried, pressing myself into the wall, wishing it could absorb me, that there was a secret gate that would open only for me.

"You see, promises were made, Mabel. I do not agree on a whim to help someone. Do forgive me, but, *especially* not a dwarf. Commitments were made, and they need to be honored. Do you not agree?"

Not yet. It was far too soon. I had nothing to offer.

"Carving? Statuary? A career as an artist. It is a decent start. I heard your meeting with Olin went very well. My percentage from your earnings will do nicely, for now."

I never should have gone out on my own. What was I going to do? All the homes were set too far back from the road. Even if they weren't, the wall would stifle any noise from my screams. No one would come to help me. Sevrin wasn't home and neither was Mam. They wouldn't know to look for me.

I felt myself sagging. He was manipulating me. I forced myself to straighten.

He leaned in. "Do I destroy your loving Mam, Mabel? She has so much more to lose now. More wealth, more friends, higher social standing... so much more than a litter of dwarflings," he snarled.

A sudden, sharp, stabbing pain ripped through

my shoulder. I cried out, sinking to my knees. He hadn't touched me and he still triggered his magic.

"It is up to you," Aubrey said. He backed up and the moment he did the pain was gone again. "Think about it."

"MABEL." BRENT nudged my leg.

My attention snapped back to Brent, and the cart, and the agent we were about to go see. "Sorry, what?"

"Are you all right? You've been distracted and you completely went somewhere else there for a few minutes."

No, I wasn't all right. I'd been distracted and horrified since Aubrey approached me two days ago. "Yes, I'm fine. Just nervous about seeing…" Which one was it again? "Fion."

"Varv. Fion was yesterday."

Right. I knew that. This was the third agent meeting. I wanted this, I did, but every meeting, just spending time with Brent, was a risk to all of them. The meetings attracted Aubrey's attention. "Sorry."

"No need to be nervous. Both Olin and Fion were impressed by you. Varv will be just as impressed, I'm sure. You're a brilliant artist. They'd be fools not to offer to represent you."

It meant the world to me that Brent thought so highly of my carvings. He was such an expert in the field. It reminded me a lot of when I began mining and axe-throwing, and how impressed my brothers were of me and my work. It wouldn't matter how talented I was. I couldn't possibly accept an offer if one was made. I had to stay hidden if I wanted Aubrey to leave my new family alone.

Not to mention my concern about what Aubrey may or may not have done to me. I wouldn't tell Mam or Sevrin until I knew for sure. I wanted to see Dr. Thora the moment Aubrey left me that day, but to make an appointment that wasn't already scheduled... I didn't know how to do it without telling Mam or Sevrin what had happened. Thankfully I had an appointment to see her in a couple of days. I hoped she had some good news for me, that she could somehow remove the elven magic.

With my debt to Aubrey, it felt pointless to still meet with Varv. I'd only kept it, and the one with Fion, because I didn't want to let Brent down. He'd gone to so much trouble to set up these meetings. To bow out now would also make him look bad. Realistically, though, even if all the agents wanted to represent me, I wouldn't expose them to Aubrey.

Maybe, if one of them wanted to represent me, there could be a way to make some kind of arrangement that wouldn't hurt anyone. I am nothing, if not a dreamer.

"Mabel." Brent nudged me again.

"Sorry."

Brent squeezed my hand.

That caught my attention. What was happening?

Did Brent like me? I hoped so.

We pulled up in front of an office building not far from Dr. Thora's. There was no sign to indicate who occupied the space. Brent let go of my hand and it was all business again.

Maybe he didn't like me.

He helped me out of the cart, but instead of walking to the office, he stood there for a minute, standing so close. He caressed my cheek, my stubbly beard, which was finally starting to grow back.

Oh. Oh! He did like me! But I hadn't done anything. I hadn't flirted. I didn't even have braids in my beard! I'd just been myself—exactly the way Dr. Thaddeus said I should be.

"We should go in." He almost sounded reluctant to say it.

I smiled and relaxed. Brent liked me!

I took my bag of carvings from the cart and held it close. I really hoped Dr. Thora had some good news for me. I needed to be free of the elven magic so that all of this would be all right.

I'd expected Varv's office to look much like Dr. Thora's, with a receptionist and a few smaller offices off of the waiting room. Instead, there was only the one room with two large desks facing each other in the middle, though only one was occupied, and a smaller table with a few chairs around it in the corner.

Varv's thick shiny silver hair and beard suggested he was old, but his unlined face hinted otherwise. He rose from his desk and greeted us. We were the only ones in the room. "It's good to meet you, Mabel," he said, ushering us to the small table in the corner. "Brent has told me a lot about your work, and I'm excited to have the opportunity to see it firsthand. Let's have a look, shall we?"

He didn't waste any time on small talk. I liked that. I supposed I should want an agent who was interested in getting to know me, but Varv seemed to already know. I passed him my bag with the carvings and sat there quietly while he pulled them out, setting them on the table. I wondered if I should say anything, but I thought it best to let him take the lead, so I kept my mouth shut. I was being myself, just a quieter version.

He lined up the carvings on the table, looking at them as a group. Then he picked up the carving of Aramis, holding it close to his face, as though if he could touch it to his eye, he would. Like Olin and Fion, he touched every etched line and filed surface. He held it like he was weighing it, tapping it like he was checking the quality of the stone. He mumbled every now and then, what sounded to me like "excellent craftsmanship" and "elegant simplicity," but that might just have been wishful thinking on my part.

He picked up the next carving and studied it just as closely. And then he looked at the third. When he finished, he looked at me. "I think your work is fantastic. It's obvious you have a gift and the skill to have a great career. I'll be in touch soon."

I stood, and packed up my carvings. "Thank you for your time."

Minutes later I was back on Brent's cart. "This is incredible, Mabel. I expect the offers to be rolling in very soon."

"Thanks." That was all I could get out, and even then, barely. The possibilities of it all overwhelmed me.

Brent rubbed my back. "What is it?"

I shook my head. I couldn't tell him. He'd been so kind, so sweet, such a good friend. "It's nothing. Just can't believe it's happening."

"I thought you'd be happier about it."

If it weren't for Aubrey, I would be. "I am. I just feel unworthy. I only have three-and-a-half carvings. That's nothing. It's going to take me a while to make more carvings. What if it takes too long for them?"

"Doesn't matter how long it takes. They'd rather you take your time and produce beautiful work than rush yourself and have poor quality work."

Maybe taking my time was a good idea. Aubrey would lose interest, or at least figure out that I have nothing for him.

Stabbing pain ripped through my shoulder. I cried out and grabbed at my arm. Where had the pain come from? Why was it happening now?

"Mabel, what's wrong?" Brent reached for me.

The pain didn't stop. It hurt too much. I couldn't speak or I'd cry.

Out of the corner of my eye, I saw Aubrey

standing on the opposite side of the street. He smiled. When I blinked he was gone. The pain remained.

CHAPTER 6

THE PAIN was so severe I thought I was going to pass out. I should have. It was worse than when I shredded it at Regionals and I'd briefly passed in and out of consciousness then.

"Mabel, talk to me," Brent said. "What happened?"

Dr. Thora's office wasn't far. My official appointment with her wasn't for a couple of days. I couldn't wait. I had to see her now. The pain was overwhelming. I couldn't talk. It took all my energy and focus to stay conscious. "Dr. Th—" It was all I could get out. Tears fell and darkness edged my vision.

"Dr. Thora. Got it," Brent said. He snapped the reigns and within moments we stopped outside her office.

He helped me out of the cart, and walked me inside, his arm around me to keep me upright and moving.

Stacie said nothing when she saw me. She simply ushered me straight into Dr. Thora's office. If there was anyone in the waiting room, I didn't notice. I didn't care.

Brent waited with me until Dr. Thora came, which probably was only a minute or two, but even that was too long. "I'll be just outside," he said softly.

The moment he was gone, I tried to speak. "Aubrey—"

"Triggered it," Dr. Thora concluded for me. She looked down at the parchment in front of her for a moment. "Then this won't be necessary, not that it was helpful anyway. I consulted with a number of my colleagues and as advanced as our medicine is, we have no way of freeing you of the dormant magic. Obviously that is irrelevant now. Let me have a look, see if I can assess the extent of the damage done. Perhaps he removed his magic, in which case we may have some options."

That seemed a little optimistic, though it would have been nice. I couldn't imagine Aubrey would give up his means of controlling me.

Dr. Thora put a hand on my shoulder and gently massaged it, feeling the scar tissue and the extent of the injury and determining my mobility which was non-existent.

After some more tests, she said, "The damage is extensive, and the magic is still there. I am going to prescribe you some medicine made of pixie dust, which has a special healing quality to it. It is a salve you'll need to rub on your shoulder three times a day. It will keep the damage from spreading and hopefully reduce the pain. It should be able to work around the magic. In the meantime, I will go back to my colleagues. Perhaps there is something else that will work.

"I won't lie, Mabel. This isn't good. I will still do what I can for you with the physical damage, but this may be beyond any of our capabilities." She scribbled something on a small parchment and handed it to me. "Take that to the apothecary on your way home."

"Thank you, Dr. Thora." I didn't feel thankful. I felt like all the good things that had happened to me since I'd arrived in Leitham were being torn away from me. I felt trapped. Precisely the way Aubrey wanted me to feel.

"While the salve is working, you are at risk of causing greater damage to your shoulder so I need you to be extra careful. Keep your arm in a sling at all times. No exceptions, and I do mean *no* exceptions."

It would have been difficult to go back to immobilizing my arm if I'd only been able to use it for one day. By now I'd had too much freedom. I'd used it for a couple of weeks. Even back in Gilliam, when I was still in a lot of pain but had started to heal, I could use it on occasion. This was such a setback. At least Dr. Thora was giving me something to improve things, a salve we didn't have access to in Gilliam. "Got it."

"Good. I want to keep a close eye on this. Come and see me the same time next week."

Brent drove me home. We were both silent. I thought about the agents we'd met with. I was expecting to hear from them in the next few days. Would they still represent me now, with my wounded shoulder? I wouldn't be able to carve. Did I want them too? If Aubrey controlled me, he would control them.

Was that really so bad? So I gave him a cut of my earnings? I wouldn't hurt any more, I could have a life, and he would leave Mam alone.

I WAS grateful neither Sevrin nor Mam were home by the time I got there after my appointment with Dr. Thora. I had no idea how I was going to tell them what had happened. They knew about the trigger, of course, but Sevrin believed his friends were protecting me so this shouldn't have happened. Aramis had added reinforcements. How could I tell them that their efforts hadn't worked?

I just had to say it. That's all I could do. Or simply be in the living room with my arm in the sling when they got home.

I had yet to get comfortable in front of the fireplace—without a fire—when Mam walked in, Lillian behind her, laughing and smiling. I'd forgotten Lillian was going to pick me up and take me to the Lair.

The smile vanished off Mam's face the second she saw me. "What happened?"

"Can we talk about it later?" I asked. I didn't want to discuss it in front of Lillian, and I wanted to wait for Sevrin to be here so I only had to say it once.

"What were you and Brent doing to hurt your arm so bad it needs a sling?" Lillian teased.

"I wish," I replied, though I wasn't in a witty-banter kind of mood. It was a natural reflex developed out of every conversation I'd had with my brothers Kenneth and Ross.

"Do you, now? I'm sure we can make that happen," she said.

"Lillian, can you give us a few moments?" Mam asked.

"Of course. I need to freshen up anyway before we head out."

"I don't think I'm going to go with you," I said. I couldn't. Not with the pain I was in. What if Aubrey found me again and made things even worse? If Aubrey found me with my friends, he might go after them. What would I tell them, about any of this?

"Yes, you are," Mam said. "Just a few minutes, Lillian. You can freshen up upstairs. I'll call you when we're done."

Mam waited until we heard Lillian's footsteps on the second floor before turning to me. "When and where did he do this to you?"

"This afternoon. I'd just left my meeting with an agent." My voice hitched. I paused a moment to get it back under control. Mam was so composed. I wanted to be as strong as she was. "I'd just gotten onto Brent's cart. Aubrey was on the opposite side of the street."

Mam cursed. "Sevrin will look into it and figure out how Aubrey got near you. I'll talk with him. Don't you worry about it. Just go out and have a good time with your friends," she said with a smile, curling a lock of my hair around her finger.

"I can't," I said. "I mean, I'd like to, but it hurts too much." The pain was so much more excruciating than when I'd shredded it during the regional competition in Mitchum.

It had been a brutal trip home from Regionals, riding in the cart, constantly banging my shoulder against my brothers or the edge of the cart with every bump or turn. At least then I'd had some proper medication from the medics at the competition. I wished I had some of it now. I almost wanted the poison Emma had given me. Sure it had made my injury worse, but at least it left me completely numb to the pain. The salve from Dr. Thora hadn't made any difference in the pain yet, though I supposed it needed more than one application before it would have any real effect. Without some kind of relief,

I couldn't bear the thought of going out in a cart. It had been bad enough just getting here after my appointment with Dr. Thora.

"Did Dr. Thora give you anything to help with the pain?"

"She did." I showed Mam the pixie-dust salve. I was willing to be patient about it this time. At least I'd learned that much; that proper medicine takes time to be effective, and the results are much longer lasting, and way more beneficial, than some quick fix.

"That's good stuff, there. Excellent." Mam was quiet for a moment. "What about if you were to invite your friends over here? This place is big enough to fit all the tavern's patrons three-fold. Sevrin and I will stay out of your way."

A part of me liked the idea, but most of me was terrified and upset. I just wanted to go to bed and sleep off the pain. It didn't help that I rarely had more than one or two friends over back in Gilliam. I wasn't very good at hosting parties and I wasn't really in the right mood for it. But there was one thing that overshadowed all of that. "Is that really a good idea? Aubrey's watching me. He has to know who I'm friends with. It's only a matter of time before he goes after them. He's already proven he can get to me whenever and wherever he wants. Nothing is going to stop him. I agreed to letting him heal me. I will deal with the consequences. But I won't let him hurt anyone else."

"Which is probably why it is better to have your friends here," Mam said. "Within these walls we can protect you. When Aubrey did this to you, did he say what he wants from you?"

Not this time, but he had before, when he threatened me. I hadn't told Mam about that, I could use it now. "He wants a portion of whatever I earn off my carvings. He didn't say how much he wanted, just that he expected more from me but this was a start. He did this as a reminder of what he would do if I refused." I motioned to my shoulder. I didn't bother to mention his threats against Mam. It was unnecessary, and I would find a way to stop him from carrying them out.

"Sweetheart. I understand your concern. I really do. But I am not going to allow him to ruin your new life in Leitham. You did not come here to hide out in our home forever, alone, with no friends."

I appreciated everything she said, but the pain and Aubrey's threats made it difficult for me to think about anything else.

"You just sit down here, make yourself comfortable. I'll talk with Lillian, have her bring your friends here. I'll make sure they understand that they are not to stay long. All right?"

I nodded. I could see there was no point in arguing. She had the same intractably determined look and tone as my brother Mikey.

"Lillian," Mam called up the stairs. "Come down when you're ready. There's been a change in plans."

Moments later, Lillian was in the living room, her hair freshly brushed and braided, and wearing a clean gold tunic and trouser set. "Everything all right?"

"I'm just not in a good place to go out," I said. "So Mam said it was all right if I invited you all over here for a bit. You don't have to, of course, but would you mind going to the Lair and seeing if the others would like to come here instead?"

"There are plenty of drinks and snacks in the kitchen," Mam said. "If you don't mind being the host for Mabel?"

"Aww, that would be brilliant," Lillian said. "A great change from always being at the tavern. It will be so much fun. I'm sure the others will love it. I shouldn't be long," she said and left.

While we waited, Mam built up the fire and prepared some food.

I hadn't moved from the time Lillian left to the time she returned with the others. The only thing that had changed was that Mam had brought me an as-yet untouched tankard of ale which I'd set beside me.

I was glad that everyone had agreed to come here instead of staying at the Lair. It really made me feel like I was one of them. I had a good set of new friends.

Lillian issued a quick instructional tour, pointing out where the key rooms were, then disappeared into the kitchen with Sam to gather food and drinks. I was grateful she was here to show everyone around and look after anything they needed.

"Lillian told us you were hurt and that you'd seen Dr. Thora," Chris said, sitting beside me. "What did she say?"

I gave them the general gist of it all without going into any details about Aubrey or elven magic.

"Can she fix it?" Hannah asked.

"She isn't sure," I said.

"What happened, anyway?" Sam asked, coming in with a tray of tankards.

"My axe-throwing injury," I said. "I'd thought it had gone away, but apparently not. I must have been using it too much."

Brent stood behind me and squeezed my good shoulder as I talked. He knew I was lying.

"Frerin's your mam, right?" Jeff asked from the middle of the living room.

I noticed for the first time that he'd been standing there and was turning in slow circles, studying every element in the room, the furnishings and the architecture. "Yes, she is," I said.

"Where is she?" he asked.

"Out back," I said.

"Hmm, I see," he said, nodding.

Lillian came in carrying a platter of smoked pork, cheeses, and apple slices. "I'll be right back with the mushrooms," she said, disappearing again, this time only for a few seconds.

"What's happening here?" Sevrin said, entering the living room. His gaze went straight to my right arm and sling.

Behind me, Jeff choked on his drink.

"Mam said it was okay," I said, then introduced Sevrin to my friends.

"A great idea," he said. He tore his eyes off my arm. "Have yourselves a wonderful time. Mabel, where's Frerin?"

"Out back," I said. I felt like asking if anyone else needed to know where she was.

Sevrin kissed me on the top of my head. "I'm going to talk with her and Aramis about this," he whispered. To the others he said, "Wonderful meeting you all."

"Nice meeting you too," Chris and Hannah said.

We had a good time talking and laughing, coming up with ideas for the movie Lillian and I were still apparently going to make. It didn't take long before I started to fade. At first I'd been right in on the conversation, now I couldn't work up the energy to speak.

Brent noticed right away. "I think it's time we get going," he said. "Let me know the minute you hear from any of the agents, all right?"

"I will," I said. There was no point to getting an agent now, not until my shoulder was at least a little bit better and certainly not until Aubrey had been dealt with.

"Yeah, I should get going too," Sam said. "I have an early call time tomorrow on set."

"Me too," Chris said. "Thanks for having us over,

Mabel. I say we do these house parties more often. Next week, you're all invited to my place."

"Love it," Hannah said. "We'll be there." She hugged me and said, "I hope your shoulder gets better soon."

The four left, leaving Lillian and Jeff. Lillian cleaned up the food and dishes while Jeff sat beside me. He didn't say anything, just sat there, staring at my family portrait over the mantle. I didn't want to be rude, but all I could think was, *would you leave already?*

"Jeff," Lillian said, tapping him on the shoulder. "Come on. Let's go. Mabel's exhausted."

He looked surprised by this revelation. "Oh, oh, right. Yeah." He looked to the kitchen, in the direction of the back door.

He was waiting for Sevrin or Mam to come back. I was pretty sure that after Mam had told Sevrin about Aubrey triggering his magic, Sevrin had gone to talk with Aramis and their friends who were supposed to be protecting us. I presumed Mam had gone with him. While I didn't know for sure they'd gone, if they had, I had no idea when they would be back. I wasn't going to wait up for them, and I had no intention of sitting with Jeff or anyone else while they waited for Mam and Sevrin.

If Jeff was that keen to see them again, though, I would give him a few minutes more.

"I'm going to bed," I said. "Lillian, before you and Jeff leave, can you help me?"

"Of course."

She followed me to my room.

"Sorry about Jeff," she said. "I'll get him out of here as soon as possible."

"No worries," I said. "I just wanted to thank you for tonight. You've been so understanding and helpful."

"Hey," she said with a smile. "That's what friends are for."

Emma had been my friend. Even when she was decent to me, she would never have been as under-standing as Lillian.

"Thank you," I said again, this time hugging her.

"Listen. You get some sleep and I'll check in on you tomorrow, okay?"

I nodded.

"Do you need some help changing?"

"No, I think I've got it," I said. "Maybe."

"Let's be sure," she said. She helped me undress, then reached under my pillow, pulling out my pajamas, and helping me into them. I was too exhausted to be embarrassed. "I'll leave a note for Frerin, thank her for the food and drinks, and let her know you're safely tucked in."

I groaned and cringed as I climbed into bed. The mere act of moving, of lying down, was pure agony. The pain overwhelmed me. I had no choice but to give in to it.

"Sleep well, Mabel. I'll see you tomorrow."

"'Night," I said.

I closed my eyes, grateful that even with the threats, the pain, the delay of, or potential loss of, my carving career, I had Mam, Sevrin and Aramis to look after me. And even more important, that I had friends, especially Brent and Lillian. With their help, I could get through anything.

I SAT in the living room setting up my recording fork and wizard's crystal. The pixie dust salve started working a lot faster than I'd thought possible. Within two days, the worst of the pain was gone. It was still bad enough that I couldn't do anything with my arm and it was best to keep it immobile, but at least I wasn't in constant, unbearable agony.

I decided not to go with Mam to Studio City, at least not for a little while. I asked her to let Aramis know I appreciated the lessons in editing, but I just wasn't up to going out. I was still practicing with the crystal, and wouldn't mind having more time with it.

I wasn't feeling sorry for myself, though it would have been easy to do, and sitting around the house, nursing my pain, was incredibly tempting.

Home felt like the safest place for me to be. It was the one place where I was certain Aubrey couldn't reach me.

Staying safe and giving the salve more time to work while I figured out what I was going to do, those were my priorities now. When I was finished practicing, I planned to read Dr. Thaddeus again.

On the one hand, being injured made things a lot easier for me. I could stay this way and I would never be able to work which meant I would never have to pay Aubrey anything. Indeed, I had no need to now. He'd nullified the agreement.

Except I had a pretty strong feeling Aubrey wasn't going to leave me this way. He would be an idiot if he did.

Then again, maybe I had just been a play thing to him. He healed me, had a bit of fun threatening me and when he tired of it, he'd hurt me again. I could only hope he'd lost interest in me.

If that was the case, then I would happily take my time, let Dr. Thora and her pixie-dust salve do the job. I'd be pain free enough to work eventually.

If I was just Aubrey's play thing, and he did lose interest in me, I'd be happier if I had no more of his elven magic in me. As long as it was in my shoulder, Aubrey could always come back and control me.

I refused to think about that. I would just think about taking my time to heal and enjoying Mam and my friends, for now.

I jumped in my seat when someone knocked on the door. My first thought was that it was Aubrey. I had to stop allowing thoughts of him consume me. If it really was Aubrey, he would not have the courtesy to knock.

I shuffled to the door, still not sure I should actually answer it. I peeked through the window beside the door and breathed a sigh of relief. It was Brent, preparing to knock again.

"Brent," I said, opening the door. "Come in. What brings you by?"

"A couple of things. How are you?" he asked, following me into the kitchen.

"All right. The salve from Dr. Thora is working some, but I have a long way to go before I'm even close to being as well as I was when I first arrived, which wasn't particularly good." I pointed out where the glasses and ale were.

Brent poured two tankards and we sat at the table. "What really happened, Mabel?"

My instinct was to deflect, but I felt I owed Brent an explanation. I hated others playing with my future, making decisions for me. Da had tried. Aubrey was doing it. I wouldn't do that to Brent. He needed to know everything so that he could use all the information to decide if he wanted to be my friend.

I took a deep breath. "Aubrey, Lord of the Elven Mafia." I explained everything to Brent that had happened and Aubrey's threats.

He took it all in stride, with no judgment, no fear. He simply asked, "Dr. Thora believes she can help?"

"Some. Neither of us know how much. I hope I'll be able to carve eventually, but it won't be for a long time."

"I'm so sorry," he said. "Your carving was the other reason I came here. I've heard from Varv and

Fion. They were both in my gallery this morning on other business. They are both very interested in representing you."

He fished in his pocket and pulled out two envelopes. He opened them for me and passed me the letters. Their offers were incredible. They were both so flattering of my talent and skill. They said my work would show in the best galleries and that they had connections to those who would pay impressive commissions. They each listed their plans to represent my work.

"Wow. That's all I can say. Just... wow." I put down the letters. "I'm sorry."

"For what?"

"I wasted your time, and theirs. I knew Aubrey would come after me, and he did. Of course I didn't know he would do this to me, but he did, and now I can't carve, so there's no point to it."

"Your shoulder will improve."

"That's true, but that's not the point. When I am able to carve, Aubrey wants a cut of my profits. Once he's taking a cut from me, what's to stop him from threatening whichever agent I choose until they start having to pay him?"

"That does make it tougher. Something we should give a lot more thought to. Don't make any decisions just yet. We still need to hear back from Olin. In the meantime, think about how you want to respond, which agent you'd prefer to work with. We can go back to them, explain the injury situation, not in detail, just that it is going to take time before you can carve again. We would have to leave off the part about Aubrey for the moment. When we do tell him, whichever agent you choose will want to work in some additional financial protections for themselves, and whatever galleries show you or commission you into your contract."

It sounded entirely reasonable. If the agent was willing to wait for me, then I could be patient with this. "Varv," I said. "I liked him the most. I don't need to hear from Olin. I think Varv would be the best one for me. I'll stop in and talk to him in a few days, after my next appointment with Dr. Thora."

CHAPTER 7

TRAVELING TO see Dr. Thora wasn't quite so bad this time. It wasn't that I'd become accustomed to the smell, because the stench of the city was as bad as ever. It was because I was pre-occupied. I hadn't noticed my shoulder improving much with her pixie-dust salve. The level of pain had lessened a bit at first, but had leveled off quickly and was still too much. This did not make me happy and certainly did not give me any hope for any actual healing to take place. I was thinking about the lack of progress in fixing my shoulder, and about Aubrey, as always. He consumed me.

Dr. Thora was the best doctor in Leitham. I had to be patient.

"I know this is difficult for you, Mabel," Sevrin

said, turning the corner and parking in front of Dr. Thora's office. "But I promise, you will get better."

"I know. I'm just not very good at being patient."

Stacie welcomed us and ushered me right into Dr. Thora's office. "I like your tunic," she said.

"Thanks." It was one of the new ones Lillian had helped me pick out. The thin material was remarkably comfortable, especially on my injury. It didn't put any extra weight on my shoulder when any touch, never mind an ounce of pressure, was too much. And the seams were negligible so they didn't irritate it either. "How are your studies going?" I asked.

"Fantastic," she said. "I'm almost ready for my internship."

"Great news. Maybe you can practice on me."

"I'd love to."

A few minutes later, Dr. Thora walked in, smiling. "How are you doing, Mabel?" She asked.

"I don't know how to answer that. I think I feel worse than before."

"Really? In what way?"

"The pain hasn't changed. It isn't worse, but it isn't less either, which I guess is all right. What's bothering me is that my shoulder feels weaker. I know it sounds strange because the pain stops me from using my arm entirely. Somehow I feel like even if I could use it, I wouldn't be able to."

"Hmmm. Let me have a look." She put one hand on my shoulder, feeling the scars, the tears. She massaged it in what I assumed she thought was a gentle touch though it made me cringe and bite my bottom lip to keep from screaming. I turned away so she couldn't see the way she made me cry. She then rotated my arm a little, testing my range of motion, of which there was still none.

"The salve is working very well. There is a lot of scar tissue which the salve is breaking up. It's also working on the extremities of the reach of the elven magic, trying to reduce its effects. I need you to keep using the salve, for several more weeks at least, to give it time to work. Your concerns are reasonable, however. Your muscles are starting to atrophy.

"Continue to keep your arm immobile, but I want you to do some exercises with it twice a day. By exercises, I don't mean using it. What I want you to do is rest your right hand on your left, and using the strength in your left arm, raise your right and lower it, only as much as you are comfortable with. Like this." Dr. Thora showed me what to do, then helped me with it until I'd raised my arm five times. "These exercises are just to give you a bit of mobility and help the blood circulate into those muscles. The rest of the time, keep your arm in the sling. The muscles will be better able to heal that way, with the help of the improved circulation. Once your muscles have been strengthened, and we've reduced the scar tissue, we'll discuss what options you have. All right?"

"Sure."

After she made a few notes, Dr. Thora closed my file. "I will see you in a week."

"Thank you, Dr. Thora."

I made my follow-up appointment with Stacie then walked with Sevrin to our cart. I glanced in the direction of Varv's office. I had to do something about that soon. I just couldn't deal with it today.

Both Sevrin and I were quiet all the way home. I should not have been so sullen, but this whole thing was depressing me. The constant pain and weakness was exhausting enough. What was really wearing me out was worrying about Aubrey.

By the time we arrived home, I could barely keep my eyes open. "I think I need a nap. Can you wake me up in an hour?"

"Sure, honey," Sevrin said.

I liked that he called me honey, like we were family. A real family, where he would look out for me, and protect me, and always want the best for me. Not that my family in Gilliam didn't do all of that. They did, as long as I fit into what they expected of me. Sevrin was seeing me at my very worst, with no set path in life, and yet he still cared about me. He didn't expect anything from me. His silence, his just letting me be, was proof of that.

"Thanks." I climbed the stairs to my room. This was unusual for me, I never napped. Something was wrong with me.

"Are you all right?" Sevrin asked from the bottom of the stairs.

I shook my head, unable to give voice to the "No" my brain and heart were screaming.

"Do you really want a nap, or would some ale by the fire help?"

I didn't really know, but thought the ale might be better. Sleeping wouldn't make this go away. Maybe not being alone was what I really needed. "Only if you join me." I walked back down the stairs.

Sevrin smiled and put an arm around me and kissed the top of my head. We walked to the living room and I sat in front of the fireplace while Sevrin fetched us some ale and built up the fire.

I caught Sevrin looking at the family portrait. "Does it bother you?" I asked. "Having that there?"

He was quiet for a moment. "Not really. I won't lie, it isn't my favorite thing in the house. I think far too often it only serves to remind Frerin of her loss. At the same time, your family is very much a part of her. They will likely never know it, but everything she does is for them, for you. Everything."

I could see it, now that I knew her. I nodded and sat back.

Within minutes we both leaned back and closed our eyes. It reminded me of home, with my da and brothers, though it was never this quiet. At any given time, half my brothers were working, and the other half sleeping and snoring loud enough to rattle the house. Still, it was nice, it was family, even if Sevrin was old enough to be my grandda.

———

I HATED being patient. Especially if I didn't really have to. Sure the solution would be messy, but the more I thought about it, the less messy it seemed.

Staying home and being unable to do much of anything but read Dr. Thaddeus and practice with the wizard's crystal had given me nothing but time to think about Aubrey. I was becoming sorely tempted to just go out for a walk alone, in hopes that it would lure him into finding me. I would confront him then, and tell him that he'd breached our agreement by injuring me, thereby nullifying it. I owed him nothing.

It wouldn't fix the injury, but it would end the threat and I could get on with my life.

I lay in bed and pulled the blankets closer around me. For the third day after my appointment with Dr. Thora, I had no energy to get up, to do much of anything.

"Mabel?" Sevrin asked, knocking on my door.

I sat up, wiped my face, took a deep breath and said, "Come in."

He poked his head in. "Hiya, pet. A letter came for you." He handed me an envelope with a big grin. "It might help cheer you up."

It was a letter from my brother Max!

I tore it open, unfolded the pages and sat on my bed. Dear gods of family and foes, it was good to see the handwriting of someone familiar. I missed Max so much. A part of me hoped he was writing to tell me he wanted to come and visit. I knew that couldn't possibly be true—he wouldn't dare risk the wrath of the family. If he did, though, he could stay here with Mam and me and Sevrin, and it would be fantastic!

Dear Mabel,

Hey, Sis! I've missed you so much. Things just aren't the same around here. They won't admit it, but I know Da and the others miss you too. I see Da reading the news from Leitham every now and then. I think he's hoping to hear how you're doing. He's just too stubborn to sit down and write to you. Mikey's been throwing axes a lot in the back garden. He's even participated in a few competitions at The Prospector. His form is definitely nowhere near where it used to be. Sometimes he's done great, sometimes he loses big time. He doesn't seem to care either way. I think it's his way of keeping a connection with you.

I don't know what Frankie's up to, exactly, but he's been setting aside his first gems and a few others from each extraction. I know, we all set aside our firsts, but this is different. Frankie always had his on display, now he seems to be tucking them away like he's either saving up for a trip or he's sending them to someone. My guess is he's either going to come visit you, or you might receive a large package of diamonds some day.

As for me, I've been promoted to rubies! That's much quicker than I expected. I'm enjoying the new challenge, but my mining mates are, well, a little old, and we don't have anything in common. I'm hoping to have a word with the foreman and try to get shifted to another team as soon as I've learned the details of ruby mining.

Yesterday was a day off from the mines so we held our annual family mage-stones tournament. Danny won. He beat Kenneth in a best of three. It was a fun tournament as always, but it just wasn't the same without you. I was eliminated early, like you and I usually were. I needed you to hang out with and make fun of the others the rest of the day.

Nothing here has changed. I don't know that it ever will. I guess I'd hoped it would after Aramis and the movie crew were here, but no such luck. It's all mining and socializing at the tavern after, then sleep and back to mining again.

I miss you, Mabel. Phillip, Ben and Zach wanted me to tell you they've been thinking about you. Jimmy does too. He also wanted me to tell you that his offer is still open, if you're interested. Whatever that's about. What is that about, Mabel?

I wasn't going to tell you about Emma, but maybe you want to know. She keeps telling me to tell you how sorry she is for what she did. It's up to you if you want to believe her or not.

She and Zach are back together, but I don't know for how long. Given their history, I doubt it will last. What is this, the third or fourth time they've gotten back together? Who knows? Maybe this time it will work out. I kind of get the feeling she's turned her attention to Jimmy, though. Poor guy. He really doesn't like her, especially because she's the one who told Da where to find you on the movie set. I don't think he'll ever forgive her for that. Neither will I.

I've got to go, and get this to the trading post before work. I can't tell you how much we all miss you. Da will change his mind eventually, and when he does, so will the others. If they don't, I'll find a way to come see you, I hope, but I can't promise anything.

Please, please, please write to me. Tell me how you are, what you're up to, all of it.

You are still family to me.

Loads of love,

Max

I pressed the letter to my heart. Max was mining rubies! Gods I missed Max, and the mage-stones tournaments, and Ben and Zach and Phillip and Jimmy, and oh, poor guy. He didn't stand a chance now that Emma decided she wanted him. No one ever did.

And yet it all seemed so distant, not a part of my life. They were characters and stories, that were entertaining, who I felt fondness for. With everything going on now, Leitham felt like home. Mam, Sevrin, Aramis, and my friends, felt more like family than Da and my brothers ever had.

I had to do something about my situation. I couldn't live in fear anymore. I wanted Da to read about me and know I was doing great without him and I wanted Max to know I was fine.

CHAPTER 8

"YOUR CARRIAGE awaits, my dear," Sevrin said
with a flourish and a bow, when I met him at the door
for my appointment with Dr. Thora.

"You're in a particularly good mood," I said.
"What's up?" I took Sevrin's hand as he helped me
into the cart.

"It's a beautiful day, my dear. A beautiful day.
That is all."

His smile told me there was something more to
it, a secret he was holding in. As much as Sevrin was
a gifted storyteller, and loved to talk, he could also
be very quiet. If he didn't want to talk, there was
nothing I or Mam or anyone could do to make him. I
had a feeling this was one of those occasions.

There was only one thing I knew of that ever

made anyone that happy for no apparent reason: he was going to propose to Mam.

Max would hate it if Mam said yes. As much as I loved Max, he was still fairly traditional. He didn't know Mam like I did. He never saw her with Sevrin. He remembered Mam living with us. I didn't. And I'd seen how happy Sevrin made her. I would love it if he officially became my step-da.

If Max ever visited us, if he gave Mam a real chance, he would be happy for her and Sevrin. He couldn't really have a problem with Sevrin becoming our step-da.

The ride to Dr. Thora's was quiet and I quickly forgot about Sevrin's secret. I didn't like the silence. It made me paranoid. I kept hearing Aubrey's voice in my head telling me that I needed to pay my debt. That being an artist was a good start to re-payment. I kept feeling his hand on my shoulder, sending searing pain into me and taking it away just as quick. Seeing him across the street, smirking as, with a twitch of his finger, my shoulder exploded in pain.

He was an immortal elf who was bored, and I was his play thing. He was never going to leave me alone. I didn't want to be in his debt or control, but was it really possible to get out of this?

There was nothing in Dr. Thaddeus's book that could help me. I'd checked. Several times.

I scanned the faces of the elves in the streets, certain that one of them was Aubrey, or one of his minions, watching me.

I huddled a little closer to Sevrin.

"Everything all right, love?" he asked.

"Mm hmm," I said, positive the group of elves waiting to cross the street worked for Aubrey.

How was I going to get rid of him? What more would he do to me before I was able to pay him back? Would it ever be enough?

We pulled up in front of Dr. Thora's office. "I have to run a few errands," Sevrin said. "I'll be a few hours. Here's some money for a taxi."

I was going to be alone? I couldn't be alone. Could I ask Stacie to walk with me to the taxi stand?

"Oh, okay." I took the coins from Sevrin and did my best to fake a smile, though I didn't think it was particularly convincing.

"You have nothing to worry about, love. I promise. You are safe now." Sevrin smiled, waved goodbye, and snapped the reins, leaving me standing outside of Dr. Thora's office.

There weren't any elves on the street here, only a handful of dwarves, and they weren't looking at me. I had to trust Sevrin and believe I was safe here. For now.

I may have been safe, but the longer I stayed out here, exposed, the more I felt like I would invite harm from Aubrey or his minions. I hurried inside.

"Hiya, Mabel," Stacie said. She was always so cheerful. "Come on in." She ushered me into Dr. Thora's office where Dr. Thora waited.

For a specialist in high demand, she sure didn't

have a lot of patients—none, actually, from what I saw, on any of my visits.

"How are you doing, Mabel?" she asked.

"All right, I guess," I said. My right arm hung limp at my side.

As always, she massaged my shoulder, assessing the damage or improvement. Then she walked me through the exercises she'd asked me to do. There was some movement, but not much. "Very good," she said. "It's a good start. Keep up with the exercises. I'd like to try something new, something to help with the pain. Are you open to it?"

"Why not?" I had nothing to lose.

She pulled out a rolled up cloth and opened it. There were dozens of hair-thin needles. "One of my colleagues I consulted about the elven magic recommended acupuncture. He said it wasn't likely to eliminate the magic, but it works around it, repairing the tissues. He said it isn't perfect, but for now it is our best option and will certainly compliment the salve."

The needles were long and terrified me but I was willing to try just about anything. "What do I need to do?"

"I'll need to remove your tunic from your right shoulder. I'll put the needles in, and they need to stay in place for twenty minutes. And then we'll be done."

"That's it?"

"That's it."

Sounded easy enough. I could handle twenty

minutes of sharp things actually stabbing my shoulder. It might be a nice change from just feeling like that's what was happening. "Let's do it."

It took a few minutes for her to tap the needles into place. If I hadn't watched, I wouldn't have known they were in at all.

"There you go," Dr. Thora said. "Don't move, and I'll be back in twenty minutes."

The office was warm, and I kind of liked having the time to myself. It was time to feel safe, and have some peace and quiet. Time to breathe.

Twenty shockingly pain-free minutes later, Dr. Thora removed the needles. I didn't notice any improvement. Dr. Thora asked me to perform the exercises once more. I did, and much to my surprise, I had slightly more mobility than before, and the pain was marginally less.

Coming to Leitham had definitely been the right decision. The doctors here really knew what they were doing.

SEVRIN AND Aramis arrived home soon after I had. I was still smiling, pleased with the progress made courtesy of the acupuncture treatment. Seeing Aramis brightened my mood further. I hadn't seen him in a while. I did think it was odd that he would be here, assuming Sevrin planned to propose to Mam tonight.

"Frerin should be home soon," Sevrin said. "We can strategize then."

So, no proposal?

"Very good," Aramis said. He said nothing about my shoulder, but clearly he knew what Aubrey had done. I assumed they were going to strategize about what to do about him. "Mind if we join you until then?" Aramis asked me.

"Of course not," I said.

They sat beside me by the fire. Two of the greatest legends in dwarf and elf history were sitting beside me! How did I get to be so lucky that they were now my friends, my family? How many times had I day-dreamed scenarios similar to this? Where I fought or went on adventures with Aramis and Sevrin? A giggle escaped my lips.

"What?" Sevrin asked.

Would it be terrible if I told them how surreal all of this was? "Nothing," I said. I had to think of something else. Movies, of course. I turned to Aramis. "I've been practicing daily with the wizard's crystal, and I'm starting to get it. I can do the sound and I can get the pictures, but not at the same time. Can I come see you for another lesson?"

"Of course," he said. "I am always in my office these days. Come by any time."

"You haven't finished the editing yet?" Sevrin asked. "Fiddle with that movie of yours much more, Laddie, and you will have nothing left."

"No, Old One, I am not still editing. I am working

on a new script. But thank you for the reminder. I have finally been given a date for the premiere. It is set for eight months from now."

"Eight months? Why so long?" I asked.

"To give me time to finish up, make any last minute changes. But mainly because there are just so many movies being made now, the release slots fill up fast so we are booking times farther and farther ahead."

In eight months, my friends in Gilliam would see me on the screen. I'd love to write Max, maybe even Phillip and Jimmy, to let them know. Too bad they wouldn't likely be allowed to travel to Leitham for the premiere. They deserved to be a part of it as much as I did. This was depressing me. "You said you're working on a new script. What kind of movie is it?"

"A time travel movie."

"A what?" I asked.

"Time travel, into the future. An imagining of what our world would be like five hundred years from now, with the re-emergence of the Evil Lord of Darkness."

He had an amazing imagination. "Where will you record it?"

"I am not sure yet. I have to finish writing the script first, and scout out locations, start figuring out my ideal cast, sets, hire crew. I have written an initial draft of the script. It is quite good, but it needs some revision before I can officially announce I am making it."

It fascinated me how much there was to do before a movie was made. I leaned forward. I never seemed to get enough when it came to the process of making movies. "How many drafts of the script do you write before you decide to use it?"

"Three or four, though there are many rounds of edits that go into each draft. There will likely be revisions during recording. What is written does not necessarily work in the actual movie. And then when I edit, things might get cut or rearranged. Nothing is finished until it is in theatres. Even then there are things I wish I could go back and change."

Working with Aramis on set, he'd seemed so relaxed, most of the time, but everyone talked about what a perfectionist he was. I'd thought he was impatient sometimes, but not unreasonably so, and perfection was a reasonable demand from a director, especially since it was Aramis's directorial debut. He had every right to want it to be perfect. But this was the first time I'd ever witnessed him suggest that he expected perfection from everyone, including himself. He was on a constant quest for it and each new project was one step closer.

I liked that work ethic in Aramis. It wasn't un-like mining, finding the right amount of pressure and strokes to find the gems. I'd love to work with Aramis on his next project, but I didn't quite know how to tell him. It was his choice, of course, and I didn't want to work as an actor. I could do set pieces, maybe help with the recording like I had in Gilliam, or help with the editing since he was teaching me how to do it.

"So what happens in five hundred years when the Evil Lord of Darkness returns?" I asked.

"It is a little soon to know for sure," Aramis said, like he was researching an inevitability. "But in general, no one knows who he is. He is a stranger walking the land, charming dwarves and elves alike, trolls, maybe even some sprites and ogres, turning them into his minions. It is not until he has amassed an army that the rest of the world realizes who he is. The question is, who really populates the world five hundred years from now, and will they be able to fight him, or will they believe he is good rather than evil?"

"How would they not know he's evil?"

Aramis smiled. "If you had disappeared for thousands of years, reduced to the shadows, what might you learn from watching the world? If you could come back to dominate, would you use what you learned? What form would you take?"

He'd given this a lot of thought. The possibility of the Evil Lord coming back, the way he suggested, terrified me. "He can't really come back, can he?"

"No," Aramis said, sounding confident.

"How can you be sure?" I asked.

"I was there when he was destroyed," he said.

That was a story about Aramis I didn't know. How did I not know this? "You were?"

"I was." He shifted.

I understood; he didn't want to talk about it. I couldn't begin to imagine the things he must have seen in his lifetime. I had so much to learn from both him and Sevrin. "Sounds like this movie is something you have a personal interest in."

A shadow fell over him, deadening his eyes, hovering for several seconds as he dipped into the memories which must have haunted him all of these years. "I think you are right."

I RE-READ the offer from Varv. It might not have been quite as lucrative as the others, but it wasn't all about the income. It seemed to me that he understood me best, and because of that, he would make sure my carvings were put in the hands of purchasers who would appreciate them, not just pay the most for them, though that would be nice too.

I couldn't put it off any more. My inability to write made it all the more difficult to deal with. I would have preferred to write so I didn't have to see Varv, or the others, in person. That was the only option I had.

After my next appointment with Dr. Thora, I told Sevrin I had one more thing to take care of before we went home. He agreed to wait in the cart while I paid a visit to Varv.

I knocked, and at his bidding, I entered his office. "Ah, Mabel Goldenaxe, I was hoping to hear from… oh!" He stopped when he saw my right arm in the sling. "Is everything all right?"

He was kind to ask, even though he could see the answer. "Not really," I said. Sadness, anger, and disappointment threatened to overwhelm me. "I, um… I was very pleased by your offer of representation. I would like to accept it. Before I do, I feel there is something I need to discuss with you. I owe it to you." My words felt stilted, planned, like I was reading them off a page. They weren't planned. Speaking carefully, methodically, was simply the only way I could keep my emotions under control.

"Of course. Please, sit."

I sat in the chair across the desk from him. The same one I'd sat in just three weeks ago when I'd shown him my carvings, when he'd been so impressed with my work.

"Tell me what's happening."

His patience and kindness was what I'd liked so much about him. "As you can see," I motioned to my shoulder, "I have been injured. It happened soon after I met with you. Well, the original injury happened some time ago, but I thought it had been healed. In any event, my shoulder was re-injured. I am seeing Dr. Thora about it. She is doing all she can, but it doesn't look like it will be taken care of any time soon."

He leaned back in his chair. "I see."

"I have hope that it will get better, but I don't know how long it will take. In the meantime, I am not able to carve. I'd thought for a moment, that I could agree to your offer, and then just not have any work for you for some time, but that didn't seem professional to me."

"No, it wouldn't have been."

"Right. So, I was wondering, hoping, that by telling you, well, that I could still sign with you, and you would be willing to wait for me." I cleared my throat and looked down.

Varv was quiet for quite some time. I refused to fidget even though every muscle begged to move. To move would be to give myself permission to cry, and I would not show weakness in front of anyone as important as Varv.

At last he spoke. "I appreciate you coming to see me, Mabel. It takes a lot of courage. It is quite a predicament you have found yourself in, and it all becomes much more uncertain when there is no set time frame, or outcome. Here's what I can offer you: once you are well enough to carve again, come back and see me. Assuming your carving will be at the same standard as it was before, I will consider representing you again."

"Sure," I nodded. "That's fair."

"Please know that I do not doubt that your talent and skill will remain." He got up and moved around the desk and sat in the chair beside me. "I do, however, question whether or not the healing will be adequate or how it will affect your abilities. Even so, I want to be the first agent you see when you are able."

"Okay. I can do that."

"Let us hope this does not last much longer and that any and all healing goes well." He patted my knee.

I nodded again. "Thank you for your time."

I walked out of the office without looking at him. I leaned against the closed door and squeezed my eyes shut, pushing down the pain and tears.

Varv was right, it had taken a lot of courage to ask him to wait for me. The outcome wasn't perfect, but it gave me hope. I began to think that there might be a way to get my life back. If I could hold on to this courage.

All I had to do was confront Aubrey and demand that he remove his magic and threats. I had to find a way to make that happen.

CHAPTER 9

I SAT in the living room in front of the fire doing the exercises Dr. Thora had asked me to do. Thanks to the acupuncture, I wasn't in constant, excruciating pain. While most of the pain relief was temporary—at its best in the hours after the treatment—I had noticed that it was taking longer for the full extent of the pain to return.

The pixie-dust salve helped too. When I rubbed it on my shoulder and arm, I could feel the damage slowly diminish.

The effects of Aubrey's magic were receding. While I doubted the treatments would eventually reverse all of it, this made me more determined to make him remove it. Whatever the results of the magic's removal, Dr. Thora could help me with it.

Aubrey may have thought he was just threatening me by hurting me, but he had nullified the agreement. I owed him nothing. I was done with him.

To me, that changed everything. I had the power now.

I would meet up with Aubrey when and where *I* wanted to.

Sevrin walked into the living room, interrupting my wild dreams of confronting Aubrey.

"Here," he said, casually setting a chunk of onyx on the table beside me. I tore my eyes away from the fire and glanced at the rock and then Sevrin as he sat beside me, a mug of coffee in hand.

"What's this for?" I asked.

"Carving," he grunted.

It was a gorgeous piece of stone. Immediately images flashed through my mind, ideas of what I could do with it. "I can't carve. Not with my arm like this," I said.

"Aramis said you carved on set in Gilliam all the time, even with your arm in a sling."

I had, but that was also before Aubrey inflicted his elven magic on me, rooting it in my muscle. The treatments were working, but I was still far from being able to carve. "I know, but…"

"Honey, I know you're in a lot of pain, unable to carve. I don't expect you to be able to be fully able to work the stone just yet. The thing is, I've seen you with your carvings. I see how much you miss it. Why don't you try? Just take it easy, do what you can. A little bit here, a little bit there, for yourself, when you're ready."

The stone was so beautiful. Such a perfect shape and size. I could see a dragon in it—Dakkar, to be specific. Back home, when I'd carved on set, I'd been able to do it by keeping my arm immobile, all but my wrist. It was difficult and slower than if I had full mobility, but my carvings were small enough it didn't really matter. Except that even then, in Gilliam, there had been some relief from the pain. At the moment, I wasn't sure I could hold one of my lightest carving tools.

I picked up the stone with my left hand. If I could carve it, make it into the spectacular piece of art I knew it could be, there would be no doubt that I had to rid myself of Aubrey and his threats. "I'll try," I said.

"Good. Here." He pulled out from one of his pockets a leather pouch tied together by a thin leather strap.

I untied and unfurled the supple leather. It was a new set of carving tools with jade and opal handles with diamonds and gold inlay. These kinds of tools must have cost a fortune. "Wow. Sevrin. I don't know what to say. Thank you so much."

Sevrin put up his hand to stop me. "It will be thanks enough when you carve something beautiful like I know you can."

In spite of all my bravery for thinking I now had the power over Aubrey, I wished I'd never talked to

Radier about my shoulder. I would have still come to Leitham and seen Dr. Thora and I'd be able to carve.

I cursed the moment Radier had mentioned Aubrey. Why would he make me indebted to the Elven Mafia?

Unless he was working for them.

Why would Radier, the greatest wizard ever, be working for the Elven Mafia? Boredom?

It was the only reason I could come up with. He'd said he became involved in the movie business because he was bored. Except that he'd discovered the process when he was on an adventure with Aramis and Sevrin. He'd been involved from the beginning. It couldn't possibly have been because he had nothing to do.

Of everything about this mess, Radier's actions made the least sense to me. Sevrin knew him well. Maybe he could help me understand.

"Sevrin, can I ask you something, about when you and Aramis were with Radier, and he discovered that he'd recorded your trek through the caves of Haddam on his crystal?"

Sevrin chuckled. "That was the strangest day ever."

I could imagine it would have been. "What happened with Radier after that? Was there a period of time where you didn't see him?"

"Several, but that wasn't unusual." Sevrin paused. "What's this about, Mabel?"

"Nothing." I shrugged. "I was just curious. All of

this talk about carving made me think about Gilliam and Radier, and I guess I'm still trying to make sense of why he would get involved with Aubrey if he was as close to Aramis as I thought he was."

Sevrin sighed. "That's a good question. Frerin and I have been trying to figure that out."

It felt like a stretch, and I didn't want Sevrin to think badly of me, but I had to ask. "Do you think Radier's working for him?"

"What, you think he's indebted to Aubrey?" Sevrin shook his head. "Not Radier. He's far too independent. He answers to no one. He brow-beats others into submission."

I thought back to that day, with Radier and Aubrey and Mam. Radier had stood behind Aubrey. I thought it was to hide from Mam's wrath. But if Radier was as strong-willed as Sevrin said, he wouldn't need to hide from anyone. If he was truly independent, and had brought me to Aubrey expecting Aubrey to heal me outside of his mafia business, Radier would have intervened on my behalf. I kept thinking about how he stood behind Aubrey. Not beside or in front, or away from, but behind. Like he was pushing Aubrey.

What if Aubrey was working for Radier? What if Aubrey's so-called Elven Mafia was really just a front for Radier? If Aubrey was really in control, wouldn't he have sent his minions to hurt and threaten me? Instead, he came himself. What lord of anything would do that?

I had to know exactly what the relationship was

between Radier and Aubrey. I had to talk to Aramis.

I LEFT Mam's studio dressing room to go see Aramis. The movie lots and roads connecting them were bustling as always. I never tired of seeing the variety of species walking around together. It was a colorful sight. I remembered feeling the same way about the entrance cavern of the Gilliam mines. It was beautiful but static. Studio City was an ever-changing specter of sights and sounds. My enjoyment of Studio City was dampened by the purpose of my walk to Aramis's office.

Now that I'd started to think about Radier being the one ruling Aubrey, I couldn't get it out of my head. It made so much sense except for one thing: Radier might be a long-lived wizard but he was still mortal and elves were not. Why would Aubrey be indebted to Radier at all? Why not just get rid of him somehow? The only answer I could think of was that Radier had some kind of magical control over Aubrey.

Aramis sat at his desk, head bent over parchment, quill in hand. He dipped the quill in ink and scribbled a few lines down. When he picked up his hand, his skin was smudged with the black ink. Was it really possible for elves to get dirty? By the time I'd finished the thought, the ink had disappeared and his skin was as perfect as before.

"How do you do that?" I whispered in surprise.

Aramis looked up at me, bewildered until I pointed to his hand.

"Where did the ink smudge go?" I asked.

He smiled. "Ancient family secret," he said with a wink.

Elves. Always talking in riddles. Even Aramis did it when he felt like it. It was so annoying. "Is that the time travel movie script?" I asked.

"It is." Aramis set the quill down and leaned back in his chair.

"How is it going?"

Aramis shrugged. "All right. I am at a tough spot so it is slower than I would like at the moment."

"It didn't look slow to me."

Aramis waved at the page. "Just a few rough notes, nothing solid."

It was difficult to read the upside-down script but I did catch something about the Evil Lord of Darkness reappearing, confronting the unified army, and the word fear was underlined three times. No wonder it was going slow for him. He was having to imagine what it would be like to confront the Evil Lord again.

"Do you have a moment?" I asked.

"Of course. Are you here for another editing lesson?"

"Maybe in a bit. I need to ask you something first."

"Would you like some mead?" Aramis pulled out

two goblets from a drawer, and a bottle of mead. He didn't wait for me to answer, he simply filled the two goblets and passed me one. "Ask away."

"It's about Radier," I said hesitantly, fully expecting him to throw me out.

Aramis pursed his lips, looked down, drained his cup, and poured himself another. "What about him?"

"H-how long have you known him?"

"All his life."

I tried to imagine Radier as a small boy but only managed to shrink his stature, which made his gray beard look ridiculous. "You mean since he was much younger."

"He was born in our woodlands, and raised by my family."

"So he's like a brother to you? Or was?"

"At times. I was away from home a lot when he was younger, so it was not until he was a full-fledged wizard and we went to war together that I really got to know him."

"War? But that was a millennia ago, or more. He isn't immortal. He shouldn't still be alive, should he?" Unless he was much older than I'd thought. It wasn't possible for him to have lived that long. Not even if he was at the very end of life, which he hadn't seemed to be.

"Funny you should say that." Aramis laced his fingers together and leaned forward, elbows resting on the desk top. "Because he was raised by my family and because of his heroics during the Great War, he was gifted with elven immortality."

Well that would explain why Aubrey hadn't simply rid the world of him, whatever Radier's role was in the Elven Mafia.

"Heroics?" I asked. The tales all dwarves were told growing up about our heroes were apparently greatly lacking. Not telling us that Sevrin saved dragons I could understand. If we were told, he would not hold the same stature in our legends. We wouldn't have been told about Aramis killing the Evil Lord. Why would any dwarf make an elf the hero of the Great War? But Radier, he was a legend to all. Why diminish his stories?

Aramis shuffled a few pages of his script. "He and I are the ones who destroyed the Evil Lord, and he saved my life."

My jaw dropped. "Immortality is an appropriate reward for saving the world."

Aramis cocked an eyebrow and tilted his head to the side for a moment. "We thought so."

"You don't think so now?"

"Immortality is a long time."

"And he does seem to get bored." I sipped my mead. "How do *you* not get bored?"

Aramis smiled. "Elves, in general, have a patient disposition."

I didn't think so of Aubrey, but if I was right about Radier, that might explain it.

"We like to take our time, care for the earth, the woodlands. Or if you are like me, you explore, take risks, get curious about life and being creative."

"But Radier?"

"He is a wizard, not an elf." Aramis refilled our goblets. "For a while we thought he had adopted our disposition, but even when we went on adventures, he was less patient than he should have been, often disappearing for periods of time, occasionally instigating more trouble than we needed though we could never prove it was on purpose. Why do you ask, Mabel? Is this still about your shoulder?"

"I just can't understand why Radier would take me to your father if he knew what Aubrey had done. And if Radier is that close to your family, your father, he had to know, not just about Aubrey's involvement with my family, but about everything."

Aramis frowned. "He certainly knows my father better than I do, or have ever cared to. I suspect that it is that relationship that blinded him to the truth. Knowing what I do about Radier, he probably believed it would be different, that he was bringing you to Aubrey, asking for a favor as a family member, not as a business deal."

"So it has crossed your mind, that Radier took me to your father for reasons other than simply wanting me to get help?"

"It has."

"Why do you dismiss it?"

"Because as much as we argued over him taking you to Aubrey, Radier is a part of my family. He was convinced Aubrey would heal you as a familial favor, and he tried to persuade me of the same."

"It didn't look that way. If that's what he really thought, he would have intervened when Aubrey suggested payment and threatened Mam. Instead, Radier stood behind him and did nothing."

Aramis sat back, his eyes narrowed, his lips pressed together. "Do you think Radier is behind... is the one controlling my father?"

I bit my bottom lip. It felt dangerous hearing it out loud. I didn't have all the answers, but it was the only reasonable explanation for Radier's actions. "I think it's possible."

Aramis didn't say anything in response. He closed his eyes and rubbed his forehead.

"What could he have over Aubrey?" I asked.

Aramis closed his eyes and shook his head. "Nothing I can think of. Unless... "

"Unless what?"

"Unless this was all his idea to begin with."

"What do you mean?"

"Radier is the one who has traveled, made connections, witnessed... things." Aramis was silent for a while, then said, "I was on an adventure when my father shifted into organizing his criminal behavior. I do not know if Radier was with him then. All I know is that Radier was not with me."

If Radier was behind the Elven Mafia, then he was the key to making all of this end for me. But Radier was long gone. No one knew where he was. I had to deal with Aubrey first. I needed Aramis's help more than ever. "I want to meet with Aubrey to stop the threats," I said. "But if Radier is behind it all, what do I do?"

"I do not know. But we need to be absolutely certain he is before you meet with Aubrey. You need to be as prepared as possible. I will get you as much information as I can about their history, and the workings of the organization."

I breathed a sigh of relief. "You're not angry with me?"

Aramis shook his head. "I would rather you stayed as far away from Aubrey as possible, but as I said to you when we talked at the White Rabbit, I will not let him harm you the way he did Arienne. I would rather you go in ready for battle, with support and knowledge, than without. It will be your only chance to survive. I will do what I can to help."

"Thank you."

Aramis cursed. "I am so sorry Mabel. I was so blind to it all because he was family. And yet, for that very reason, I should have known better. I knew something was wrong before we left for Gilliam. I was not going to bring Radier with me, but my first choice had cancelled due to sudden illness, and Radier was my back-up. He insisted on it. He probably made it all happen. Probably had it all planned from the beginning."

CHAPTER 10

LILLIAN AND I joined our friends at the Lair. It was great to feel well enough to go out again, but as I always seemed to be lately, I was preoccupied. I laughed along with the others at the story Chris and Hannah told but if anyone were to ask me a question about what they'd said, I'd be at a complete loss how to answer.

After my conversations with Sevrin and Aramis the last few days, all I could think about was contacting Aubrey.

The easiest thing for me to do would be to sit back and wait for him to come to me, but I didn't want that. He'd made me go to him on his turf, then he'd ambushed me twice, taking away any control I might have had.

He'd nullified our agreement. He wasn't even in charge of his own mafia. I had the knowledge, thanks to Aramis, and I had the power. I needed to be free of him and I wanted him to know it. If I let him find me, I had no control of when or where that would happen and I would feel like I was at his mercy. He should feel like he was at mine.

The problem though, was that I had no idea how to set up such a meeting. Aramis and I had talked about it and he was convinced that Aubrey had gone back to his side of the Haddam Mountains. He said he'd made sure the elves protecting me from Aubrey had driven him back, and that communication with Aubrey would be difficult at best.

Lillian got up to get another round of drinks and Jeff slipped into her vacated seat next to me. "Hey, Mabel," he said. "Everything okay? You're quiet tonight."

"I'm fine, thanks," I said. "It's just been a long day, I guess."

"How's your shoulder?" he asked.

What about Jeff? Would he know how to contact Aubrey? Lillian had said he liked to know everything about everyone. Not likely. I knew blokes like him. They talked like they knew everything but they usually knew less than most.

"My shoulder is getting better, slowly," I said. "Thanks for asking."

"You see Dr. Thora, right?" he asked, inching his chair closer.

"I do."

"She's hard to get in to see. It took my neighbor a year before he got an appointment with her. How did you get one so fast? If you don't mind me asking."

I did mind, but I wasn't going to be rude about it. "My mam is already a patient of hers. I guess she accepts family members as new patients." It may or may not have been the truth. I didn't actually know how Mam got me the appointment but I didn't really care. Jeff didn't need to know. It also, I hoped, cut off any expectation on his part, that I had some connection to getting his neighbor in to see Dr. Thora.

I looked across the table at Sam who now had an open seat beside her. Excellent. I'd wanted to talk with her. I'd heard she'd had an interesting day. "Excuse me," I said.

I moved to the empty seat. "Hey, Sam," I said. "How was your day on set? Are you really working with Dakkar? Is she as tame as Sevrin says?"

Sam smiled, her posture melting like she was about to talk about a cute furry pet. "Dakkar is the sweetest thing. Today we recorded the scene where I have to ride her. I'd worked with her already but I was still a bit terrified—I mean, she is a *dragon* after all. She totally nudged my shoulder, nuzzling me until I was comfortable with her. Then, when I was on her back, she kept her wings in such a way that there was no way I could possibly fall off, even if she flipped over, which she did, doing this looping maneuver. It was incredible. Afterward, she followed me around the set. The trainer eventually took her away. It was the most amazing day. You really should come visit and see her up close. You would not believe how gentle she is." Sam shook her head. "It's amazing how wrong the stories were that we grew up with."

"Wait," Jeff said. "Back up a minute. You rode a dragon?"

"Three times." Sam took a tankard from Lillian who had returned with a tray of them. "If I'm still alive when they decide she needs to retire, I want to adopt her."

Jeff and I weren't the only ones awed by Sam's feat. Everyone at the table was now listening.

"Wow." Lillian said. "You're my new hero, Sam. Ooh, Mabel, we should have dragon riding in our movie."

"I love it," I said.

"If you do, then I want to be the one to ride her," Sam jumped in.

"No, I want to do it," Hannah said.

"We could have a flock of dragons," I said.

Jeff moved over to sit beside me again and cut in. "Mabel, didn't you say that Sevrin was the one to have tamed Dakkar? How did he do it?"

"He said something about removing a gem from their hearts," I said quickly. "What was it like, Sam? To fly? On a dragon."

"I felt like I was in one of those stories I'd been told as a dwarfling: an adventurer taming a dragon, getting it to do my bidding, conquering all others.

I kind of hated coming back down to the ground, knowing it was all just pretend." Sam chuckled. "I guess that's why I like acting. I like living in imaginary worlds."

I did too, I just didn't like my imaginary worlds to be scripted for me. Maybe that's why Aramis wrote his own scripts. Maybe it was his way of controlling his adventures and the villains, when, in real life, he didn't have that control, especially over his father.

"It must be amazing living with Sevrin," Jeff said. "He's such a legend. Does he tell you stories of his adventures all the time?"

Maybe Jeff's interest in Sevrin wasn't a bad thing. Normally I wouldn't appreciate someone using me to get to family and friends, but maybe I could use his interest to my advantage. If Jeff *did* know how to get in touch with Aubrey, maybe I could offer up a chance for him to meet Sevrin in return. At the very least, it couldn't hurt to see if Jeff knew anything about Aubrey?

"Not usually," I said. "Only if I ask. He's actually kind of reluctant to talk about his past. He doesn't mind telling me, but he isn't one to offer up without invitation."

"That's kind of un-dwarflike, isn't it?" Jeff asked.

That was an odd thing to say. "What do you mean?"

"Aren't we all storytellers of some kind?" Jeff continued. "Aren't we always anxious to talk about our exploits in the most dramatic fashion? If you were to go to any table in any tavern, you'd hear stories told without invitation. Even Sam does it."

So? "Maybe when we're Sevrin's age, we won't care so much for entertaining everyone."

"I suppose. But you're a bit like that too. Reluctant, I mean. We hardly know anything about you, not even how you injured your shoulder except that it was from throwing axes. You worked with Aramis on the last movie he and Radier paired up on. You know what happened there, but you won't tell us. Even when we invite you to. You're here with your mam, but what happened to your family? Why is your mam with Sevrin and not your da?"

Lillian leaned over Sam and said, "It's none of your business, Jeff. Mabel will tell us what she wants to, when she wants to. If she wants to."

If Jeff wanted information from me, he was going about it the wrong way. He was nosy, bordering on rude. What Jeff really wanted to know was what happened between Aramis and Radier. He was constantly asking about it. By the rest of his questions, it sounded to me like he was starting to figure out all of it was connected: my injury, Mam, and Radier. I was tired of his questions and his gall to ask them.

"I thought you knew everything about me already," I said. I braced myself against the back of the chair, ready for an onslaught of hate. I kept myself looking casual, my hand loose around my tankard. I was exhibiting more attitude than I was comfortable with. "I thought you knew everything about everybody."

Lillian snickered. Okay, I wasn't totally adverse to having attitude. I'd done it before, when Ricky had challenged me to an axe-throwing rematch early in my axe-throwing training. I could pull it out when I needed it, but that didn't mean I enjoyed it.

"And why is it so important that you know what happened between Aramis and Radier?" I asked. Jeff's face was starting to contort and I couldn't decide if it was because he was trying to come up with an answer, or if he was angry at me for challenging him. "What do you care? Do you think Aramis is going to hire you if you tell him what you know? Like it's some big secret he wouldn't want to get out?"

Jeff shook his head. "I just find it odd how many of us are so enamored with you and yet we know nothing about you."

"So you know nothing, then. I guess you're not as important as you think you are." Gods, I wish I'd said something like that to Emma when she couldn't find her first-ever emerald. I should have known she would turn my help against me. She'd done it enough before that. I'd just thought our friendship was still a good one. I'd hoped our friendship meant more to her than it did. But being nasty to Jeff wasn't going to help me figure out if he knew anything about Aubrey. "Look, I don't know what happened between Aramis and Radier. Everything was fine on set so whatever it was happened after, on the trip back to Leitham. What I can tell you is that I suspect it had something to do with Aubrey."

"Who's that?" Lillian asked.

"Aramis's father," Jeff jumped in, clearly eager to share his wealth of knowledge to prove me wrong. "Lord of the Elves and the Elven Mafia."

At least he knew who Aubrey was. But what else did he know? "I've heard of this Elven Mafia, but that's just something they tell us dwarflings to scare us. It isn't possibly real," I said.

"Those aren't just spooky stories," Jeff said.

"How do you know?" I asked.

"I've heard—"

"Stories," I interrupted Jeff. "Exactly. Do you know anyone who was supposedly hurt by them? I mean, Aramis is super nice. He can't be so different from his father."

"If he's not so different, why would he and Radier fall out over him?" Lillian asked.

"I just said I suspected. I don't know for sure."

"I do," Brent said.

At least I thought he said something. We all turned to him now.

"Say that again?" Jeff asked.

"I know many who have been harmed by the Elven Mafia. In Gypsum, where I grew up, several of his clan lived in the neighboring forest. They'd done significant damage to our businesses. It's one of the reasons I left."

Why hadn't Brent told me any of this earlier, when I'd told him that Aubrey had triggered the magic in my shoulder? I hated that my friend might have been harmed by Aubrey and his minions. "Did he, or his clan, do anything to you?" I asked.

"I'd left before they had a chance." He said no more about it.

Moments later, conversation had started up around the table, this time talking about the fast approaching Dwarf Games.

Brent came around to me and said in my ear, "You look tired. Can I take you home?"

I wasn't tired, but he sounded worried about something, like he wanted to talk, away from anyone else. I wanted to talk to him, too. Let him know I understood about Aubrey and that I was so sorry to hear it. "I'd like that."

"WHY WERE you asking about Aubrey? Acting like you knew nothing about him?" Brent asked, helping me onto his cart.

"Why didn't you tell me about your experiences with Aubrey?" I asked.

Brent snapped the reigns. I grunted from the jolting pain in my shoulder. "Because then I would have also tell you that he's one of my top clients at the gallery," Brent said. "And I didn't think you'd like it."

"Are you serious? How long has he been a client? After all that your city went through? After he drove you out?"

"He's been a client for at least ten years. Maybe more. He sent a buyer early on. Now he comes himself, usually once or twice a year. He doesn't know it was me and my family his people were pressuring. I take advantage of that and charge him a little extra each sale."

Aramis would not be happy to hear that his father has been breaking their territorial agreement for years, not just the few weeks he'd been after me like Aramis thought.

"I didn't tell you," Brent continued, "because it isn't exactly a connection to be proud of. Quite frankly, if it gets out, I could be questioned for money laundering, which I'm not, by the way. Nonetheless, other clients would suspect it. Even if I'm never officially put on trial for it, that suspicion would always be there and I would lose many clients because of it."

Was Brent the reason Aubrey found me? Had Aubrey been coming in to the city to go to the gallery and saw me with Brent? It didn't matter. Brent was my way to Aubrey. He must have seen me with Brent that day outside Varv's office.

It was now or never. "I have a huge favor to ask."

"What is it?"

"If it's going to put you in a difficult situation, just say so. It's not a problem."

Brent leaned a little closer. "Mabel, just ask it and I'll decide if I'll do it."

"Right." I took a deep breath. He smelled wonderfully of stone and oak and varnish. I stretched my neck the way Mikey had taught me to before throwing an axe. It helped me calm down and focus. "I need to meet with Aubrey. Can you help me?"

Brent looked around for a moment. "What are you talking about?"

"I want the threats to stop, to go away completely. He's immortal, he can wait forever. I can't. I want to make him take away the elven magic."

"Mabel, no. That's a terrible idea. Can't you live with the way things are? Dr. Thora's fixing your shoulder as best she can. It won't be perfect, but it will be all right."

"This isn't about the injury. I don't want to live in fear. I want to be able to go out when and with whomever I want. I want to be able to work and not have his threats and henchmen in the shadows, constantly threatening to take away everything from me and my family. I've lived with that once. He practically destroyed my family in Gilliam. They had almost recovered from what he'd done when they exiled me. I let him heal me because I didn't want him to destroy my mam, but this constant threat is the same as if he was actually stealing from us."

"Sounds like you've made up your mind. Have you talked to Sevrin or Frerin about this?"

"No. I'm not going to. Neither are you."

Brent sighed. "I'll see what I can do."

CHAPTER 11

WAITING TO hear back from Brent was excruciating. The impatient part of me wanted this mess with Aubrey to be done quickly. The rest of me wanted to never hear his name much less think about him again.

I was happy Lillian had a few weeks off between acting jobs and she was willing to spend some of her free time with me, without the others around.

I held the door to my house open for her as she carried in over a dozen bags. We'd both had a successful shopping trip in the dwarven shopping district. Only four of the packages were mine. I didn't need that many clothes, though it was wonderful to be able to buy so many things I liked, that were new, all for me, and never worn by my brothers.

"I could get used to this," I said, following Lillian up the stairs to my room. "Having a servant carry my things for me. When you've finished putting the new clothes away, do you think you could do some dusting? You're letting this place go."

"Shut up." Lillian grinned. "That's what you have male servants for. I'm your shopping servant only, remember?"

"Right. You'll need to help me shop for a male servant then."

"I bet Brent would do it," Lillian said, putting the packages on the floor by my closet.

"What? Help me shop for a male servant?" I flopped on my bed, exhausted.

"No! *Be* your male servant."

"Excuse me?" I sat up.

"I bet Brent would do it," Lillian said again. "He'd do anything for you."

I knew Brent liked me. I mean, I knew I was fairly clueless about romance and attraction, but I was not an idiot. He'd practically kissed me outside of Varv's office. But he hadn't done anything like that since, and certainly not around our friends. "What are you talking about?"

"Come on, Mabel." Lillian put her hands on her hips. "Are you telling me you haven't noticed—"

"Yes, *I* have. How do *you* know about it?"

"It's obvious to all of us. The way he's always trying to sit next you, how he's been driving you home a lot more…. So spill it. What's going on with you two?"

I remembered all the things Emma had done to me because she'd thought I was a threat for the attention of the fellows. I should have stood up to her. But I was new here. I didn't want to cause any trouble. I didn't know the rules here. "Are you upset? Do you like him? If you do, I'm sorry. I didn't know—"

"Relax. I don't like him. I mean, I do, as a friend, but nothing more. I promise. I'm not going to poison you over him. Though Hannah might."

My jaw dropped and my eyes felt like they were going to pop out of my head. I had to make it right.

"Kidding. Kidding!" Lillian said hurriedly.

I breathed a little easier. Thank the gods.

"You do like him, though, don't you?" she asked.

"I think so," I said when I could breathe again. "There isn't really anything going on. He was helping me find an agent to represent me with my carvings so that's what we talk about, mostly. It would probably be seen as a conflict of interest if we had a romantic relationship and a business one at the same time."

Lillian sat next to me. "I suppose. Do you want one? A romantic relationship with him, I mean."

I hadn't given it much thought. There were far too many other things going on right now. "I don't know."

"But you have considered it, right?"

It was weird and wonderful to talk about a fellow with a friend who didn't get jealous. "Maybe," I said with an embarrassed giggle. "But I don't want to jinx it."

"There's no way you can jinx it. Brent is smitten with you. Jeff too, for that matter."

"What? Jeff? Now you're just making this up." I nudged her.

"I kid you not!" Lillian nudged me back.

"After the other week at the Lair when he was grilling me about Sevrin and accusing me of keeping secrets, or something? What was he accusing me of?"

"I have no idea. All I know is that since you've been around, Jeff has never been so decent. Ever."

Yikes. "Well, if that's his decent behavior, I'd hate to see what he's normally like. Why do you let him hang out with you all?" I was horrified by how nasty that sounded. "Oh, I'm sorry. I didn't mean it the way it sounded. I'm just curious. Obviously you can be friends with whomever you want."

"It's all right." Lillian blushed. "He and I dated for a while. It was an amicable split, and we've stayed friends. He can be kind, but he does have a tendency toward manipulation."

"Is that why you split?"

Lillian chuckled. "Surprisingly not. He's just not what I'm looking for."

"You're looking for a mate?"

"Don't sound so surprised."

"It's just that you don't have braids in your beard. None of you do, and this is the first time I've really heard you talk about fellows. So who do you like?"

"Sam," Lillian said, lying back on my bed.

"Sam? But, she's a *she*."

"It does happen, you know."

"Well yes, among the fellows." I lay back with her. "But we're females. We need to mate and have dwarflings. We can't do that with other females."

"Oh my gods, Mabel. What kind of backwards town did you grow up in? Frerin ought to be ashamed of herself for not rescuing you earlier." Lillian sighed. "We have as much right as males to find love with whomever we choose. It doesn't happen as often, but there are those of us out there who prefer females over males."

"Huh," I said letting it sink in.

"So in Gilliam, you had to find a male to mate with and have a few dwarflings?"

A few? "By now I should have at the least been courting someone with the inevitability of a golden-ring in a year or less. Gotta get started on having those dozens of dwarflings."

"Dozens? Ugh!" Lillian groaned. "I'm in pain just thinking about it. How many brothers and sisters do you have back home?"

"We were a small family. I have eleven brothers, all older than me. I'm the youngest. Didn't Mam tell you about us?"

"She talked about you and Max the most. There were others she mentioned, but I don't remember her specifically mentioning that they were her dwarflings. Mind you, I've only known her for six or seven years. Now that I think about it, as long as I've know her, she's been obsessed with news from Gilliam. She was super proud of you for your axe-throwing. She also talked about your coach, Mikey, saying how brilliant he was."

"She talked about Mikey?" I couldn't imagine how Mam felt about my brothers, especially Mikey, after all these years. If I was her, I'd think I'd be furious still. It sounded to me like, if Mam really had been so complimentary of Mikey, that she had forgiven him, or chose to remember the happy times rather than dwell on the hurt he'd caused.

"Yeah. She was proud of him. Said he'd been Dwarf Games Champion, and that you were in great hands with him."

"Did she say anything else about him?"

"No. Though she seemed a bit sad when she talked about him. Why?"

"He's my brother. He took me out of her arms when Da exiled her."

Lillian swore. "How old were you then?"

"Barely walking."

"Do you remember Frerin at all?"

"No. I was told she'd died giving birth to me."

"Good gods of truth and… How are you so calm about this?"

I snorted. "I wasn't when I first found out she was alive. I turned on my friends, I ranted at Da, it wasn't a pretty sight, believe me."

"I'd still be freaking out if I were you."

I smiled. "I have my moments." Most days I still found it hard to believe I was with Mam, in her house, sitting with her in front of her fireplace, or watching her on a movie set.

"What was it like growing up without a mam?"

"It was fine, until I came of age."

"Then Emma's antics and your injury happened."

"And acting and not being interested in finding a mate so soon. I tried, but I just wasn't as into it as Da wanted me to be. I'm so happy Mam is alive and was there to rescue me. It's like she knew I needed her most when she showed up. Without her, I'd have had nowhere to go. Well, I could have accepted Jimmy's offer of a golden ring, but I didn't love him. We would have been miserable together."

"Oh, honey, I'm so sorry. I promise never to even jokingly pressure you to find a mate. I'll tell Brent and Jeff, and anyone else, to back off, if you want me to."

"Jeff, please." I paused. "But not Brent."

"You got it," Lillian smiled. "We're your family now. And you are definitely in the right city. You can love who you want, when you want, or not at all. And you can have any career you want, including acting, with elves."

I smiled.

Lillian gently leaned into me. "I'm so happy Frerin rescued you."

Lillian was right. Leitham was the place for me. Dr. Thaddeus was right about being myself. It was incredible to have a female friend who liked me for me, who didn't feel some absurd threat from me.

ALL THIS extra time to kill was the perfect opportunity. After Lillian left the night before, I'd decided to work through more of Dr. Thaddeus's book. As I flipped through it, I noticed how frequently I mentioned movies in the lists I'd made. I could make one particular dream happen. I was in Leitham, home of the movie archives. Sevrin agreed to take me there.

It turned out the archives weren't that far from Studio City, so after we dropped Mam off, we drove a mile farther. We stopped in front of a large three-storey, white-marble bricked building. The windows on each floor were at least seven feet tall. Gold-gilded lettering over top of oak double-doors read *Center for the Creation and Preservation of Motion Pictures.*

"This is it?" I asked. I knew it was a stupid question.

"Where else would it be?" Sevrin helped me out of the cart.

Aramis had challenged me to find it, suggesting I wouldn't be able to. I thought it would be more hidden. "I don't know. I just wasn't expecting it to be so... visible. It's right here, in the middle of the city, where anyone can find it."

"That was the point of building it here. It is supposed to be accessible to anyone." Sevrin pulled on the brass door-handle and held the five-inch thick door for me.

Inside, marble covered the walls and the floor, with the exception of onyx and gold inlay in the shape of a twenty-one point star on the floor. The ceiling was ornately carved wood of abstract shapes and gargoyles.

"The gods of creativity," Sevrin said, pointing to the gargoyles. "The shapes are their blessings bestowed on us, the twenty-one peoples in the industry, represented by the star."

Twenty-one? I hadn't seen that many species here in Leitham, or ever. How amazing to know I still had so much more to see and learn.

Beyond the star was a centaur standing behind a desk, blocking the way to the offices.

"Good morning, Percy," Sevrin said, walking us toward the centaur.

"Morning, Sevrin. What brings you by?" Percy's voice was sonorous and rumbled through me. He was massive and muscular. Smooth-skinned and russet-haired. His deep-brown eyes were framed by elegant lashes.

"Percy, this is Frerin's daughter Mabel. She'd like to see the archives."

Percy bent one knee and leaned down to my height, his face a few inches from mine. He grasped my hand in his, smothering it, shaking it. "It is lovely to meet you, Mabel. How long are you visiting Leitham?"

My mouth was suddenly very dry and my heart was racing. I was actually meeting a real centaur! I'd seen centaurs in Studio City, but I'd never thought I'd meet one. "I moved here to live with Mam."

"Very good. And how do you like Leitham so far?"

"It's…" I was having a conversation with a centaur! "I love it. So much excitement, so many new things."

Percy smiled. "That's wonderful. Welcome to Leitham, Mabel."

"Thank you."

"We'll see you later, Percy," Sevrin said, leading me away.

"It was nice to meet you," I called back over my shoulder.

To the side we entered through a door labeled, conveniently enough, *Archives*. The door led to a stairway heading down. Sevrin made sure the door was closed behind us before we took the stairs. Twenty feet down, we came to a second door, which opened into a tiny vestibule and a third door. "The archives are sensitive to sunlight and outside elements," Sevrin said.

We emerged into a plain room dimly lit by a handful of candles. A counter stretched across the room, dividing it into two, and a bell sat on top. Everything was ordinary wood. No stone, no marble, just plain, utilitarian wood. Sevrin climbed onto a stool in front of the counter to ring the bell.

What kind of creature would I see now? Another centaur I hoped.

A pixie flew out of the shadows, which, upon closer inspection, was an open doorway, its frame barely visible in the dim light, and even then only when I looked closely.

"What can I do for you?" he asked.

I cleared my throat. "My name is Mabel Goldenaxe, daughter of Frerin Goldenaxe. I would like to look at the first movies made, please."

The pixie opened up a large book and quill. He dipped the nib of the quill into some ink and hovered over the book. "For what purpose?"

I looked at Sevrin, panicking. I didn't suppose "just for fun" would be a proper purpose. "I am studying under Aramis, and he suggested I have a look at the earliest movies, to compare the subject matter, and the production methods."

The pixie nodded and wrote it down.

"I have to go look after a few things," Sevrin said. "I'll be back in about two hours. Will that be enough time?"

Probably not, but hopefully I'd have many more opportunities to come back. "Sounds good. See you then."

The pixie glared at Sevrin as he left. "Are we done chit-chatting?" the pixie asked me.

"Yes, sorry." I felt my face flush.

"Good. Do you have a particular artist's work you'd like to see?"

I hoped they had the very first one, of Aramis and Sevrin in the Haddam Mountains. "Radier's, please."

"Any one of his in particular?"

"The very first ones, if possible."

The pixie wrote some more then dropped behind the counter. He popped up moments later and tossed a pair of white gloves at me. "These must be worn at all times. I will take you to a viewing room where you will wait for one of my assistants who will bring you the crystals. Understood?"

"Yes, perfectly." I put the gloves on.

He flipped open a section of the counter I could now see was on hinges. I passed to the other side and through the doorway into the dark.

Small candles burned in sconces along the stone walls. It was cool and dry, much like the mines, but darker. There were no stalactites or stalagmites, no gems waiting to be excavated. We passed an open doorway that from my quick glance, appeared to be to a room full of cupboards with drawers. I could only guess that was where the crystals were stored.

At last I was ushered into a small room with a chair, a table with a projector's fork on it, and a screen.

"Have a seat. Someone will be with you shortly." And with that, the pixie was gone and I was shut in.

The furniture was fairly plain. The chair had some padding on it, but not enough to be sink-into-it comfortable. It would be fine for the next couple of hours.

Minutes later, someone knocked on the door. "Jeff?" I asked. He stood in the doorway holding a small partitioned box with half-a-dozen crystals in it. "What are you doing here?"

"Hey Mabel," he said, coming into the room. "I work here, part time."

"You do? I thought you were an actor?"

He set the box of crystals on the table. "I am, but I haven't been getting a lot of work lately, so I needed to find something else to do that helps pay the bills."

"I'm so sorry to hear that."

Jeff shrugged. "Things will turn around soon, I'm sure."

"I hope so."

"Listen, you're all right, so I don't mind you knowing, but please don't tell the others. I don't want them to know I'm having a bit of a tough time right now."

"Of course."

"Thanks." Jeff sat on the edge of the table. "So, Radier, huh? Looking for anything particular in his work?"

"Not really. I've always wanted to see the early recordings. It just fascinates me."

"Have you heard from him lately?"

"Who?"

"Radier?" Jeff crossed his arms, like he was settling in for a long conversation.

"No, I haven't. Thanks for bringing these to me. What should I do with the crystals when I'm done?"

"Just put them back in the box. I or someone else will clean them up. So, not a thing from him then?"

This was getting annoying and seriously cutting into my time. "Not a thing. I hate to be rude, but I have less than a couple of hours, and I'd really like to watch these."

"Oh, sure. You know how to work them?"

"I do."

"Great. Is Sevrin picking you up?"

"He is. And I don't want to keep him waiting, but I really want to get through as many of these as possible."

"Right. No problem. I'll see you later then."

Finally Jeff left and I was alone to watch the treasures I'd once only dreamed of seeing.

Next time I came here, I'd have to bring some almonds and smoked meat. Of course, given I had to wear gloves at all times, I suspected food wasn't likely allowed.

I picked up the first crystal, set it in the fork the way Aramis had taught me to, and tapped the tines. They vibrated against the crystal. Light grew from within the crystal and projected silent images onto the screen.

I gasped.

This was it! This was the first movie ever made. This was what Radier and Sevrin and Aramis saw in the caves of Haddam that started the whole movie industry.

I exhaled in awe. The movie wasn't of great quality—it was rather blurry and shaky, but it was old, and before Radier knew what he was doing.

Good gods Sevrin looked young. Aramis looked at Radier, right at the crystal on the wizard-staff, and smiled, laughter lighting his eyes.

When that movie ended, I picked another crystal at random. The label said "Red Sun Rises." This one had sound. This movie moved up and down in a regular motion, like Radier was using his staff for walking, perhaps not realizing he was recording.

The entire cast was elves. I didn't recognize any of them, only Radier's voice.

A few minutes in and there had yet to be opening credits. So far the actors had maintained an air of panic and fear. Their dialogue was choppy at best and it was difficult to understand what they were talking about.

Radier entered a tent where a beautiful blonde she-elf lay on a mattress, her skin a sickly pallor. As Radier neared, I could see bruises, old and new, marked her skin, deep shadows circling her emerald-green eyes. Her long blonde hair was thinning, patches were missing.

"My dear Arienne, how are you?" Radier asked.

Arienne? Aramis's sister? This wasn't a movie. This had really happened.

"Radier." Her voice was raspy. She smiled

weakly. She looked like Aramis. "Have you seen my brother? Does he come?"

"I have spent much time with Aramis. I am so sorry. He will not come to your aid."

"Did you tell him, Radier? Did you tell him father is killing me?"

"Not fast enough," Radier muttered. Louder he said, "I did."

Had I heard him right?

"Go to him again. I beg of you. Make him believe you." Her voice was weak but her desperation was strong.

"He believes me, Arienne. But your brother, he does not care. He chooses adventure with a dwarf over you."

I jumped out of my seat. That was not true. Aramis had loved his sister. He would have gone to her. He'd tried to help her. He'd said he was too late.

Tears glistened in Arienne's eyes. "No. Aramis would come if he truly knew."

"He does not care." Radier's voice lowered to a whisper. "And neither do I."

Arienne's sad eyes widened in fear.

The picture went blank. When it flickered back on, Aramis and another elf were reading lines from a script, practicing their acting.

I stopped the crystal. Stunned at what I saw. Unsure of what to do. Should I tell Aramis about the crystal? Should I take the crystal and show him? I didn't want to steal it, but I couldn't leave it here and risk anyone else seeing it. Perhaps my panic was unnecessary; it wasn't like anyone had seen it until now. If they had, they hadn't said anything. Certainly if Radier knew about it, he would have never allowed it to be archived.

I had to leave the crystal here but I would tell Aramis. He had to know the truth. That Aubrey had tried to kill Arienne because of Radier. That Radier was the one who had actually killed her.

My stomach turned over and clenched. I regretted ever befriending Radier. Not all elves were evil like Da thought, but their world was far more dangerous than the one I'd grown up in, in Gilliam. I may not have been super happy there, but at least I'd been safe.

I removed the crystal from the projector's fork and held it in my hand. It would be so easy to tuck it in my pocket and take it to Aramis. He had to see this sooner rather than later.

I decided to keep looking at the crystals. Radier may have left other bits of recording on them, something I could use against Aubrey. As long as no one else knew I'd been looking at them, then it should be fine and the crystals would be safe.

"Mabel," Jeff said, knocking on the door. "Sevrin's here."

I glanced at the door. "Thanks. I'll be right out." I placed the crystal in its slot. Arienne's terror haunted me.

———

"DON'T BE a stranger," Percy called after me as I left the archives with Sevrin.

"Can we go to Studio City?" I asked. "I saw something I need to ask Aramis about."

"Sure," Sevrin said, snapping the reigns. "Can I help you with it?"

I didn't want Sevrin to hear what I had to say. Maybe Aramis wouldn't mind, but if he wanted Sevrin to know, that was up to him, not me."No. It's about the editing process."

"Are you sure? You look worried about something."

I tried to look cheerful. "I'm fine. Just curious about some of the methods used."

We rode the rest of the way in silence.

"Do you mind waiting for me?" I asked. "I shouldn't be long."

"Not at all. Frerin is two studios over. I'll go look in on her. Meet me there."

"I will."

Aramis was in his office working on his screenplay. He looked up, surprised to see me. "Is everything all right?"

I saw Arienne in his face, his eyes. I shook my head, unable to speak, and closed the door.

"What is it, Mabel?"

I took a deep breath and told him everything "I was in the movie archives, and I saw one of the first recordings Radier did. I don't think it was intentional. It couldn't have been from what I saw. It was your sister, Arienne, and she was dying. She asked Radier to get you. He said you didn't care, that you refused to help her."

Aramis's jaw clenched and his eyes darkened.

"I could be wrong, but when she told him Aubrey was killing her, Radier said 'not fast enough.'"

Aramis sagged in his seat. His natural breeze that continually rippled through his hair, stopped. The sadness I'd seen in Arienne and in Aramis at the White Rabbit, returned tenfold.

"I'm so sorry, Aramis. I didn't know what to do. I had to tell you. You need to know."

"Which one was it?"

"The label said 'Red Sun Rises'."

"Thank you." His voice was soft, distant. "When do you meet Aubrey?"

"I'm not sure yet."

He stood and walked over to the door. "I must see this recording for myself. Come back tomorrow, and we can figure out how you can get Aubrey out of your life for good, including his magic."

CHAPTER 12

"ARE YOU sure you want to do this?" Brent asked me. We stood in the back room of Brent's gallery, surrounded by statuary and paintings half in and half out of packing, some being returned to their creators or sent to their new owners, others being prepared for exhibition.

I nodded. In truth, I was terrified. Aubrey was dangerous. Arienne's desperation for help echoed in my mind constantly. I'd barely been able to sleep. Aubrey had been killing his own daughter to satisfy Radier.

There was nothing to stop him from doing the same to me or anyone else. He had much less reason to keep me alive.

Aramis had come through. I'd seen him several

times since I'd told him about Arienne. He'd spent hours with me, telling me stories about Radier and Aubrey. We dissected the stories for any detail that might help me. We pieced together bits of information about Radier that finally made sense to Aramis.

Our work became more urgent when Brent had come to me telling me he had a date arranged for the meeting.

Aramis and I still had a long way to go to figure it all out, but it was a start, something I could use against Aubrey, enough to at least make him think twice before considering taking anything from me or Mam again. I hoped it would be enough to get him to remove his magic.

I was as prepared as I could be. I had to trust what I knew. There would be time for more research if more negotiations were necessary.

I took a deep breath and let it out slowly.

"He'll be here any minute." Brent held my hand and gently squeezed it. "You don't have to do this. You can change your mind. Cancel the meeting. It isn't too late."

I thought of what Mam said to me when Radier waited to take us to see Aubrey. She'd cautioned me then with the same words. I should have listened to her then. I should have agreed to simply ignore the possibility of elven magic fixing me right away. If that had been the only concern we would ever have about Aubrey, it should have been enough to stop me.

Because I hadn't listened to her then, Sevrin's and

Aramis's friends were trying to help protect me but they had failed twice. They may well be succeeding now but who knew what risks they were taking thanks to my impatience? If I didn't do something about this now, it could go on indefinitely. I wished I could change my mind, not meet with Aubrey, and forget all of this. It was too late for that now.

"It will be all right," I said. I had a wealth of information from Aramis that I could use against Aubrey. And I had Brent's support, which meant the world to me.

Brent had chosen his gallery as the place to meet Aubrey.

My first thought was that this could potentially ruin Brent. He promised it was the safest place for such a meeting. He'd told Aubrey he was just making the connection and providing a neutral meeting place. Brent also assured me that here, he could stay out of the actual meeting, but he would be near me if I needed help.

Being surrounded by all this beautiful art helped calm my nerves. It reminded me of the freedom I would have once Aubrey was out of my life.

"I can't believe I let you convince me to allow this," Brent said.

I faked a smile. "My brothers always said I could be very persuasive."

"Yes, well, next time try using those powers for good, will you?" He was teasing and serious at the same time.

"That's what I'm trying to do now."

"I know, and that's what concerns me. For now, please focus on getting Aubrey to leave you alone, with minimal repercussions, and that's all. Promise me, Mabel."

"You make it sound like I intend to dismantle the entire Elven Mafia in one meeting." I tried to laugh it off.

"Aren't you?"

"Please. It will take at least two meetings for that."

"Mabel."

I looked into Brent's dark brown eyes. "I just want to be able to live my life. I don't want my family or anyone else to get hurt because of me. That's all I'm doing. If he can't do that, then nothing changes and I will deal with it. That's all. I promise."

There was a delicate knock on the back door. Aubrey had arrived right on time.

Brent kissed my forehead and caressed my cheek before answering it. "Aubrey, good to see you again. Come in."

Aubrey bent nearly double to get through the door. Once inside he could stand straight but the top of his head grazed the ceiling. It was also one of the reasons Brent picked this place. He said because the space was dwarf-sized, it would make Aubrey uncomfortable enough to be reminded he was in my territory.

Aubrey smiled when he saw me. "Mabel. How

good to see you again. I must say I was a bit surprised to hear from you so soon. I had planned to give you more time to think, but I guess," he waved dismissively at my shoulder, "you've had enough. Have you?"

"I'll be in the office if you need me," Brent said, looking at me pointedly.

"Thanks, Brent," I said.

I waited until the door closed behind Brent before I turned my attention to Aubrey. "Thank you for meeting me," I said.

"Yes, well, please let Sevrin know I admire his efforts at keeping me out of the city and away from you, pitiful and ineffective as they are."

Mind games. It reminded me of when I competed in axe-throwing. Competitors played all kinds of mind games, from Ricky stalling and complaining, to that fellow at Regionals who tried to have Mikey coach him instead of me, right there, during practice sessions. I hadn't let either of them distract me then, and I was far from allowing Aubrey's games to distract me now. It was time for the direct approach.

"By re-injuring my shoulder, you've made our agreement obsolete. Remove your magic, end the threats against me and my family, now."

Aubrey cocked an eyebrow. "You have no idea what kind of pain I can, and will, inflict upon you, until you agree to repay the favor I granted you. For indeed, I did grant you a favor. I did heal your shoulder. There was no agreement as to how long that healing had to last."

Inside, I cursed. My stomach turned. I couldn't let him see how he was affecting me. But I couldn't deny that he was right. "What do you want from me?" I asked.

"Payment, of course." Aubrey's voice was so condescending, like I was a stupid dwarfling.

I rolled my eyes and spoke slowly. Two could play this game. "What do you want as payment?"

"Does it matter? Is there really a price you wouldn't pay to be able to have full mobility? To be able to carve and throw axes? To have your family fortune restored, as well as their faith in you? I should think you would be willing to do anything for that."

The part about my family, that was new. Could he possibly do that? Wrong question. Why would he do that? Why would he offer? He must have been getting desperate. Radier must have been pressuring him. "It sounds to me like you're willing to do an awful lot for me, even though I have very little to give, if anything at all."

"You underestimate yourself, Mabel."

"You want my carvings? They're hardly valuable, but if you're that desperate, they're yours to do with as you please. If I became the wealthiest artist in the world, I doubt the entirety of my income would be enough payment for what you're offering. Which makes me wonder why you're bothering with me at all. So I will ask you again, and you will answer, with no riddles, no deflection. What do you want from me?"

"You."

His answer threw me off my plan. "Me?"

"Yes, you," he sighed. "I control the elven population and now I want to expand my operations into the dwarven territories. You will be my access point."

"Didn't you try that once? You and your friends came to Gilliam. You befriended Mam, but you took everything from us and were on the run." Why was he constantly targeting my family?

"That was rather foolish of me. I had not thought things through then."

I snorted. "You're Lord of the Elves. Do you really expect me to believe you did something like that without thinking? Maybe a few millennia ago, but not seventy years."

Aubrey shrugged off my incredulity. "Nevertheless, I believe you are the perfect means. You are insignificant enough that it would not be noticed, but you are talented enough to gain me the right access."

"Excuse me?" Was that what I was to him? Weak and gullible? It had worked with Mam if only briefly. Why shouldn't he try it with me too?

"We would start with your axe-throwing, having you fix tournaments. It's quite simple, really. I place wagers on certain competitions you have entered. You lose those competitions. I win and I pay you enough to make it attractive to your other competitors. You flash your extra income around, particularly to your fellow competitors who perform well enough but are not likely to win the big prizes. Tell them how they can earn as much. I then pay them for fixing their tournaments and they flash their income to more competitors, until a number of them have joined the operation."

"They wouldn't do it."

"They will. For a while. And when they want out, I threaten to expose them. They will stick with the tournament fixing rather than be publicly ruined. Then we move on to the mines. You dwarves have been hoarding your wealth for far too long. Once you are back home in Gilliam, you will tell the city council that they are to pay me a certain percentage of the mine's production, or it will be destroyed. I will send in a few enforcers with you, to make sure your council complies. We can do the same with your artist community. I already do this with the elves, sprites, and trolls. You see, Mabel? You are in all the right places for me. You, my dear, are perfect."

This was so much bigger than hurting me or Mam. He'd tried to get Mam to betray her family and maybe all of Gilliam. Now he wanted to use me and make me betray all dwarves everywhere.

"It would not be for long. Only until I have a firm hold in all those areas, with strong connection to others. A few dozen years or so."

A few dozen years? Did he really believe I would be willing to turn on my entire species in return for the removal of his magic and the return of my family's fortune? I loved Da and my brothers, I loved Mam, but I would rather see us all suffer extreme loss and pain, even death, before I would sacrifice every dwarf in return for some gems.

I paced, pretending to think about it, trying not to look at Brent's office door where I had no doubt he was listening. I wondered what he was thinking. I could have asked Aubrey why he didn't use Brent as his access to the artist community but if nothing else was successful, I needed to keep Brent out of Aubrey's clutches. Brent, and Gypsum, had suffered enough at the hands of the Elven Mafia. I needed to get back into control. This was *my* territory, *my* meeting.

"Why not use Radier? He has connections everywhere, with all species."

Was that a flicker of fear I saw in Aubrey's eyes?

Aubrey shook his head. "Far too conspicuous."

"And why would you, Lord of the Elves, be interested in such small takings? Even after a few dozen years, as you say, I doubt your connections would be significant enough to take over the dwarven people. I mean, I understand you're immortal, but I don't think even you would risk angering the dwarves, instigating a war, for a few pieces of art and small earnings from sporting competitions."

"Need I remind you what is at stake for yourself if you do not agree to my terms?" Aubrey asked. He quirked his finger and fire blazed in my shoulder.

I bit back my cries. "You think I can't live with pain?"

He turned his wrist and the pain spread through my body, bringing me to my knees. Then, with a snap of his fingers, it was all gone. It was euphoric.

"You could. But why should you have to?"

Radier. I had to turn the conversation back to Radier.

Aubrey snapped his fingers again, restoring my pain to what it had been after the meeting with Varv.

"You wouldn't want to take the risk of war," I said through clenched teeth. "Just like you weren't really foolish enough to steal from dwarven families as a means to expand your operation. You have been around far too long, you have seen far too many wars. This isn't for your benefit. You're working for someone else. You're indebted to someone else."

"And who would that be?" He wasn't as confident as he tried to sound. I detected a slight tremor in his demeanor.

"The one who fought the Evil Lord of Darkness and saved your son's life. The one who then convinced you to bless him with the elven gift of immortality. The one who is bored and restless and who has become irrelevant in our world. He made you exile your son and wanted you to murder your daughter. He's the one who murdered her." I had to stop there. I saw sadness chip Aubrey's defenses. He regretted losing Aramis. He now knew who was responsible for Arienne's death. I wished I had definitive proof of what leverage Radier had over Aubrey. No matter how much Aramis and I talked, after all the stories he recounted, we came up with nothing. Our best strategy was to hint that we knew. I had done that. "It's Radier who wants the war, not you."

Aubrey chuckled but I could tell it was a nervous laugh. He didn't deny any of what I'd said. I pressed on. "What would your people think if they knew that their king was the puppet of a wizard? What would your organization do if they knew you weren't really in control? Seems to me you have far more to lose than I do. So here's the deal I offer you. You will remove your magic from my shoulder and all damage you have caused me. You will leave my family alone, including my mam and me. You will never set foot in Leitham. In return I will consider not telling your people what I know."

Aubrey glared at me. "You would never…"

My pain remained the same. "How long do you think it will be before Radier tires of you too? What will you do then, when he decides to openly take over your organization? I'm surprised he hasn't done it already. Where is he, anyway?" I walked to the door and opened it. If I was right, Aubrey would be eager to leave and safeguard his position. "No one has heard from him in a couple of months. While you're over here, are you sure he isn't taking over your people west of the Haddam Mountains?"

Aubrey was speechless. I could tell he was calculating what he knew of Radier and comparing it to what I'd said. He knew I was right.

"Think about it." I closed the door before he could say or do anything else.

Brent burst from the office and hurried to my side. I let out my breath then, and collapsed to the floor.

CHAPTER 13

I WAS still in shock a week after my meeting with Aubrey. I stayed home. I'd angered Aubrey and likely Radier. Home was the only place I felt safe. And yet I was excited. I had done something I never thought I could—I'd stood up for myself. I was tired of hiding.

I wanted to tell someone about it. I was desperate to tell my brother Max but I still couldn't hold a quill. Both Mam and Sevrin had offered several times to write the letter for me if I told them what to say. But a letter was far too personal, even if I mentioned nothing about Aubrey, or Brent, or living with Mam and Sevrin.

I found myself pacing with too much energy. I had to be careful not to do it when Mam or Sevrin was around. I needed to get out of the house, to do something, anything. Maybe Aramis needed some help. Studio City should be safe for me. At least Aramis had never said Aubrey ever contacted him there.

Had I really threatened Aubrey? Lord of the Elves, leader of the Elven Mafia?

Maybe I should just stay home and stay in bed.

"Mabel, honey," Mam said, knocking on my door.

"Come in."

Mam stood in the doorway. "You've been in here the last few days. Come to the studio with me. We're shooting a big scene today, we need lots of extras, and you could be one of them."

It would be nice, something to do, something to distract me. "Sure, sounds like fun."

Thankfully I was mostly dressed. Mam helped me tie the belt around my trousers and fasten my tunic. Minutes later we were in the cart and on our way to Studio City. I remembered what Sam had said a few weeks ago, about riding Dakkar. I knew I wanted to carve a dragon, but I needed details. "Hey, Sevrin, do you think it would be possible for me to see Dakkar? Sam was telling me how she rode her. I'd love to see a dragon up close."

"Sure, I can take you to where she lives," Sevrin said. "It's been a long time since I've spent time with her. It would be nice to introduce you."

Sometimes I wondered if Sevrin wasn't just a bit abnormal, talking about a dragon like she could speak to me. Then again, he knew best.

After we dropped Mam off and promised to be back in an hour for me to be cast as an extra, Sevrin and I continued on to the back corner of Studio City. At first I thought we were on an elaborate set, with a large stone mountain and a stream surrounding it, like a moat. Sevrin led me across the bridge over the moat and to the entrance to the mountain.

"This is where she lives?" I asked. "Wow, this is impressive." It was like something out of the stories I was told as a child, the kind of mountains dragons lived in, as yet untouched by dwarves.

"We wanted it to be as much like her first home as possible, so she'd feel comfortable here."

It was like she heard Sevrin's voice and remembered it with affection. Dakkar came bounding out of the recesses of her home, and stopped inches away from us, licking Sevrin's face.

She was massive this close up. And so beautiful. Her eyes sparkled like the most perfect emeralds. Her scales were a pearlescent green, with intricate criss-crossing and swirling patterns. Her claws, which were still sharp, and likely just as deadly as they had always been, also had details on them, lines and runes I'd never thought possible. I pointed them out to Sevrin. "Who did that?" I asked.

"They're born that way," he said, stroking Dakkar's lowered cheek. "It's part of their power."

There was a low rumbling coming from Dakkar. It sounded like she was growling, ready to roar and breathe fire. I was about to step back but Sevrin said, "You like this, don't you?" The rumbling grew. It was a sound of affection.

"Dakkar," I said, hesitantly. "May I touch your scales?"

She eyed me for a moment then lazily swung her head in my direction, nuzzling me with her snout and licking me with her surprisingly velvety soft tongue.

"I'll take that as a yes," I murmured. Her scales were hard, almost like metal, but they felt like glass, like they were made of some kind of gem. I traced the patterns of the scales with my fingers, and the fine lines. "Amazing," I said. "What do the runes on the claws mean?" I asked.

"It's what gives them their strength," Sevrin said. "You'll find similar runes on their wings, which is what gives them the power to fly."

"And of fire?"

Sevrin smiled. "On the inside, I think. We never looked."

"Dakkar, may I look at and touch your wings?" I asked.

Dakkar settled on her hind quarters, raised her chin and unfurled her expansive wings. She knew she was on display, proudly showing off her beauty.

"Thank you," I said with a smile. They were a fine leathery skin with tiny pebbles of scales in the same green as her regular scales, so small yet so impenetrable. This was going to be the most intricate carving I had ever attempted. It was going to be a huge challenge. If I could pull it off, it would be incredible.

All the more reason to get my shoulder fixed, at least to a place where I could hold a carving tool without wanting to cry.

I walked back to Sevrin's side. Dakkar snorted and bent down, this time breathing warm air on my right shoulder. Had she read my mind, thinking about my shoulder, or could she sense I was in pain? The heat felt wonderful. It didn't take away the pain, and yet at the same time it soothed me. "Thank you," I said again.

"DID YOU get to see Dakkar?" Mam asked when Sevrin and I joined her on set.

"I did," I said. "She let me touch her and look at her wings. She's spectacular. I think Sam's going to have some competition when it comes to adopting Dakkar."

"She loved you, that's for sure," Sevrin said.

"Perfect," the director, an elf I didn't recognize, said, approaching us. "Hiya, Sevrin."

"Hiya, Allain," Sevrin grunted.

"You two want to be extras?" Allain asked. "Payment is five diamonds for a hall-day."

"Mabel will," Mam said on my behalf.

"I'd love to," I said.

Sevrin shrugged. "Sure. Why not."

"Fantastic," Allain said. "Wardrobe will help you out. It's just back there." He pointed to a door at the back of the studio.

Sevrin and I walked to wardrobe. He'd been in a few movies, but I knew this wasn't really his thing. I had a feeling he was doing this mostly to keep an eye on me and Mam. I didn't care. And I didn't care what roles we were to have. I was acting with Sevrin! It was almost as amazing as acting with Aramis.

Sevrin wasn't just a legend in stories. He was also a hero in the first movie I ever saw. It was that movie, and Aramis, which made me fall in love with movies.

I grinned. This was a welcome break from all the worry.

"It's wonderful to see you smile, love," Sevrin said as we entered our respective dressing cubicles.

We emerged moments later in warrior costumes, complete with battle axes. Our armor was dark leather and iron. The hair and makeup artist added charcoal to Sevrin's beard and back-combed it. She glued a thick matted beard on me. It was a much better job than the one Emma had done when she'd glued tips of her own cut hair onto her chin to make it look like she was growing a beard when we first came of age. I wasn't sure if it was the glue, but I'd forgotten how itchy it was to have a beard.

We met the other extras back on set to rehearse. Allain's assistant moved us into a block formation that would give the best impression of a massive army. We practiced marching and some fighting moves against an invisible enemy. I looked over at Sevrin. It was like we'd traveled back in time and I was seeing Sevrin in his youth on his adventures and in battle.

After an hour of rehearsal we were loaded onto wagons and taken to a rolling field just outside the city. We got back into formation and Allain shouted action.

Sevrin pounded his fist against his breastplate. The rest of us joined in. We roared a battle cry. Over the hill came another dwarven army, led by Mam, in spectacular armor of silver that looked indestructible. Her helm had horns which I would have normally thought simply inconvenient, but I could now see how they could be useful as an added weapon. A war-horn blew and the two armies charged.

Mam flew through our ranks, taking down our numbers with ease. She fake-hit me and I fell to the ground. Allain shouted directions and I crawled one-armed to my fallen battle axe. Mam kicked it out of the way and stabbed me with the spear-sharpened end of her axe-handle. I groaned and gurgled and died. It was a brilliant death scene.

She faced off against Sevrin. It was better than watching a battle axe competition. They were brilliant, thrusting and parrying. Finally she moved in and pierced his armor with her axe-head. Sevrin's eyes went wide and I thought for a moment she had actually killed him. His body shook a few times and he breathed one last rattling breath. Mam pulled out her axe. Sevrin remained standing. Mam blew at him and he fell over.

"Cut." Allain yelled.

Mam helped Sevrin up and we all cheered.

Best. Day. Ever.

CHAPTER 14

AFTER MY appointment with Dr. Thora, I headed straight for Brent's gallery.

Sevrin was on another one of his secret errands. I'd given up hope he was going to propose to Mam. There were far too many errands for a proposal. He couldn't possibly be meeting our so-called protectors from Aubrey, since they'd been so ineffective. I'd stopped asking him where he went, and I'd stopped caring. Sevrin's errands gave me time to see Brent after my appointments. This was my first time back in the gallery since I'd met with Aubrey.

"Hi, Mabel," Brent said, coming out of the back room to meet me, arms outstretched. "How's my hero?" he asked, hugging me.

Hero? Me? Hardly. "Um, fine?" I loved his hug.

I didn't want him to let me go. When he did, I felt a tiny bit chilly.

"You're not sure?"

"About the hero part. I'm fine. Just wanted to pop in, see how you were... if there was any word." It wasn't really why I'd come here, but it was a safe conversation. I really just wanted to see Brent. I hadn't been up to going to the Lair since meeting with Aubrey. The acupuncture was helping, but I still hurt too much. It also just felt too risky to go out. The couple of times I had gone, Brent hadn't been there. Chris said Brent had been traveling on business for the gallery. I'd been worried Aubrey had done something to him.

"None yet, I'm afraid."

"Maybe I should have given him a deadline," I said which made Brent smile. I'd made him smile!

"Because you weren't forceful enough," he said. "On the other hand he has left you alone, right?"

"For now." I half shrugged. "That's not the only reason I came by. I thought I'd ask you to join me for lunch."

"I'd love to," Brent said. "Just give me a few minutes."

"No problem."

I looked around at some of the onyx pieces on display, examining the intricacies of the tool-work. At least I tried to. I kept glancing toward the back, to Brent's office. I thought about what Lillian said, that Brent was smitten with me. I really liked him. As I looked at the carvings, I considered asking Brent to be my date to my movie premiere, even though it was still months away.

I never tired of studying the art in the gallery. They were beautiful, the technique inspiring. I looked forward to pushing myself to do the same, or better. I'd been the same way, challenging myself with axe-throwing, and before that, when I'd been doing my masterwork, a special advanced project only a chosen few were asked to do before they were hired to work elsewhere, usually the mines. I'd loved spending hours a day on my stone-work carving, perfecting it, learning new skills, making it the best possible. I should have felt the same way in the mines, but I never had.

The door opened and my heart sank. A client meant Brent would have to look after them and not be with me.

"Mabel," Sevrin said.

I looked up then, eyes wide. He was supposed to be running errands. "Sevrin, what are you… is Mam okay?"

He was cold as stone, emotionless. "We have to talk, now."

"Ready to go?" Brent asked, coming out of the back. "Sevrin, hello."

"Brent, close the gallery and send your assistant out. We need to talk, somewhere private."

"O-okay. Sure. Head on back to my office and I'll lock up. Mabel, you'll be all right out here?"

"All three of us," Sevrin said.

As Sevrin walked past me, he grabbed my good arm and hauled me with him. His grip was like granite. Mam had to be all right. He wouldn't include Brent if it was about Mam. What was wrong? Was he angry? I couldn't tell, not like when Da was mad. Everyone knew when Da was mad. Maybe he was anxious about proposing to Mam, since he hadn't done it yet. He had to know I was all right with it. My brothers might not be, but they weren't in our lives. The gallery would be a lovely place to propose, but Mam would know something was up, she never came here.

Brent joined us a few moments later. Sevrin closed the door.

"You should have left things alone, Mabel. Brent, I'm sorry she involved you in this, but she did, and there is nothing I can do about it. You are in this now."

"What are you talking about, Sevrin?" I asked.

"Aubrey," he said and sucked in his bottom lip.

My jaw dropped. How did he know?

He scratched at his moustache with his thumb nail and leaned back against Brent's desk. "You have stirred up all kinds of trouble."

He still didn't sound upset. He sounded more like he was thinking, calculating, plotting. "Sevrin, I—"

He held up a hand and silenced me. "We had our boundaries. I know Radier violated them by taking you to Aubrey, and Aubrey violated them by coming to see you, but to instigate contact… Mabel, this is so much bigger than you know."

This wasn't right. "You know I met with Aubrey?"

"Of course I do," Sevrin said.

My heart pounded, and heat filled my face. "Does Mam know? Does she know you know?"

"Of course not."

He was too dismissive, like it was no big deal. If I hadn't been betraying Mam by contacting Aubrey, I would retract my approval of Sevrin. Even so, he'd known her a lot longer than I had. How long had he been lying to her?

"And she isn't going to know," Sevrin said. "I really wish you'd trusted me. It was under control."

How could he possibly believe that? "It was far from under control. I am in constant fear he will do something to Mam, or my friends. I am at Aubrey's mercy. He can do what he wants, when he wants. I can't live like that. I won't live like that. Defenses are great if they work, but they clearly didn't," I said, waving at my shoulder. "If they were successful, how long would we need them? Aubrey's immortal. I won't ask others to risk their lives for me forever."

Sevrin's coldness dropped and for the first time since he walked into the gallery, he showed some emotion, I just didn't know if it was concern, or acceptance. Sevrin looked down, rubbing his forehead with his thumb and forefinger. "Tell me exactly what your plan was?"

I told him my demand that Aubrey remove his

elven magic from me and that if he didn't, I would make sure the elves and especially those in the mafia would know that Radier was the real boss, not Aubrey.

"You truly believe Radier is in charge of the elves?" Sevrin asked.

I told him the evidence I had. "Aubrey didn't refute it either. He just walked out."

"And right at us," Sevrin muttered.

"Us? What do you mean *us*?" I asked.

"How do you think peace was established and maintained for so long between dwarves and elves? Aubrey encroached on our territory once, with your family, and the peace nearly broke down. His threats against you and Frerin are straining relations, but we were taking care of it."

We? Territory? I didn't want to believe what I was sure I was hearing. Who was Sevrin, really?

"I understand why you thought you could handle this, but—" Sevrin shook his head. "I didn't want to have to do this, but you've left me no choice. You both work for me now. I'll try to spare you the worst of it so Frerin won't know. I'll do my best to protect you."

"Excuse me?" Brent said. "Work for you?"

Sevrin crossed his arms and casually leaned back. "The elves aren't the only ones who are organized."

My knees gave out and I sank to the sofa. "How is this possible? You're joking, right?"

"This is no joke," Sevrin said. "Cooperate and

your involvement will be short. We'll do what we can to re-negotiate the peace, but right now, Aubrey is pushing for an all-out-war."

I couldn't breathe. My vision darkened. What was happening? Was this Sevrin's way of trying to teach me a lesson? "Okay, okay, I apologize, I shouldn't have made contact with Aubrey, I'm sorry."

"I appreciate and accept your apology. And now you can help reverse the damage.

"Brent," Sevrin continued. "I understand Aubrey has been purchasing art from you. It would have been better if you hadn't used your gallery for the meeting with Aubrey, but you can still be useful. We want you to use your connections to Aubrey. Keep your eyes and ears open, and tell me everything you see and hear about his movements, his actions. Everything. Don't leave anything out. And continue to cultivate your connections in the elven community."

Brent's eyes were downcast, his shoulders slumped. "Yes, sir."

Because of me, he was now caught between the two organizations. Exactly what I'd hoped to prevent. Was his business ruined because of me? My stomach churned and I was thankful I hadn't eaten anything yet.

"I'm so sorry, Brent," I said.

He didn't look at me. He didn't give any response. I didn't blame him.

"As for you, Mabel, right now, just sit tight. Ideally I'd like you to take back your threat, but in this case, I don't think that's possible. We'll have to investigate your claims about Radier. If it's true, it could change things, in our favor. Gods, I hope you're right. We'll cancel all your appointments with Dr. Thora until this is resolved, and you will stay home. You will not wander or be alone at any time. Not only are you a prime target, so are all of your friends. I can protect you best at home. Let's go."

CHAPTER 15

I TOSSED and turned in bed. Sleep escaped me as it had for the last few nights. I couldn't stop thinking about Mam's relationship with Sevrin. He said that she didn't know about his role, his leadership in the Dwarven Mafia. It didn't make sense.

Sevrin knew about Aubrey and yet he let us go see him. When we returned, he denied knowing anything. He said he was surprised about Radier possibly running the Elven Mafia, and yet when I'd asked him about Radier, he'd been unconcerned. If tension was so high between dwarves and elves, why were Aramis and Sevrin such good friends?

What made sense to me, if it were true, was that maybe, when Mam left Gilliam, she had actually found Aubrey, the one who had stolen everything, and she needed protection, so she found Sevrin. Except she took me to see Aubrey, and was genuinely shocked and outraged at the encounter, at Radier, at everyone.

Or was she really just that good an actress?

Why involve me? Why?

That was exactly what it felt like: that all of this was on purpose, that somehow I'd been set up. That Mam and Sevrin had planned this from the start. Had Aramis been a part of it too? Was that why he'd wanted to make the movie in Gilliam? How could they have known I'd want to be in the movie? How did they know I would leave my family? Mam knew nothing about me then. For all she knew, I was exactly like Da and my brothers, against her, against acting, and against everything that wasn't respectable, everything that wasn't mining. Was I that easily manipulated?

I didn't get exiled by my family and come all this way, go through all this pain, just to be used. They were taking my choices away from me.

No more.

I wasn't standing for it with Aubrey, and I wasn't going to stand for it now.

I got out of bed and found Sevrin in the back garden, chopping wood. Couldn't he have hired someone, or had one of his minions do this work?

"What do you want from me?" I demanded between swings of his axe.

With a two-handed grip and a strong downswing,

Sevrin embedded the axe-head deep into the log, jamming it there. He eyed me for a few moments, longer than was comfortable.

I stared back, one hand on my hip. Did Sevrin care at all about me or Mam?

Sevrin looked around as though he expected elves to be peeking around the corner or from behind the neighbor's fence a good hundred feet away. He worked at maneuvering the axe-head out of the log. "I said I'd tell you when I needed too."

I moved closer before he had the axe swinging again. My stomach muscles clenched involuntarily. I was grateful for the sling because it kept my arm from visibly shaking. I lowered my voice. "I think you've made up all of this Dwarven Mafia business." I raised an eyebrow, not so much as an accusation as a dare for him to prove me wrong.

He smirked, casually working the axe handle back and forth, loosening its position. "I assure you, I did not."

"No? Prove it. Give me something mobster-ish to do. Should I threaten someone? Intimidate some business to pay up their debts? Is there some movie director refusing to give a part to Mam or someone else we like?"

Sevrin shook his head. "That's not why you're here."

"Here?" I was right. Oh good gods, I was right. "So it was the plan all along. Mam does know. You all planned this before she even came to Gilliam with Aramis. Is that why you and he were there? Pretending to scout locations so you could actually see Mam's family? See if I'd be amenable to coming here and being a part of your organization? To use me as your pawn in the war with Aubrey?"

Sevrin left the axe and put his hand on my good shoulder. "Mabel, listen to me. It isn't like that at all. Not exactly."

"Tell me what it is like, *exactly*."

Sevrin sighed and walked me to the back step. We sat down and he sighed again. "Everything about the movie, scouting locations, Aramis knowing about Frerin's family, wanting to reunite her with them, you, was entirely legitimate and true. You were right about one thing, Frerin does know about me. That is why we connected. She came to me for protection."

"I knew it!" I felt triumphant that I was right, but it didn't make me feel any better about the situation I was in.

"Aramis knew that Aubrey had been breaking their agreement, coming into Leitham to purchase art and other things. It has put us on our guard."

"Wait, you mean Aramis is working with you? He knows?" My Aramis was a part of this too, from the beginning? Was he really my friend at all?

"Of course. We'd been friends long before I became boss, while I was working my way up the ranks. He was our inside man on the elven side for a long time. And while he has been out of it for some time, he's still in the know. He can't not be. As for your mam, Frerin was ecstatic that you wanted to come back to Leitham with her. You are her daughter. You are all she has ever talked about. She loves you more than anything. You also became helpful to our cause when she heard that Radier had promised to take you to Aubrey. We saw this as our chance."

Mam willingly used me too? "Chance for what?"

"We've suspected for several years now, that Radier is really running things, not Aubrey. We need proof. Once we have it, we can hopefully put a stop to the impending war before it begins."

I hated that they were using me, but, if I could be useful… "What impending war?"

"With Aubrey pushing the boundaries, there had to be a reason for it. He'd respected them for too long for there to be any real reason for him to break them now. Yes, your friend Brent showcases amazing art, but Aubrey could have continued to send one of his workers. There is no reason for him to come in. He isn't doing this of his own free will. Someone is pushing him. Then Radier takes you to see him? It could be argued that he did so because you're so likeable, he doesn't want you to hurt, and he thought that Aubrey would do it out of friendship. I would have said as much, if Frerin hadn't told me about the way Aubrey greeted Radier, and Aubrey coming to you, instead of sending for you. All of what I said about Radier liking you is probably true, you are wonderful, so don't take this the wrong way, but we don't think that was his real motivation."

And I'd helped him do just that. "With me con-fronting Aubrey… how bad did I make things?"

Sevrin smiled for the first time and shook his head. "You sped things up a bit, perhaps, but that's all. We are concerned, though, for your safety. You confronted Aubrey in Brent's gallery. Thankfully you didn't say anything to him to make him think you are a part of our organization, though you did come awfully close with your assertions about Radier.

"From the moment she said you were going to come to Leitham, I promised Frerin I would keep you safe. To do that now, I need to keep you and Brent separate. It is the only way I can see right now."

"Have I endangered Brent? What about Lillian? Or my other friends?"

Sevrin shook his head. "Brent knew what he was getting into the day he agreed to start selling art to Aubrey. He knew this was bound to happen."

Except that he'd been doing it to get back at Aubrey for destroying so many in Gypsum. Brent had offered the gallery as neutral territory. He'd kept quiet about his connection to Aubrey so he wouldn't draw any unwanted attention and lose clients. Because of me, he'd received that attention but not from whom he expected. "Is he in trouble for selling to Aubrey?"

"Ha. No. Money needs to be made. Who cares where it comes from? Actually, that the money comes from Aubrey, is fantastic. Brilliant young fel-low there, that Brent. I should have recruited him earlier."

"I don't understand. If it was perfectly fine for Brent to be taking money from Aubrey, and I didn't know who you are, or what you do, why tell me? If I didn't know, Aubrey couldn't possibly think that I did. Why keep me away from my friends? Why tell me?"

"While your actions are of some benefit to me, you have stirred up some trouble. We'll protect your friends as much as possible. The more time you spend with them, the greater the danger you, and they, will be in. Aubrey is now tracking your movements. If he sees you with your friends too much, he may start to show more interest in them. You were right about the ineffectiveness of our defenses. I am the only one who can protect you from Aubrey. I can't do that when I am not with you. I love Frerin. I want you to be my step-daughter. I will do absolutely everything to keep you safe."

Sevrin paused a moment, looked to the sky then down at the ground before continuing. "As for why involve you? Why tell you? We need you. You've put Aubrey on notice that you're aware that he isn't in charge. We want you to dig deeper, get actual proof that we can use. By you confronting him, you've also made him believe that you know nothing about me, or your Mam, which is also the reason she took you to see him in the first place. So, Aubrey thinks you're an innocent in all of this."

"Why not leave me ignorant of it all?"

"Frerin and I discussed it at length. In the end, we would rather you know just what you're getting into, and have proper protection and backup when you need it. I would have preferred to tell you some other way, but this was the best, for all of us."

"Why make it so public? Even if it was just you, me, and Brent, someone will know, and it will get back to Aubrey. That will just make my job more difficult."

"No one saw, we made sure of that. And we've let Brent get away without too much notice for too long."

Oh gods. They were going to start taking money from Brent. "What does that mean?"

"We should have asked for his cooperation earlier. It was about time we asked for, and got it."

"Cooperation?"

"He has Aubrey and other clients that we want access to. He has had those clients for a long time, and has built strong relationships with them. We can now utilize those connections."

"What about his business? Are you going to take it from him? Hurt him?"

"We don't hurt our own, as long as they cooperate."

Sevrin was being too vague. I was going to have to apologize to Brent. "So, what do you want from me?"

"We want you to keep after Aubrey. Follow up on your threat if you have to, about telling his people about Radier running the organization. We need to expose Radier. Once we do, we can take care of him. Then Aubrey will be back in charge, and we can negotiate a decent settlement."

"What if his people don't want him in charge because he'd relinquished his power to Radier? What if they don't trust him?"

"They don't have a choice. Aubrey's their king."

"What if they rebel?"

Sevrin smiled. "Then it will be war."

AFTER SOME lengthy negotiations with Sevrin, I joined my friends at the pub. Mam and Sevrin agreed with me that I should act normal, do my normal things. It was the only way to go on, to keep my involvement with Sevrin's organization a secret, and to make Aubrey believe I still didn't know about Sevrin being Lord of the Dwarven Mafia.

Going out, having a normal night out, was a bit of a relief. Once I stepped through the pub door and inhaled the pipe smoke and ale, everything else in my life melted away.

I was the last to arrive at our table and everyone stopped talking. They just stared at me. All but Brent, who sipped his pint and looked at the wall behind Jeff. Great. They all knew I was trouble. They weren't going to have anything to do with me now. I'd lost my friends in Gilliam because of my family.

Now I was losing my friends in Leitham because of my family.

Not this time. And I wasn't. I realized then that they weren't looking at me with dread or disdain or loathing. They were looking at me with expectancy. Of what, I didn't know. I took a deep breath, made sure I was smiling as I approached. "Hey. Got a pint for me?"

Lillian reached for one, not looking, missed a few times before grasping a tankard and handing it to me. Jeff pushed out a chair for me.

"Thanks," I said, taking a sip and sitting down. "What's going on?"

"You tell us." Jeff said.

"I-I don't know what you're talking about," I said, looking at each of them in turn, trying to figure out what they were thinking, what they wanted me to say.

"We heard you talked to Aubrey," Chris said.

I glanced at Brent but he hadn't moved, not even a flinch or a nod of recognition. "Who told you that?" I asked. Brent wouldn't have, I didn't think.

Lillian blushed. "I'd heard it from some of the elven actors on set."

So Sevrin's plan was working. Pressure was being put on Aubrey. Word was getting out that maybe he wasn't all he said he was. "What? How?" I had too many questions. I couldn't get them out quick enough.

"I heard them say you threatened Aubrey," Lillian

said.

"Why would I do such a thing?" I felt the heat rising in my own cheeks. I had essentially threatened him. It felt so weird to lie about it. I turned to Lillian. I couldn't imagine Aubrey was open or even wanted any of his people to know he'd been threatened by anyone, much less a dwarf. Were the elves happy about the threats to Aubrey? "What exactly where they saying?"

"They said that Aubrey has been quiet for the last several weeks. No one has seen him. Then, as of a few days ago, there has been a lot of activity in his territory, and that rules are tightening up. His soldiers are closing ranks, being more firm-handed with their people. They said it could only be because he was confronted by someone, that his position was being threatened, and he had to re-group."

"But they didn't say who had threatened him." I relaxed a little. No one knew anything. Brent's and my secret was safe.

"Not exactly," Lillian said. "But it had to be you."

"Why? Because I asked about him? That's ridiculous."

"That's what I said," Brent said. It was only then that he looked at me. He was still my friend. The knowing look he gave me and the relaxation of his shoulders told me we were on the same side.

"Well, I've never felt so popular, so talked about, since I shaved my beard." I stroked the short bristles speckling my chin. "I hate to be the one to disillusion you, but it wasn't me."

"You expect us to believe it's pure coincidence you asked about Aubrey and then we hear that someone confronted him?" Jeff asked.

"Yep."

"Nope. No way," Chris said.

"Come on. Why would I confront Aubrey? That would be crazy. I was just curious. Just trying to figure out how everything works here. Leitham is so different from Gilliam." I wasn't just trying to protect myself and Brent, I was also, maybe rather clumsily, trying to do what Sevrin asked of me, to perpetuate the story that I was an innocent, that I didn't know what I was doing, that I wasn't aware of Sevrin's or Mam's involvement in the Dwarven Mafia. "Very sorry to have disappointed you all."

"So much for you being the hero of dwarves everywhere," Lillian said with a smile. "And some of the elves too."

They wanted things to change? It might not mean they would want Aubrey back in charge, but maybe they would help us depose Radier.

"Yeah, and here we all thought you were the chosen one," Hannah added.

"Chosen one? Now I'm disappointed," I said. I loved being able to joke around with my friends like this. It also made me warm with pride, that even though they didn't know, I was working with Sevrin and the Dwarven Mafia to bring down Aubrey and Radier. Maybe it wasn't exactly delivering all dwarves from some evil tyrant, but it was still protecting our people. There was no prophecy or any need for a chosen one, but it kind of felt like it was me anyway. "We should put that into our movie," I said to Lillian.

"Brilliant," Lillian exclaimed. "Prophecy and a Crime Lord. I love it."

As the night wore on and our usual pattern of switching seats carried on, I eventually ended up next to Brent. "How are you doing?" I asked in a lowered voice.

"I'm all right," he said.

"I'm really sorry," I said. "I had no idea about, well, you know."

"It's okay. Honestly," he said.

"Has anyone contacted you? Is the gallery okay?"

"Yes, on both. It's nothing I can't handle. I'm just surprised it hadn't happened earlier. And maybe I'm a bit proud to be helping out. How are you?" he asked, reaching over and grasping my hand, holding onto it, leaning toward me, like we were the only two at the table, in the room.

My heart thumped in my chest, the blood pulsing through my ears. "Um, yes, I'm fine. Feeling proud too."

"Good," he said and scooted his chair closer to mine. He squeezed my hand then let go.

For the briefest of moments I panicked, until he rested it on my knee. He'd freed my hand so I could still drink. Sweet and thoughtful. Maybe I should pressure Aubrey to fix my right shoulder again so I could hold Brent's hand all the time.

"Thank you for not telling everyone about, you know," he said.

"I wouldn't dream of it."

"I didn't think you would. How about you? Seriously. How are you? Is everything okay at home? I haven't seen you in a while. I've been worried."

"Everything's fine. I had a talk with Sevrin. This was not my plan when I moved here, but," I half shrugged. I couldn't help but feel I was playing with fire, in both my relationship with Brent and my role in the mafia, "I feel like I have so much more to gain by helping Sevrin than I have to lose."

CHAPTER 16

AFTER A routine and oh-so-necessary appointment with Dr. Thora, which Sevrin reluctantly reinstated, I walked to the taxi stand and hired a cart to take me to Aubrey's.

Just over a month had passed since I'd met with Aubrey and I still hadn't heard from him. He hadn't given me that kind of time between his threat to me and finding me after my meeting with Varv. Maybe I should have been grateful that he was leaving me alone. But that wasn't my role any more.

I now had access to resources I never thought existed. I could now do what Aubrey did to me. I could go into his territory, slip past his henchmen, and remind him that I had a demand he had yet to answer.

The plan was simple. Sevrin had found out where Aubrey lived, just outside of Leitham. I was to go to him, without warning, and remind him of my demand to remove his magic and leave my family alone. It was necessary to go to Aubrey to prove that we could find him and that we could get past his defenses, just as he had done with ours.

When I'd pointed out to Sevrin that by doing this, it would become obvious that I worked for him, he shrugged and said it couldn't be kept secret forever. He also thought if Aubrey knew about my position within the Dwarven Mafia, it might give me more negotiating power.

I hadn't wanted to use just anyone to take me to Aubrey's. It was going to be difficult enough for me to hide how I found out where he lived. I didn't want to get anyone else in trouble. Sevrin assured me he had the perfect solution: someone who was in the organization but knew enough not to have attracted any notice of his involvement.

One of the newer members of the Dwarven Mafia had been placed as a taxi driver to be at Sevrin's disposal. I recognized him and I suspected he'd also been the one to tell Sevrin I'd been seeing Brent after my doctor's appointments, and probably also that I'd met with Aubrey. He would take me to Aubrey's and wait for me. Because he was an unknown, while he waited he could study the location and the guards both visible and hidden, and be seen as a mere taxi driver, without raising any suspicions.

Unlike when Radier took me to see Aubrey, this time I paid attention to where we were going. My first thought, as we left the distinctly dwarven business district, was that I was actually getting used to the smell and size of the city. We traversed through the neutral business district, shops and other offerings for all manner of species, and into a pixie neighborhood. From there we headed south, through another dwarven residential area and then a troll area, and finally out of town, toward the forests on the eastern edge of the city.

Elven territory.

This was not the same as where I'd gone with Radier. That home must have been a decoy, a stand-in, some place he wanted me to believe he lived in. This was his real home.

The moment we turned up the path leading to Aubrey's home built into the trunk of a gigantic beech tree at the center of the forest, lit by elven glow-lamps, we were stopped by elven guards blocking the way.

I waited for them to speak, but they didn't. Finally I said, "Aubrey asked to see me." It was a lie I hoped they wouldn't catch.

"He is not here," the one on the right said.

I knew he wasn't, that had been a part of the plan, to arrive several minutes before Aubrey. "I guess I'm early. My apologies. I didn't think I was. I'm sure he wouldn't mind me waiting inside." I pretended to shiver. It was chilly, but not that cold. I hoped they'd let us pass. I'd love to get a look at Aubrey's home up close, maybe even inside. Who knew what all I might find that could help our cause? I shivered for real this time at the thought of what evidence there might be to prove that he worked for Radier. I might find out what Radier used to control Aubrey.

"You can wait here," the one on the left said.

I half-shrugged. "Fine. No problem."

It wouldn't be so bad. Aubrey was due back soon and it would interesting to see his reaction when he saw me with his guards. He wouldn't know if I told them anything. Not right away, anyway. It wouldn't be long before he figured out I'd said nothing, not with the elven power of reading the minds of their own people. But that first moment of not knowing could be worth it.

I considered leaving the moment Aubrey approached, letting the momentary belief I had followed through with my threat of telling his guards Radier was really in charge be enough. I needed to stay and see this through, not just because that was what Sevrin wanted of me, but because I needed to get Aubrey to remove his magic from my shoulder. At the root of all of this, I still needed to get healed without the lingering possibility of the injury being triggered at his whim.

So I stayed, and I waited.

Minutes passed and turned into an hour. Aubrey should have been back by now. All reports were that he rarely went out and when he did, it was only for short periods of time. I hoped today was not the day he finally changed his routine.

The guards finally stood aside and without a word, let us pass.

I thought it was because they'd kept us waiting so long, until we arrived at the base of the beech tree. Aubrey stood at the door.

Had he been here all along? Or had he come back a different way so we couldn't see him? It didn't matter. He'd known I was waiting, thanks to that crazy mind-reading ability elves had with each other, and he made me wait on purpose to show he had the power.

"Sorry to have kept you waiting," Aubrey said with the subtlest upturn at the corner of his lips. "Please, do come in."

He was trying to take control back from me.

My taxi driver helped me down.

"Leave your chauffeur here," Aubrey said.

Wordlessly, the driver got back onto the cart. I swallowed hard and followed Aubrey through the door to a stairway.

"I was wondering when I would hear from you," Aubrey said.

I stopped a few steps down. I wasn't here for a friendly chat and it irritated me that he was treating it as just that. "Will you do what I asked?"

Aubrey kept walking, forcing me to go with him.

At the bottom of the stairs was a large room, with a bar, some chairs, and a large mirror. Aubrey walked over to the mirror. "I do not think so." He waved his hand in front of the mirror. The glass swirled and when it cleared, there was Jimmy and Phillip, my two best friends in Gilliam, bound with vines, arrows dripping poison aimed at them.

I gasped.

Aubrey waved his hand again and they were gone.

I didn't know if it was real, if that was happening right now, or if that was just what Aubrey wanted me to see.

I took a few moments to collect myself. I wasn't in this alone. I had Sevrin and his entire organization behind me. I would tell Sevrin about Phillip and Jimmy the moment I got home. He would make sure my friends and family were protected.

"Retract your threat and no harm will come to your friends," Aubrey said, his voice cold, heartless.

How interesting, that he was most concerned that his people might be told Radier was truly in charge. "Remove your magic from my shoulder, leave me and my family alone, and I'll be happy to let you do whatever you want, for whomever you want."

It wasn't an unreasonable request, I thought. In fact, I thought it made it clear to Aubrey that I wanted out of this whole mess, that I wanted everything to go back to the way it was before we ever met.

Aubrey sneered. "Your shoulder will remain as it is." He crooked his finger and excruciating pain flared in my shoulder.

I clenched my jaw and breathed into the pain. "I will not betray my people to you, and most certainly *not* to Radier."

Aubrey came within an inch of my face. Out of the corner of my eye I saw him twist his wrist. Pain flooded through me, to the edge of blacking out. I stifled my cries and kept eye contact with him.

"You know nothing," he growled.

"Give it up, Aubrey. I'm of no use to you."

With a wave of his hand, all pain was gone. All of it. He backed up a step. "You are of far greater use to me now more than ever."

With another wave, I was outside the perimeter of his territory, standing next to my taxi driver and his cart.

"Was it successful?" he asked once we'd recovered from the trans-location.

"I don't know."

THE MOMENT the taxi driver left me at Mam's front door, my knees began to tremble. Mam, on one of her rare days off, met me at the door.

"Your shoulder. Where's your sling? Did it work?" She pulled me into the kitchen and sat me down at the table. Sevrin joined us, placing large, steaming mugs of tea in front of us.

"What happened?" he asked, leaning toward me. I could see the eagerness flashing in his eyes.

The first thing I did was tell them about Phillip and Jimmy. As I knew he would, Sevrin promised to send protection to Gilliam. He said it would be inconspicuous. My friends and family would be safe.

I told them how Aubrey seemed more concerned than anything about being exposed for being under Radier's control. "To me," I said, "while it isn't real proof, it's probably a pretty good indication it's true."

Sevrin agreed. "Unfortunately we will need more than that."

"What about your shoulder?" Mam asked.

I told them how Aubrey had made me hurt, then he took it all away. "He said I was of more use to him now more than ever."

Mam and Sevrin looked at each other.

"What?" I asked. "What does that mean?"

After a moment's pause, Sevrin said, "It means we need to be on our guard more than ever."

"He's using me to get to you, isn't he?" I asked Sevrin.

"Likely."

Mam buried her face in her hands. "It's all my fault. All of this. The moment I decided to act in that stupid play in Gilliam I ruined my family. I just couldn't leave it be. I couldn't just move on."

"Frerin—" Sevrin tried to interrupt.

Mam kept talking. "I found you, Sevrin. And you've helped me so much. We started fighting back."

"Frerin—" He tried again.

"But then we brought Mabel into this."

"Frerin—" This time he reached for her.

"I'm not going to let Aubrey or Radier hurt my daughter anymore."

"Let?" I broke in. Until she said that word I was all ready to say it wasn't her fault. "What do you mean *let* them hurt me?"

Mam turned to me, tears in her eyes, her jaw dropped. "Oh, honey, I didn't mean… I shouldn't have let Aubrey heal your shoulder. I shouldn't have let Radier take you to Aubrey. I should have insisted Aramis make his movie elsewhere."

"You knew they were going to do this to me before you came to Gilliam?" Aramis had told me he should have known something was amiss when Radier signed on to work on the movie in Gilliam, but he hadn't because they were like brothers. They often worked together. Sevrin told me they had only seen the opportunity to involve me after Radier had mentioned Aubrey to me. "You knew about me, my injury. You'd been following my axe-throwing career. Which one of you made it possible for Radier to step in? Which one of you made the original Recordist sick?"

"It wasn't like that," Mam said. She reached for my hand but I snapped it back.

She'd heard about me. She'd known about me all this time. "If it weren't for this feud with Aubrey, if I weren't such a grand opportunity to destroy Aubrey and Radier, would you have ever come to Gilliam?

Would you have ever come for me?" My heart ached. "Or was I just a means to an end?" I remembered her hesitation at hugging me when we first met. She'd had all kinds of explanations for it. This made the most sense.

"Mabel, love," Mam said. "You're right. We did see the movie and your situation as the chance to get at Aubrey and Radier. I had a lot of reservations. Big ones."

"She did," Sevrin said.

"You're my daughter. I love you. I had been away for seventy years. I didn't know if you would accept me if I came back."

"You never gave me a chance before you decided to use me."

"I gave her an out," Sevrin said.

Was that supposed to make me feel better?

"He did," Mam said. "I insisted on it."

"So why didn't you take it?"

"I wanted to. You have no idea how much I wanted to."

"Clearly not enough."

"Mabel, do you remember when we met, and I told you I'd gone to see your da?"

"I do."

"The out was that if attitudes had changed, then I wouldn't have a need to go ahead with the plan. I would simply watch Radier, make sure he behaved himself." Mam paused. "Your da hadn't changed. The hurt caused because of me was still so strong, like it had just happened. So I felt it best to allow it all to play out the way we intended. I let Radier lure you into his confidence. I let him stir hope for healing. I hated it. I did. I thought it was the only way I had left to make things better for your da." Mam dropped her eyes. "It was my way to stop feeling guilty. I hated it, love. I did. But I didn't stop it."

I didn't know what to think. I was so angry and hurt, and yet I reasoned that I shouldn't be. What was done was done. Except Mam had stood by and watched Radier use me. *She* used me. It made me question whether Aramis had actually wanted to cast me as his sister, or if all of my involvement with him, from being in his movie, to my editing lessons, was to keep me involved, keep me clueless. Hadn't Aramis asked Mam to tell Sevrin that he'd pierced the big one?

"The big one," I said looking at Sevrin. "The wager you and Aramis had. Was it that he'd pierced me or Radier?"

Sevrin shifted in his seat. "Radier." He cleared his throat. "You were the bait."

I couldn't believe what I was hearing. It was too much. Everything was crumbling around me. Everything I'd come to believe in was being swept away. I grasped for the only thing I could. "Mam, would you have ever come for me?"

She was quiet for several seconds. "I wanted to, every day—"

That wasn't good enough for me anymore.

"Would you have done it?"

"The movie was my only way in."

She was avoiding answering. "Without the movie?"

"I didn't know how."

I couldn't breathe. "My fist night here, you asked me if getting my shoulder fixed was the only reason I was here. It's my turn to ask: is this plan against Radier the *only* reason you wanted me to move here with you?"

"Of course not, Mabel. I love you so much. Every day I have wished all of this didn't exist."

I was lost. My heart was shattered. I felt numb. "So let's end it," I said.

"I'm so sorry, Mabel." Mam reached for me again.

I stopped her. "Give me time and space. When this is over, then I'll think about my relationship with you."

Mam sniffled. "That's fair." She turned to Sevrin. "What do we do?"

"I hope, Mabel," Sevrin said, "that you will give Frerin another chance. We both love you."

I almost believed Mam. I didn't believe Sevrin.

He cleared his throat. "I think we have no choice but to go after Radier directly. To do that, we also need to isolate you, Mabel."

CHAPTER 17

I STOOD outside the taxi stand in the dwarven business district, and looked left and right. I was on my own. I had my instructions from Sevrin. I was to find Radier. Until I figured out how to find him, I was to move out. We made it look like I'd had a falling out with Mam which was easy to do. I didn't want to be around her right now, anyway. Sevrin insisted I stay in dwarven neighborhoods as much as possible. He wouldn't be able to truly protect me, but he could have his henchmen watching and they would report back to him. The point was to make me vulnerable.

Bait for Radier once more.

Mam hated the plan. I wasn't crazy about it, but I wanted to finish this whole mess. If this was the only way, then I would do it. I didn't care what Mam thought or wanted. She'd had more than one chance to prevent my involvement and she'd done nothing. As far as I was concerned, she'd used me, willingly or not, as much as anyone else.

There were a couple of inns nearby. I could probably afford one night's stay, but I didn't think I could afford more than that. I headed south. If I remembered right, in a couple of miles, the neighborhood wouldn't be quite as important or wealthy. I hoped I'd be able to find an inn I could stay in.

My throwing axes and the handful of belongings I'd brought with me from Gilliam clanked and bumped against each other in my two leather bags as I shifted them up on my shoulder. Sweat beaded on my head. I was back in my old mining clothes. I hadn't realized how warm they were. I was also back in my mining boots. They were much more comfortable than the finer boots I'd purchased here, for all the walking I expected to do.

I'd left everything I'd bought with Mam's money. Sevrin said it would help public perception that I'd had a major fight with Mam. I was happy to leave them. To me, they were all tainted, like they had been bribes or guilt gifts for using me. I insisted on going further than Sevrin thought necessary. I would pay my own way. I would find my own place to live and I wouldn't tell anyone where it was. Sevrin's henchmen would spot me soon enough, anyway.

There was a purpose to all of this, but it also gave

me a much needed break from Mam and Sevrin and the mafia, if only for a day.

My stomach rumbled and clenched at the same time. I needed to eat something.

I passed several inns on my walk but all were well out of my range. At the three-mile mark I found the Hammer and Chisel Inn. The paint on the sign was faded and peeling. Some of the windows had cracks in them, or they just looked that way because they hadn't been cleaned in a long time. The prices listed beside the door were finally something I could afford.

The inside of the inn was little better than the outside. The sitting area by the cold, blackened fireplace was empty. The leather of the chairs was splitting in several places, the stuffing showing and spilling out. Everything, including the torch sconces, was covered in a fine layer of dust or ash. At least there weren't any spider webs that I could see, not that I wanted to look too close.

I was beginning to wonder if the place was closed when a wonderfully stout female dwarf came down a set of rickety wood stairs. Her clothes were smudged with dust and dirt but her cheeks were rosy and she smiled warmly, her eyes sparkling.

"What can I do for you, love?"

"I'm hoping you have a room you could let to me for a few nights. Three, maybe four?"

She put her hands on her hips and looked around. "Well, as you can see, we're a bit busy right now."

I looked around at the empty lounge around us. Was she crazy?

Then she laughed a most beautiful, deep, sonorous laugh. "Only kidding, love. We absolutely have a room for you, for as long as you'd like. You'll even have your pick."

I chuckled with her. I should have caught her sarcasm. "Great. Thanks. I don't have a lot of money. Some emeralds and that's about it."

"Tell you what," she said climbing back up the stairs. "We'll put you in the best room we have and if someone comes along who can pay more, we'll move you out to one of the smaller rooms. How does that sound?"

I followed her, the wood creaking beneath our feet. I was glad I wasn't as stout as my family would have liked me to be. If I had been, I would have worried about the stairs breaking under my weight. "Sounds like a lot of fuss, actually, but great. I'll take it. I'm Mabel, by the way."

"Sophie," she said. "So, Mabel. What brings you to our part of Leitham? Looking to get into the movie business are you? Here."

She opened the door to the room at the end of the hallway. It was smaller than my room back home in Gilliam, but it had a bed, a small table and chair, a closet, and a wash basin. What more did I need? "Not exactly. I'm an artist, and I hear there are some great galleries here that might be willing to show my work, maybe have it used in movies." It was the story I agreed to use. It wasn't far from the truth. As long as my shoulder was pain-free, I could use some of this time as an opportunity to get back to carving and see if it was something I really wanted to do as a career after all of this was over.

"An artist. Well. Fancy that. I hope this will do you. The washroom is next door. Come down for lunch in an hour."

I put my bags down and fished for my emeralds again. "It's wonderful. Thank you. How much do I owe you?"

"We can work that out over lunch. Just get yourself settled in here."

The bed was a thin straw mat stretched out over a wood frame. The blanket had a few small holes in it and the sheets did as well, but it was a bed. The door to the closet hung off its hinges and the table leaned to one side. I turned around slowly, looking at my pitiful new surroundings, what would be my home for the next few days, at least. Thinking of Sophie's warmth and smile were all that kept the tears from falling.

For so long I'd wanted to write to Max, tell him about all the amazing things I'd seen and done and everyone I'd met. Now, though I was physically able to, I couldn't write to him. I couldn't imagine telling him about the predicament I was in, the place I was living in now. The worst part would be telling him about how Mam betrayed me, all of us, really, and admitting I let her.

I sat on the bed and leaned against the wall. I pulled out the onyx from my pocket and the carving tools; they were the only things from Sevrin and Mam I'd dared to keep. Well, that and the wizard's crystals and recording fork from Aramis. I filed and etched. It was the only way I could relax my mind, and accept where I was. Maybe I could convince Brent to show and sell my other carvings even though I didn't have an agent. Maybe he could make an exception to that rule for me and sell these, so I could earn enough to afford a decent place to stay. If I had a few more carvings, maybe I could live off of my earnings for a while, and I would never have to go back to Mam and Sevrin.

I lay down on the bed and curled up, pulling my knees to my chest. I longed for the days when I was bored with mining and imagined myself in movies winning the love and saving the life of Aramis. Was that really less than a year ago?

SOPHIE AND her husband, Otto, were lovely. They asked for two emeralds as payment for a week's stay including lunch and dinner, which I thought was very generous of them. I would have liked to stay in the lounge, sitting in front of the fireplace, but I needed some time to think. I also thought it was best for at least a couple of days, to stay hidden. I didn't want either of Aubrey's or Radier's people to find me. Not yet.

I stayed in my room, moving between the thin straw mattress to the hard wood chair, carving, practicing with the crystal, and reading Dr. Thaddeus.

Working the tools over the onyx—chiseling, filing, etching fine lines—helped me think about what I needed to do.

I had come to Leitham so I could choose freely what I wanted to do with my life, choose who I wanted as a life-mate, if I wanted one at all. Mam, Sevrin, Radier, even Aramis, had taken it upon themselves to decide my fate for me, without me knowing.

This was their life, not mine. I was no mobster. I had no interest in being one. I wouldn't betray all of dwarf-kind. I wouldn't steal from them either. I was not a thief or a traitor. I may have dreamed of adventures where I destroyed evil like Radier and Aubrey, but it was never by partnering up with someone just like them.

What I really wanted was a career that made me happy. It didn't matter what I did. I wanted a life full of love and laughter with good friends who accepted me regardless of what I looked like, how much I earned, or what my social standing was.

I thought I'd had that with Brent and Lillian and the others. I couldn't be sure if Lillian was a part of the Dwarven Mafia. Surely she had to know Mam was because they'd been so close. On the other hand, I hadn't known and I'd lived with her. Brent had been a genuine friend. He hadn't known about Sevrin. He was a part of it now, though. They'd been my friends. If I could find accepting friends once, I could, and would, do it again.

As much as I enjoyed working the stone to create a beautiful piece of art, I decided that carving wasn't going to be my career. I wouldn't mind selling my carvings if it helped me earn enough to live until I found something more permanent. But it would never be more than a hobby. I didn't want the pressure of having to produce work on demand, to someone else's schedule or specifications. I didn't want to be stuck in a room, no matter how beautiful it might be, and do nothing but work with stone. It was too much like mining. Except that even in mining I had coworkers to talk to. No, I loved carving, but it would not be my career.

Acting wouldn't be it either. Aramis and Mam had been very complimentary about my acting skills. I'd enjoyed it, especially being an extra, but not enough to spend my life doing it. Of course, given that I didn't want to be near Mam or Aramis, doing anything in the movie business might be impossible.

I'd enjoyed the archives, though. And it didn't appear that Mam or Sevrin went there very often. Perhaps I could work there.

I didn't have to decide just yet. I had to deal with Radier first. I had to get out of this situation once and for all.

———

TWO DAYS later and I had my carving of Dakkar completed. I began to pay for my room and board by working for Otto and Sophie, pouring and delivering drinks to the few customers they had. When there was no one around, I was free to sit in front of the fire or in my room. It was wonderful.

I didn't care that my bed was missing most of the straw it should have had, that there were cracks in the walls, or about the ever-present layer of dirt on the floor, no matter how often it seemed that Sophie swept.

For the first time in my life, I was free to do what I wanted. There was no pressure from anyone to get out and find a mate or get a job or be sociable. The only thing I had to do was serve drinks every now and then and when those times came around, I was usually grateful for the distraction and a bit of social company. The rest of the time I spent alone, and instead of carving, I found myself practicing with the wizard's crystals. I was getting better at it every day, becoming more consistent at adding sound to the visual.

Repeatedly cursing in elvish definitely helped elevate my mood.

I allowed my imagination run wild the way I used to. Except this time I wasn't imagining myself in any fantastical story.

I was living one for real.

I imagined the events of the last few months, how

they would play out on a movie screen. To be honest, I'd rather be acting it than living it. At least then I could go home to normality at the end of the day. Though I didn't like acting because I didn't want to live other people's stories, I was beginning to think that, for this case, I felt differently. It would be so much easier if this was someone else's life and I could just step out of it.

If my life were a movie script, I wondered what the main character would do. I could imagine several fantastical outcomes, none of which were a real possibility for me. The one I had the most fun imagining was me discovering a magical power to give me super-strength where I crushed everyone and ended up controlling both the elven and dwarven organizations, and persuade my friends and family back home in Gilliam that I was wonderful and accepted and respected. I replayed that scenario in my head a lot. The magical power varied from pure physical strength, to mind manipulation and hypnosis, to the gathering of all kinds of magic in my hands so I could make everyone and everything bow to my will.

I kind of really wished it could be possible. The only magic dwarves really had was our craftsmanship and skill with stone.

I knew that every day I spent in front of the fire carving and serving drinks was another day I hadn't looked for Radier. I couldn't stay hidden forever. It was time I made a concerted effort to do the job I was supposed to do. When it was done, then I would have true freedom.

With my latest carving of an elf mining completed, I took it and my tools up to my room to prepare for the dinner crowd. Hopefully we would get the full complement of our ten regulars tonight. I set my carving on the table alongside my others. I shifted it to be between my carvings of Antinae and Radier.

I picked up my carving of Radier. Until I'd carved Dakkar, it was probably my most detailed piece of work, with the laugh lines and his beard and wrinkles in his hat and robes.

Finding him would be the challenge of a lifetime. He could very well have gone off on one of his adventures which meant no one would hear from him for years. Simply asking around wasn't going to do it.

I looked around my room. I was alone, living on my own. I didn't have to rely on my family and friends. I was fully capable of figuring this out by myself.

The prospect terrified me, and yet, I had a confidence I didn't think I'd ever had, not even when I was throwing axes. I thought about Dr. Thaddeus and his book, *Living Your Authentic Life*. Maybe this wasn't my authenticity yet, but at that moment, I would have bet that if Dr. Thaddeus could have seen me, he would have approved.

CHAPTER 18

FOR BETTER or worse, I had only one real talent that would be useful in figuring out how to find Radier, and that was my imagination. Sure I'd have to use it for more practical purposes this time, but I still thought it was my strongest asset.

If I could figure out how Radier thought, if I could think like him, I could find him. I needed to know everything there was to know about him.

I dug through my bags. Max had only managed to save one of my movie magazines. Fortunately it had an article on Radier. It wasn't the one with the in-depth interview which I'd hoped for but it was a start. I read the article through several times, memorizing every detail. Any one of them might be relevant, no matter how small. What I learned was that he liked tea, a good pipe, and long conversations about the merits of pity versus mercy. And he was in really good shape from walking everywhere, though he'd never met a horse he didn't like.

I remembered from my time working with him that though his reputation was that he was grumpy to the point of being obstinate, he also had a good sense of humor. He was bored, and he once told me that he liked working with us younger folks. He liked our energy.

Was any of that relevant? Maybe, but not likely. Still, it was a good place to start. My next stop was the Movie Archives. That meant I had to go outside.

I stood at the door, my hand on the knob. The last few days had been bliss, hiding in here, cut off from everything. It wasn't like I was expecting anyone to be waiting for me outside. The possibility was strong that I could run into someone, or that one of Radier's, or even Aubrey's, minions would see me and my hiding place would be uncovered. I wasn't ready to see him and I didn't want to have to move.

"Heading out, are you?" Otto asked from behind the bar.

I practically jumped out of my skin and did a quarter-turn. I had thought no one was around. "Um, yeah. Is that all right? The dinner crowd won't come in for a while."

He chuckled. "Honey, you and I both know there ain't no real dinner crowd. You can come and go as you please. You're doing us a favor. It ain't like we're paying you."

I smiled. "Right."

I made to open the door but got no further.

After a few moments, Otto said, "I don't think I've seen you leave here since you arrived."

"I haven't."

"Huh."

I waited for more from Otto but that was it. "What, no words of wisdom?" I asked.

"Sure. Studio City is several miles to the east. If that's where you're going, it'd be best to hire a taxi. You'd never make it walking at this time of day."

That was Otto. Practical about everything. "Thanks."

I turned the knob. I had nothing to fear. I opened the door a crack. I could do this. I opened it all the way. There was the usual bustle on the street. No one stopped to look at the inn or at me.

At last I stepped outside and closed the door behind me. The sunlight and fresh air was a bit dizzying but I didn't wait to get my grounding. I just turned north, kept my head down and started walking until I bumped into someone. I apologized and stepped to the side. Walking was slow and awkward. I ended up bumping into more than one dwarf. So much for keeping a low profile.

Finally I reached the taxi stand. The fellow who had taken me to Aubrey's was there. I didn't like it, but it was bound to happen that one of Sevrin's henchmen would see me. Maybe this wasn't so bad.

Sevrin was probably wondering when I was going to do something and go after Radier. Now he would know.

The taxi driver nodded in greeting. "Where can I take you today?" he asked.

"The Center for the Creation and Preservation of Motion Pictures, please," I said.

"You got it." He helped me into the cart and we started off. He cut through some back roads and minutes later we were outside the archives building. "Take as long as you need, I'll wait for you," he said.

"I can't afford that."

"No cost," he said.

I was stunned, ready to protest, then realized what was happening. "Sevrin, right?"

"It's my duty and I'm happy to do it."

"You really don't have to," I said.

"Not a problem."

I didn't have a choice but to accept it. There were worst things that could happen. I shrugged. "Fine. I don't know how long I'll be."

I left him outside the Archives building. I missed the freedom I had at the Hammer and Chisel.

"Hello, Mabel Goldenaxe," Percy said when I entered the lobby.

"Hiya, Percy. I'm here to see the archives again, if that's all right."

"Yes, it is."

I waved goodbye to Percy and walked down to the archives. I rang the bell.

The pixie flew to the counter. "Oh, you again," he said. "What would you like to see this time?"

"More of the same, please. Radier's earliest recordings."

The pixie sighed, wrote down the information and showed me to the room to wait. Minutes later, Jeff entered with a tray full of crystals.

"Hiya, Mabel. We've missed you at the Lair. Everything all right?"

It was good to see him. He was a friend, not close, but a friend all the same. "I've missed you all too. Mam and I had a falling out. I had to move."

"Good gods. Where are you staying? Do Brent or Lillian know?"

I waved my hand. "I'm all right. Everything's fine. I have a nice place, for now. No, they don't know. You're the first one of my friends I've seen since it happened."

"If you need anything, let us know. Are you sure you have a place to stay? Do you have enough money? What about food?"

"I'm fine, really."

"As long as you're all right. You know how to find us if you need anything."

"I do. Thanks."

Jeff put the tray of crystals on the table. "And if you need more crystals, just give me a shout."

"I will."

I watched Jeff leave. Maybe I'd been wrong about him. Sure he could be a bit abrasive, but he

was a nice fellow. A good friend. I closed the door
and set to work. I needed to find Radier and finish
this so I could be with my friends again.

I started up the first crystal, the one of Sevrin,
Aramis, and Radier walking through the Haddam
mountains. While that one was playing, I set up my
recording fork and one of my own crystals. Then I
played the one where Radier attacked Arienne. This
time I copied that part onto my own crystal as Aramis
had shown me how to do.

I played crystal after crystal, copying any little
bits I thought might help, though none of it was new
information. The most I could figure out was that
Radier controlled Aubrey before he discovered the
process of recording. The later crystals were less and
less helpful.

I returned to the first two crystals and re-played
them several times. I watched through puddles
of tears as Arienne died for the seventh time that
afternoon. There was nothing more here. I had some
evidence of what Radier had done, but nothing to say
how he had gained control over Aubrey.

Or how I would find Radier.

If I were a wizard in Radier's situation, it
would make sense to disappear, to go far away, on
some adventure. And yet, if he really was running
the Elven Mafia, he wouldn't go far from Aubrey.
I didn't know if Radier had bought Mam's act that
she hadn't known Aubrey's role in the mafia, or even
if Radier knew that Sevrin and Mam were running

the Dwarven Mafia. Radier and Aubrey were close. Aubrey had raised him, so home would also be close to Aubrey.

I didn't know if Aubrey would have told Radier to go into hiding after I confronted him, but from what I knew of Radier, running and hiding didn't seem like something he would do. He was a wizard, after all. His magic could probably overpower pretty much anyone. He couldn't consistently control others from a distance, either.

My best guess was that he was near Leitham. Near enough to Aubrey to keep an eye on him. Why hadn't anyone seen or heard from Radier since we returned to Leitham? I wasn't so sure he had been so invisible. Maybe he hadn't been in Studio City, but Radier liked to be too involved in things. Even in Gilliam he had a tendency to voice his opinion about everything. And in that recording, with Arienne, he'd said that Aubrey wasn't killing her fast enough.

Radier was close. He was putting pressure on Aubrey to make me start paying. That's why Aubrey had shown Jimmy and Phillip being captured. That's why he'd healed my shoulder a second time.

Where did I think Radier was?

At Aubrey's.

Most likely at the home he first took me to.

It was close to the city limits. But I didn't know how to get there. I could take some time to find it without Aubrey or Radier becoming suspicious. To them, I had no reason to seek out that first home because I knew that Aubrey was in his real home.

How was I going to find him, then?

I remembered the general direction and I figured if there were elves and dwarves watching me and following me, I could use their surveillance to steer me in the right direction. The closer I got, the more activity there would be. I hoped.

Sure, it could mean that Radier would be notified and he might move. But I suspected he wouldn't. He had too much to do, to control. He wouldn't want to leave it all to Aubrey. He didn't trust Aubrey.

I realized then the reason Radier had taken control of the Elven Mafia. Aramis had said it. Radier had saved Aramis's life. Aubrey had given Radier the gift of immortality, but what else had they done for him? Nothing. They had used him, asked him for advice and for help. Radier had likely felt like he was owed. And now, Radier simply liked the power, which was why he brow-beat everyone to do his bidding. He probably saw organizing Aubrey's criminal activity as being to his advantage. By the time Aubrey realized what was happening, it was too late. Radier would ruin him, just as Aubrey said he would do with the dwarves and other athletes I was supposed to lure into to his organization with promises of wealth.

Of all the video I had copied, I had nothing strong enough to hold the same kind of threat over Radier.

I had nothing.

I packed up my crystals and headed upstairs. "Thanks, Percy," I called over my shoulder.

I stopped short outside. My taxi driver was gone. Two elves stood in his place, blocking my way.

My heart leapt to my throat. I couldn't tell if they belonged to Aubrey or Radier. "Excuse me," I said, making to walk forward.

They held their ground. Without a word and with incredible speed, they had a sack over my head, plummeting me into complete darkness. I flailed. I bent over. I let my body drop to the ground. It didn't matter what I did. A hand covered my mouth smothering my screams. I was picked up and put onto what felt like a horse. Where had it come from? Was it still one of the elves, one of my captors behind me? Holding me in place?

Nothing bound my hands or feet and yet I wasn't able to move them. I gasped for air. The sack was held too tightly over my nose. I couldn't breathe. My captor must have realized because something changed. I could still feel his hand over my mouth. It didn't feel like it had moved, but the bag had loosened, I thought.

Once I could breathe I could think. They had to be from Aubrey. He had every reason to want to stop me from seeing Radier. How was I going to convince him to let me go? To not hurt my friends, if it wasn't too late?

The smell of hogs hit me. I remembered that smell from my second day in Leitham. We weren't going to Aubrey, we were going to Radier. I wasn't ready for this.

Riding the horse was awkward at best. It was way too big for me. I felt like I was being forced to do the splits. There's a reason dwarves ride ponies and not full-grown horses. I wasn't able to use my hands to hold on to anything and my legs were too sore and stretched and weak to press against the horse for stability. I was almost grateful for the elf behind me, his arms around me. Without him I would have fallen off.

After maybe thirty minutes, we stopped. I smelled the trees. We were out of Leitham. Moments later I was up and off the horse, being carried. I couldn't figure out how they did it, carrying me like I was floating, and yet keeping me bound and my mouth covered.

The wind and rain stopped and everything was much warmer. We'd entered a building, one I assumed was Radier's house. I didn't hear any footsteps from the elves, neither on the floor nor echoing off the walls.

I was set down and moments later my hands and feet were free and the bag was lifted. I looked around but I didn't see anyone. My captor had disappeared, vanished, like he was never there.

I took a deep breath. I had to use the information I had. Radier liked me. Maybe I could negotiate with him.

I was in what looked like Radier's show room. There were shelves along the walls with treasures I recognized from all the stories of his adventures.

From dragon scales, bones and skulls, to a stone ogre in the corner, and chests of gold and gems. It wasn't a comfortable room. There were no chairs. This was what Radier wanted people to see of him.

I became curious to see the rest of his home. What kind of place did a wizard live in? I'd never really imagined him in a home, just always out traveling on adventures, sleeping outside. I also didn't see a door. How did I get in and how did my captors get out so fast, so quiet, without being seen?

I meandered over to the dragon bones. I put my hand into my pocket and felt the crystals there. A plan began to come together. I didn't know if this was going to work, but I had to try. I whispered the spell and blew on the crystal. I held it in my hand and whispered into it, describing what I saw. There had to be some kind of proof here that Sevrin could use.

I was examining one of the dragon skulls, admiring its weight, size, and the magnificent strength of it, when one of the shelving units slid aside and two elves came, each with a chair, which looked like they had been made out of antlers, and intended for admiration, not comfort. I quickly tucked the crystal into my pocket.

The elves were silent yet insistent. At first they just watched me, stared at me. When I didn't move, they walked toward me from both sides, closing in and guiding me to the chairs.

Reluctantly, I sat. Vines grew out of the feet of the chair, slithering up and around my wrists and ankles.

They weren't tight, and I still had some mobility, but they were firm enough to let me know that I couldn't leave. I may be where I wanted to be, but I was now a captive.

I was at Radier's mercy. If his heartlessness to Mam was any indication, then he didn't have any mercy.

Every part of me was tense and yet a strange calmness came over me. My head lolled to the side and I fell asleep.

CHAPTER 19

MY NECK hurt and I opened my eyes. Everything remained as it had when I'd fallen asleep. I stretched my neck then tried to stand to stretch out as was my habit from when Mikey had coached me in axe-throwing. The vines tightened around me, holding me in place. I'd been sitting a long time. I wasn't sure how long, but my muscles were cramping up. I needed to stand up soon, work out the pain. My mouth was dry and my stomach rumbled.

"I understand you were quite interested in this dragon skull," Radier said behind me, startling me. From the sound of his voice, he must have stood by the wall, where the skull was. "It is a beautiful thing, this. Have you ever tried carving bone?"

I muttered the recording spell. I hoped it would

work, that one of the crystals would record the sound. I hoped to the dwarven gods that Radier thought I was merely cursing in elvish. "No," I croaked. "I haven't."

"No, I don't suppose you would have had much access to it in Gilliam. Not good bone, anyway. Dragon bone is magnificent. Very hard. Difficult to cut into, but the reward is spectacular. There is a certain texture and sparkle that shows through. It appears to give life to the creations."

While that was fascinating, I recognized that he was trying to lure me into believing he was still my friend and this was just an ordinary conversation. Under different circumstances I would have loved to chat about carving material. That wasn't why I was here, or why he had me tied to this chair. "Are my friends safe?" I asked.

"Your friends?"

"Phillip and Jimmy. Are they safe?"

"Jimmy. He's that one that was in the movie as an extra, in the mining scene. Is that right?"

"Yes."

"Oh, I liked him." Radier came around and sat in front of me. "Why do you ask about his safety?"

He didn't know. Aubrey had acted without Radier's authority. It was entirely possible that Aubrey had that kind of autonomy but I had to gamble that he didn't. "Aubrey showed me he had them, or will have them, held captive and threatened with poison if I don't do what he asks of me."

"Did he now?" It was more of a statement than a question.

He looked over my right shoulder and gave a slight nod. We weren't alone. There were others here.

"They'll be fine," he said, to me.

"I want proof."

"I understand, though it is a little difficult to give you. Short of bringing them here, I doubt there is much you would believe, and rightly so. Anything could be a trick, much like that mirror game of Aubrey's."

If Mam had been up against such manipulation in Gilliam, she hadn't stood a chance against Aubrey and Radier. I knew better now. I decided to play along. If I could convince him I didn't really know what was happening, maybe he would let something slip, something I could use against him.

He had liked me. The old me. This time, Dr. Thaddeus was wrong. I had to be my old, inauthentic self, just this once, to help my friends and family, and to help myself. "It wasn't real?"

"Oh, no. It might have been something he was planning, but no, it hadn't happened. Such a ploy is an interesting and often useful negotiating tactic. In this situation it was rather unnecessary. Your friends are fine. I would never allow Aubrey to harm them."

He had so much power. Too much power. I knew I couldn't trust him not to harm my friends, any of them, in Gilliam or Leitham. I could use this. I could try and drive a wedge between Radier and Aubrey, make Radier think he was losing control of his puppet. "I don't understand. If you wouldn't allow it, why would Aubrey think he could hurt them?"

Radier was quiet a moment. "Well, that is hardly important now. Tell me, Mabel, did you find anything interesting in the archives?"

He was deflecting. I debated the merit of telling him all I'd seen. I bit my bottom lip and looked him in the eyes. "I found a very interesting bit with Aramis's sister, Arienne."

Surprise flickered across his eyes. I'd been right. He hadn't known he'd recorded it. "Really?" he asked.

"Tell me, Radier, what was it you muttered when Arienne told you Aubrey was killing her? Sounded to me like you said 'not fast enough.'"

Radier's eyes darkened. He stood and walked out, leaving me alone.

MY MUSCLES cramped from being tied to the chair for so long. An elf came into the room and placed a cup of water and a bowl of stew in front of me. It wasn't until after he retreated that the vines fell away and vanished.

I tried to stand but my muscles were too tight. I fell to the floor. Slowly, with the care Mikey had taught me, I stretched and loosened my muscles. By the time I was finished, the stew was cold and the water was warm, but they tasted amazing. I had no idea how long it had been since I'd last eaten.

Far too soon, the two elves who had first brought in the chairs were back, taking away my food before I had a chance to finish it. They lifted me back into the chair. Once again, vines grew out of the chair's feet and I was tied to it and left alone.

MY HEAD lolled. I was so tired but my muscles were crying out in pain.

Radier returned. I barely remembered to curse in elvish. His eyes narrowed when I did. "Sorry," I said. "I've been spending too much time in Studio City around elves, I guess."

Radier smiled. "They tend to have that effect on others. It seems we got off to a bad start the other day."

Other day? How long had I been here? "Being tied to this chair isn't putting me in the best mood," I said.

"No, I suppose not," he admitted, but he made no move to release me.

"I get it," I said. I wasn't going to let him win, no how much I hurt or how tired I was. I had to knock him off balance. "You want to wear me out so I'll drop my defenses."

"That's not—"

I cut him off. "Mikey did the same thing to me

in axe-throwing. It really helped my focus and kept me relaxed when I had no endurance for anything else but the task at hand. Look, I don't know why you brought me here. I mean, I have my suspicions it has to do with Sevrin and Mam, and that's fine." And now it was time to give him just enough to lure him back in. "I don't want to play games. I'll be honest with you if you'll be honest with me. Just tell me why you chose me."

He shrugged. "Why not you?"

"I'm just a country dwarf. I have nothing of significance to offer. It isn't like I'm Aubrey, Lord of the Elves. Why are you pursuing me so hard? Why can't you just let me go?"

"I've always liked you, Mabel. Right from the start. You're sweet and kind and fun. I may have underestimated you, though. I expected you to be as naive as Frerin. Such generosity of spirit often leads to a certain innocence, which I thought I saw in you."

I'd had that innocence until he started manipulating me. It was time to push a little harder. "How dare you call Mam's desire for a peaceful world for her dwarflings naiveté? She only wanted to create understanding and tolerance for others who are different, who aren't dwarves. And you used her. You destroyed her, and you destroyed my family."

"Collateral damage," he said with a dismissive wave of his hand.

We really meant nothing to him. And by we, I meant all mortals. Maybe even elves no longer mattered to him. Arienne hadn't. Aramis was right, immortality had changed Radier.

Sometimes forever was too long.

"Collateral damage. That's interesting. So why come back for more? Why come after my family a second time? Hadn't the collateral damage been enough the first time around?"

Radier leaned back and crossed one leg over the other, like he was settling in for a nice conversation, old friends catching up. "The circumstances had changed, you see. Now that Frerin is with Sevrin, you are my way in."

That had made sense when I thought Aubrey was in charge of the Elven Mafia. "But you were friends with Aramis and Sevrin. Why not just do it yourself?"

"Because, dear Mabel, that would have been far too obvious. My position over Aubrey has been kept secret until now. I knew it the moment I saw you with your wounded shoulder. I knew exactly how I was going to get you indebted to me through Aubrey. Oh, sure, Aramis tried to heal you himself. He suspected what I was up to, but his magic is too weak, like I told you. He'd chosen a different path and therefore lost a lot of his power."

"Didn't Aubrey know you'd gone to make the movie with Aramis?"

"I would never betray my brother like that. No. Aubrey thought I'd gone with someone else."

I was dying to tell Radier that Aramis and Sevrin had planned this all along, that I'd been the bait. I held that secret in. It was one thing I had over Radier.

"You must know by now that I've moved away from Mam and Sevrin. I want nothing to do with Sevrin and his organization. I won't have anything to do with it." I was starting to have second thoughts on that, though. I wasn't prepared to forgive them for using me, but they were trying to stop this maniac of a wizard. Being tied up in this chair gave me a much greater appreciation for their cause.

"So while I may have been an in for you at one point," I continued. It was time to push harder. "Had things worked out the way you thought they would, I'm no longer your leverage. I know what Aubrey wants from me. But what do you want from me?"

I'd intentionally mentioned that Aubrey had an alternate motive for using me. I wanted to undermine Radier's authority and the more I could do it, the more I hoped to shake his confidence.

I wasn't up for playing his games. I was definitively up for mind games of my own.

Radier leaned forward. I had his interest now. "What is it that Aubrey wants from you?"

I paused for a moment. I kind of liked having this power. No wonder Radier and Aubrey, and even Sevrin, wanted it, and more. But I'd had it before, in my failed negotiations with Aubrey in Brent's gallery. I had to be more cautious this time. I had to hold back a little.

"Aramis," I said at last. It was a complete fabrication. I wanted to test Radier's loyalty to

Aramis.

Radier cocked an eyebrow. "Really. Tell me more. What exactly did he say he wanted with my brother?"

It was my turn to shrug and act all casual, like this was rather insignificant. "Not much, actually. He said he just wanted to see him."

"Really. And what did you say you would do?"

"He gave me until the night of our movie premiere. I said I would do what I could."

"Was that before or after he threatened your friends?"

"After. He'd threatened them because he wanted me to promise not to tell his people that you're the one truly in charge. And I only said I would tell them because I wanted him to remove his magic then back off and leave me alone."

"I see. And will you do what you said? Will you bring Aramis back to his father?"

I could tell he didn't like the idea. I didn't think it was truly out of any real loyalty. He didn't want them to see how he'd turned them against each other, especially over Arienne.

I desperately hoped the crystal was recording this. I relished the thought of helping Mam and Sevrin destroy Radier.

"I haven't decided yet."

"But you're thinking about it."

"I don't see that I have any choice. If I don't, Aubrey's going to ruin my shoulder forever. Not just that, because I'm sure I'd find a way to earn some kind of living, somehow, but he'd hurt my friends and ruin my family again. I mean, even though they've all turned their backs on me, and I'm not particularly fond of Mam at the moment, they're still my family. You understand that, don't you? I'll do anything to protect my family."

"As would I." He smiled at me, just a small one. "Perhaps we can work together to get ourselves out of this."

Too many proposals and threats. I had to keep him talking. I needed definitive proof of what he wanted and how much power he had. I needed to convince him to let me go. "What did you have in mind?"

"What if we were to go back to the original agreement, forget about all of this escalation? This time it would be between you and I only. Cut out Aubrey altogether. I will take care of him and his wish to see Aramis. He can remove his magic from your shoulder and I will then ensure that he leaves you alone after that. Your friends are already safe, and Aubrey will have no power or authority to hurt your family."

It all sounded too good to be true. He needed to give me more. "Go on," I said.

"In return, you deliver Sevrin's organization to me. You said yourself you wanted to have nothing to with it, so it should no longer be an issue for you. Once your shoulder is better, you start throwing axes competitively again, perhaps you lose a few tournaments here and there. You give me a cut of your winnings, and you recruit others into the scheme."

The same offer Aubrey had made. "Simple as that?"

"That's right."

I pressed my lips together and stayed silent for a while, thinking it over. If I said yes, and the recording worked, it would be there for all to hear. I'd have to assure Sevrin somehow that I only agreed to keep Radier talking. It was a risk that if I was going to take, I had to get something out of it for myself. I still wanted Aubrey's magic out of my shoulder.

"Why the hesitation, Mabel? Your family and friends will be safe, your shoulder will be better, you'll go back to competing in axe-throwing. It is everything you wanted when you came to Leitham, isn't it?"

"What if I don't want to throw axes anymore?"

"Then in a few years, you can stop. Once you have enough recruits into our new organization, we'll both be earning off of them, and you'll have enough to retire and do whatever you want. Even mining, if that's what you'd like to do."

I had to stall while I figured out my next move. "Our organization. How does that give you Sevrin?"

"Simple. You act as though you are recruiting into Sevrin's ranks, when in reality, you're recruiting for us."

So much like how things worked with Aubrey.

"What about the elves? Where do they fit into

all of this? Are you saying that you're eliminating Aubrey from the equation? That they'll report directly to you?"

Radier shook his head. "Hardly. That would never go over well. No. Aubrey will stay, he will just have his powers clipped a fair bit."

"So essentially you would be running both the elves and the dwarves?"

"We will. You and I together, until you decide to quit. Under one ruler, we can establish that lasting peace between the dwarves and elves. The peace that your Mam wanted so badly."

A peace that was long but tentative. It might have still been shaky with Aubrey in charge, but Radier was threatening it with every breath. I had the proof Sevrin needed. Now it was time for me to get what I wanted out of all of this.

"Have Aubrey remove his magic first."

I WAS alone again. No water or food was brought to me. I whimpered from the pain. I was never going to get out of here.

I leaned back and did my best to relax, which was next to impossible. The exhaustion overwhelmed me and soon I fell asleep.

———

I OPENED my eyes to see Radier smirking. I genuinely cursed this time.

"I really should be disappointed in you, Mabel," he said. "You lied."

Oh, no! How did he know I'd lied?

"You tried to use my brother against me." He shook his head. "And yet, how can I be disappointed when it was such a clever move? You have a brilliant mind for this business and I look forward to helping you develop it. When we get those skills honed, you and I could be invincible."

Radier waved to someone behind me. Moments later, Aubrey was brought in to stand by Radier's side.

He was sullen. Without a word, he touched my shoulder. I felt something ripping out of me. I cried out and glared at him. He rubbed my shoulder a little in a light massage. There was no pain, no damage. It was like there had never been an injury. My muscles even felt strong, which they shouldn't have.

I nearly doubled over in tears of joy and gratitude. Finally I was free.

Aubrey left and the vines that had bound me disappeared. I wiped at my tears and reached for my shoulder, feeling it for myself. "It isn't going to start hurting again if you or Aubrey feel like it, is it?"

"No. You would be of no use to me if that happened. Besides, I like you, Mabel. I do regret that you had to be used as a bargaining chip, but, well, that's just the way things go. It is business, not personal, you understand."

My shoulder was fine. I was going to be all right. Now I just needed to tell him whatever he needed to hear. Anything to convince him to let me go. "Sure. Of course."

"It is time for you to hold up your end of the deal. Tell Sevrin you've changed your mind. That you want in. That you want to help him, work for him, work with him. Tell him you want more involvement, that you want to move up the ranks. I will know when you're in and I will then contact you with what we do next. As for your shoulder, he knows you confronted Aubrey. Tell him Aubrey did what you asked, that you are released from that debt now."

I had him! I had the proof. I had him convinced I was on his side. Radier had no idea what he was in for, and I was ecstatic that I was the one to have done it. "Got it. Thank you, Radier."

He smiled and helped me up. It felt great to be able to stand and finally work out the cramps in my muscles. I felt faint and dehydrated. I didn't know how long I'd been down here without food or drink. I just wanted to get out of here. I'd find something to eat and drink as soon as I was free.

Radier kissed me on the cheeks. "Mabel, it has been, and will continue to be, a pleasure doing business with you."

CHAPTER 20

RADIER MOTIONED to someone behind me and almost instantaneously two henchmen were on either side of me. "I do apologize for this, Mabel. I must do this for security reasons, you understand."

"We're partners. Don't you trust me?"

"I don't trust anyone." To his henchmen he said, "Take her to the edge, then let her go."

A large hand gripped my arm and dragged me forward. The sudden movement combined with feeling light-headed caused me to stumble. The guard tightened his hold, barely keeping me on my feet. If I'd fallen, I was certain I would have been dragged.

Another hand grasped my other arm. Two guards now carried me. They lifted me by my arms, and my toes brushed the floor.

Moments later I was lifted onto a horse. This time they allowed me to sit side-saddle, which wasn't particularly comfortable and I constantly felt like I was going to fall off if it weren't for the guard holding me, but at least I wasn't doing the splits or sitting on antlers.

I was hungry and thirsty. I had no idea how long I'd been at Radier's. I wished I'd made him feed me before he sent me away. I longed for water, any water, even mud puddles would help.

My head lolled as we trotted on. I couldn't tell anymore which way was up or down, if I was flying or sitting. There was rustling around me. Was that rain in the trees? I could gather the water in the leaves. A drop. Just a drop. That was all I needed.

My guards let go of me and I slid to the ground. I blinked in the bright sunlight. The guards were gone. The ground was bone dry. The leaves were too high for me to reach, and they were too small to have gathered water if there was any. I was on the outskirts of Leitham. I didn't recognize the neighborhood. I would not make it back to the Hammer and Chisel, or to Mam's. I lay down to rest. I could have, would have cried and cupped my hands to collect the tears, but I was completely dry.

"Mabel!" I heard Brent calling me.

I thought I was dreaming. And yet I could feel the rumble of cart wheels and the hooves of ponies coming to a stop. I felt his arms beneath me picking me up, lifting me into the cart. I heard the unscrewing of a flask. He held it to my mouth, tipping sips of the lukewarm water into me.

Glorious water! I gulped it down wanting more. So much more.

"Easy there, Mabel," he said. He controlled the flask, making sure I only took in small sips. At first it was just enough to wet my lips, then my tongue, and finally my throat.

I opened my eyes and smiled. It was so good to see him. I was alive, safe in the arms of my friend. "How did you find me?" My voice was raspy at best, and my lips felt like they were cracking, but it felt wonderful.

He handed me the flask then tore up some pieces of bread and fed them to me.

"How did you know where I was?" I asked again between mouthfuls. "How did you know to come this way?"

"Aramis figured it out," Mam said coming around the back of the cart. "Percy told him two elves had taken you from the archives. Aramis figured it was Radier who had taken you. I told him about the place we had met Aubrey and Aramis figured that was where Radier was."

Mam embraced me and played with a lock of my hair. "I have been so worried about you. I am so sorry, about everything. Please, come home. We can take as long as we need to work this out. I can never undo the pain I've caused you, I know that, but please, give me a second chance. Let me truly be a mam to you."

I was too tired, dehydrated and hungry to feel anything but grateful that she had found me. "This is the second time you've rescued me."

Mam kissed my cheek then squeezed me tighter. "Oh my girl. You wouldn't have needed rescuing if it weren't for me."

After being held by Radier, I wasn't so sure she could have done anything to prevent it. "Don't be so hard on yourself," I said, echoing Aramis's words to me when I first viewed my acting on screen. "Radier gets what he wants and he doesn't care what damage he causes. He never did answer me why, but for some reason, he wanted our family's gems, and ruining you as well." Thinking back, it was more than not caring that he'd hurt her; it was more like he'd taken some kind of pleasure in it. "That was a bonus for him."

Brent stepped in. "Frerin, Mabel, we really shouldn't talk about this here. Let's get you home. Mabel, you need to eat and rest, okay?"

"Sure." I nibbled the bread. "Do you have anything stronger than water?" I asked, handing Brent the flask.

He pushed it back at me. "Finish that first."

Mam looked at me expectantly. "Let's go home," I said.

MAM JUMPED into the driver's seat and Brent

climbed in beside me. With a snap of the reins and a jolt, we were moving. I waved the empty flask at Brent who handed me another one. It was warm water. "You promised me something stronger," I said.

"You need to be hydrated first."

I was having a flashback to when I'd traveled with my family to the Regional Dwarf Games competition in Mitchum. That time, I'd been in the back of the cart with a wounded shoulder, trying to pretend I was fine. I'd tried to get drunk then, too, but Mikey insisted that I needed to stay sober.

I sighed and reached for more bread after a deep swig of the water. I had to admit, it probably was the right thing for me right now. "Thank you," I said. "For the water, the food… especially for caring enough to come find me."

"I'm just glad we found you in time. Are you all right? Did he hurt you?"

"I'm hungry and thirsty, that's all. I'll be fine in no time."

"You're sure he didn't do anything to you?" Mam asked.

"I'm sure. It was uncomfortable, but that's it."

"What about your shoulder?" Brent asked.

In spite of the nightmare I'd found myself in with Radier, that had been a joyous moment. "The elven magic is gone." I grinned.

"Really?" Brent hugged me. "That is so wonderful! I'm so happy for you." He let go of me. "But at what price? What did he ask of you?"

I couldn't tell him yet. I needed to tell Sevrin and Aramis too. They all needed to hear what had happened, hopefully from the recording on the crystal. "It will be all right. Everything will be all right," I said.

We arrived at Frerin's. She hopped out and came to the back. "Come. Let's get you inside."

Together, Brent and Mam helped me out of the cart. I was too weak to stand on my own. Mam put her arm around me and held me steady.

"I need to talk to Sevrin and Aramis," I said. "And you, too, both of you."

"Sweetheart, you need to rest," Mam said.

"I agree, Mabel," Brent said. "When you've got your strength back, then you can tell us what happened."

I shook my head. "This can't wait. Please."

"All right," Brent said. "I'll go find them."

"Sevrin will either be with Aramis at the studio, or—"

"We are right here," Aramis said, hurrying toward us from the back door, Sevrin close on his heels.

"I'm sorry Frerin," Sevrin said. "I just had to know you found her and I knew you would come back here, and I still had a key—"

"It's fine," she said.

They'd split up? Because of me? That made me sad. All of this Dwarven Mafia business aside, I thought they'd been really good together.

"Are you all right?" Sevrin asked. He stood on

my other side and helped Mam walk me into the house.

I had to lean on them as they walked me through the kitchen into the living room by the fire, helping me sit on one of the soft leather chairs. It felt so nice after sitting on antlers. I slumped into it and Frerin put my feet up. I worried that my muscles would cramp up again. At least I could stretch out my legs, but I wasn't strong enough to stand up or move.

Frerin built a fire and brought me more food and drink. "Stoutness may not be an asset in the movie industry but you're a bit on the thin side even for an actor," she said with a smile.

I returned her smile. I appreciated her attempt to lighten the atmosphere. "I think at this moment I finally have the appetite Da always wished I had."

"Where were you?" Aramis asked.

"You were right," Mam answered for me. "Radier had her."

Aramis brushed my arms, my shoulder, like he was making sure I wasn't injured. "What did he do to you?"

"Nothing," I said between mouthfuls of pulled pork on a thick slice of bread. "Well, he tied me up for a few days, but…" I fished in my pocket and pulled out the wizard's crystals and handed them to Aramis. "These should have what all of you wanted. At least I hope it worked. If it did, then it has all the proof you need that Radier runs the Elven Mafia. He wanted me to have the same kind of arrangement with him over your organization too, Sevrin. I agreed to it to get out of there. I have no intention of doing so."

"How did you know to do this?" Aramis turned one crystal over in his hand.

"The crystals were in my pocket when I was taken to Radier. I knew then I could use them to try and capture the conversation. You won't be able to see anything. I had it in my pocket, but hopefully you can hear what he said."

Sevrin's face lit up. "You are the best, Mabel! My organization needs more who have your drive."

"Sevrin." Mam glowered at him.

"Thank you," I said. "If I managed to record the conversation, then you will have your proof and you can deal with Radier. I want you to crush him."

Mam turned to me, her mouth gaping. "I'm sorry. Say that again?"

"He ruined our family and who knows how many others. Brent, businesses in Gypsum thought they were being controlled by Aubrey, but it was Radier behind it all. Aramis, you saw the recording, didn't you? The one where he... the one with Radier and Arienne?"

Aramis nodded.

"You saw how he lied to her, and he probably lied to you. I'm not saying Aubrey is innocent in all of this, but Radier made things worse between you and your father. Radier isn't loyal to you, though he still calls you 'brother.' He likes to talk a lot about mercy and pity. He pities the rest of us because he thinks we are weaker than he is, that we are his playthings, but he does not show mercy. To anyone."

"I'll be right back," Mam said.

A shadow had fallen over Aramis. I wished I had the elven magic to read his thoughts. "Are you saying what I think you're saying?" he asked.

I realized then how I sounded. Like I was out for vengeance, some kind of violent justice, for Radier's blood. I'd let the games and discomfort of my captivity, my anger over my broken family, to take over. I was angry and hurt, but I wasn't going to let it consume me the way I'd seen it consume Sevrin and Aubrey, and Radier. "I want his power taken away, that's all," I said softly.

Mam returned with a white sheet and a projecting fork. It took a few minutes to set up, but then we had our own theater in the room.

Aramis took over, setting the crystal in the tines and tapping it perfectly, making it vibrate.

My heart leapt when my face appeared on the screen, close up. It had worked. How much of that had I managed to capture? Moments later, the image turned black as my hand closed around the crystal and tucked it in my pocket. Though we couldn't see anything, we could hear muffled noises so we knew it was still recording.

Aramis whispered an incantation and the recording sped up. The sounds were only occasional for quite a while until at last we heard voices talking. Aramis stopped and reversed the recording to the beginning of the conversation. It was when I woke up and Radier began negotiations with me. There were gaps which must have been when Radier left me and some of the conversations had been cut off. Thankfully the gaps weren't too long and the important parts of the conversations had been captured.

Mam stood behind me, hovering, playing with my hair and rubbing my shoulder. It was comforting.

Throughout, I watched the faces of Sevrin, Aramis, and Brent. Sevrin let out a few incoherent shouts of triumph and a "Got you now!" Brent returned my gaze, always smiling, like he was proud of me for what I'd done.

It broke my heart to look at Aramis. Conflicting emotions played across his face. Hurt and betrayal were most dominant. His world was crumbling. He knew most of what he was hearing, but to have it all said so plain for all to hear must have been worse than the knowing.

The recording stopped. Aramis removed the crystal from the fork, and held it. His face was stolid, back to normal. "May I take this?"

His expression was emotionless, but his eyes were full of sadness and remorse. Aramis would know what to do. He would handle Radier without harming him. "It's yours," I said.

"Wait a second," Sevrin interjected. "We should discuss this."

"No, Sevrin," Aramis said. "It is over. There will be no more escalations or retaliations. I will take care of Radier and my father. I will do what needs to be done."

"Aramis, no," Mam said. "You can't."

I looked at Brent who shrugged. He didn't know what they were talking about either. "What?" I asked. "What are you going to do, Aramis?"

He opened the door and stepped out. "There will be peace and understanding between our people. I promise you that."

"WHAT IS he going do, Sevrin?" I asked.

"He's going to replace Aubrey as Lord of the Elves," Mam said.

She'd protested, but she hadn't done anything to stop him. Sevrin had said nothing. I knew Aramis well enough; he did not want to do this.

I was wobbly but I marched to the door to follow Aramis.

"Mabel, stop," Sevrin said.

"Let her go," Mam said.

I didn't hear the rest. I was out the door, running after Aramis. Though he was dragging his feet, his strides were still three times as long as mine. "Wait, Aramis. Stop!" I called after him.

He slowed enough for me to catch up to him. We were off Mam's property, standing beside the protective wall that lined the roads. The same one I'd been walking along when Aubrey threatened me and Mam.

"I know when you made the movie in Gilliam, you were using me as bait to catch Radier."

Aramis lowered his head.

"Yes, I'm upset with you about it, but I also understand why you did it. It was necessary. You wanted to be free of Radier and Aubrey as much as Mam did, and as much as Sevrin wants peace between our people. Please, Aramis, don't do what I think you're about to do. Not if you don't want to."

"I always knew this time would come. I do not have a choice."

"You do have a choice. If you were truly supposed to depose Aubrey, you would have done it long ago."

"You are right. I should have done so. Instead, I have run around playing at adventure and making ridiculous movies."

"Aramis. Your movies are not ridiculous. Without them, I never would have known Mam was alive, or have met her, or you. I never would have come to Leitham. I never would have known that I could have a life that was different from what Da expected of me. Without movies, I never would have been able to record what Radier did to me. You never would have known what happened to your sister."

Aramis bowed his head.

I reached out and held his hand. "Do you remember, back in Gilliam, when my Da stormed onto set and ordered me to choose his way of life? I refused and he disowned me. You came to see me. Do you remember?"

Aramis nodded.

"You said that Leitham was a great place for a fresh start. You can have that now."

He shook his head. "I have already started over once, look how it turned out."

"You thought you had a fresh start, but how could it be when Sevrin kept you connected to your father and the pain caused? I'm not asking you to shirk your duties. Just, please, Aramis, take some time. Think long and hard if this is what you want to be. I'm asking you not to turn away from who you are."

Aramis was quiet. There was still a shadow over him, but it wasn't as heavy.

"Think about it, please." I repeated. "Besides, it isn't like you don't have the time." I grinned.

"All right. I will think on it," he said, with a smile at last.

"Mabel?" Brent asked stepping around the corner of the gate. "Everything okay?"

I looked at Aramis. He smiled and nodded. "It is."

CHAPTER 21

MAM AND I were alone. She hadn't said anything to me since Sevrin and Brent left. She plied me with more food and drink, avoiding conversation. I didn't know if I wanted to stay with her, but I knew I couldn't decide until I had some answers.

Mam set another heaping plate of roast pork and mushrooms in front of me. "Mam, stop," I said. "Just sit with me, talk with me, please."

She did, and looked not at me, but at the family portrait over the mantle. Several minutes passed before she said, "I couldn't live with Sevrin anymore. It was time for that part of my life to be over. I hadn't come to Leitham for a fresh start. I'd come for revenge. I'd allowed you to believe you were coming here for a fresh start, when I'd done nothing but use you and allow others do the same. I want you to know how much I love you, but I don't expect you to believe me. Why should you?"

"Who all was involved?" I asked. "Lillian? Dr. Thora?"

Mam shook her head. "No. Dr. Thora and I had arrived in Leitham at about the same time. We used to room together when I first moved here. She's retiring, that's why she's cutting down on the number of patients she sees and why she's training Stacie. Lillian knows nothing. I insisted from the beginning that I keep my acting career separate from my involvement with Sevrin. He wasn't pleased about it, but I gave him no choice. Lillian and the others, they genuinely are your friends."

"Would you have ever come for me?" I asked.

"Before your injury?" Mam hung her head. "I was too consumed with hatred for Aubrey. The only thing I could see clearly was that you were necessary for destroying Aubrey and Radier. I was so wrong. I see that now. I wish I could do it all over again. I would have returned to Gilliam much sooner. I would have fought harder to stay."

I focused on the family portrait as I listened to all Mam had to say. I had a choice. I had every right to leave her, go back to the Hammer and Chisel and start a new life. Or I could do what neither she nor Da had done, I could forgive her and I could stay. If I stayed, we could build a new life together. We were family. I didn't want to turn my back on the one member of my family I had left. She and I had both made major mistakes. Could I really make her take all the blame? Was the end result of all this so bad? Radier's power was going to be limited, she was free from Aubrey's threats, and my shoulder was healed. She should have been honest with me about all of this from the beginning. Could I trust her?

"Thank you," I said, standing.

"What? Where are you going?" Mam reached for me.

"You're my mam, and you always will be, but I can't stay here."

"Mabel, love, this is your home."

"No, Mam, it isn't."

"I know I've made a mess of things, but please, Mabel, give me a chance to make it up to you."

I held up my hand to stop her. "It isn't really about that. I mean, like I said to Aramis, I'm upset with you, but I understand why you did what you did, and I will get over it. It's just that so much has happened from the time Da exiled you; we don't fit into each other's lives. Not really."

"We can, love."

"As friends, maybe. Not as family, not yet. And I do want to be your friend."

Mam was silent for a few moments. "Where will you go?"

"My things are at the Hammer and Chisel." At least I hoped they were still there. I'd been gone so long, Sophie and Otto might have thought I'd abandoned my things and thrown them out. It didn't matter. I was starting over anyway. "I'll stay there for a while."

"I'll take you," Mam said.

"No, it's all right. I need to do this on my own."

Mam hugged me, holding me tight. "I'm so sorry, my girl," she whispered, her voice breaking. Her tears dampened my cheek.

"I know," I said, pulling back. "Me too."

I opened the door and started walking.

THE HAMMER and Chisel was just as empty and musty as the first time I'd walked through those doors. "Sophie? Otto?" I called, walking up to the bar. I was worn out from the walk. I thought I'd had more than enough to eat and drink at Mam's, but now I was desperate for a drink and a steaming bowl of Sophie's fried potatoes.

"Mabel? Is that you?" Otto asked, coming out of the kitchen.

I grinned.

"It is you!" He embraced me. "We wondered what happened to you. Are you all right?"

"I'm fine. Thirsty for a nice pint of ale, but I'm fine"

"Sophie!" Otto called back to the kitchen. "Mabel's back."

Sophie bustled out of the kitchen. "Oh my goodness. Otto, pour the poor thing some ale. Where have you been, love? Are you back?"

"It's a long story, but yes, I'm back." I gratefully accepted a pint from Otto and sipped it.

"We hoped you would be," Otto said. "We weren't sure, so after a few days, we put your things in storage. They're out back. Finish up your pint and I'll help you get them while Sophie makes up your room."

I followed Otto through the kitchen to the back of the inn. It was my first time out here. They had a nice fenced in garden, with a wee shed, and what was that I saw? A throwing post? The axes felt heavy in my bag. I pulled one out; it was one that Ricky had given me in tribute in Gilliam. I weighed it in my hand. It was perfect. I set my bag down and walked to my place in front of the post. I raised my arm, reached back and launched the axe forward. It flew in a perfect line, flipping head over handle, landing with a solid thunk, piercing the dead-center of the bull's-eye.

I was home.

I CARRIED a tray of tankards to a table I'd reserved at the Lair. It was already filling up and I had to lift the tray overhead as I twisted and turned through the crowds.

Lillian and Sam were close on my heels and

grabbed a tankard each as soon as I set the tray down. "Cheers ma dears," Sam said.

"Welcome back." Lillian hugged me with one arm as she drank. "Missed you."

"Missed you too," I said.

Sam gasped. "Oh! Oh! Oh! I've just had the best idea. You both are going to love it! Okay, so Lillian, we're always talking about this movie script you've been working on. We should totally do it. The three of us. Write it, direct it, act in it. What do you think? Great idea or what?!"

"Would be but we don't actually have any real ideas," Lillian said.

"Well then, we start writing stuff down until we have something we can work with," Sam said.

"We can get Hannah to help with the script," Lillian said. "She's awesome at that kind of stuff. I love it. Mabel, what do you think? Acting? Directing? Sets?"

I loved my friends. I loved Leitham. "Brent should do the sets," I said. "If I could direct, I'm in."

"You sure you don't want to act?" Lillian asked. "Frerin says you're pretty good."

I smiled. Mam and I had talked a few times since I'd moved out, once it was agreed that Brent and I were no longer a part of Sevrin's organization. Mam and I were becoming friends, and she was also, now, more of a mam to me than I'd thought possible. "Mam is hardly objective. When you see my movie debut, you'll see I'm not that great."

"I'm sure you're wrong," Sam said. "But if you'd rather direct, that would be fantastic."

"What would?" Brent asked, joining us.

"Our movie project," Lillian said. "We've already designated you as the set designer, so start planning."

Brent rolled his eyes. "Sure, I'll start planning, like I have been for the last three years."

"Mock it all you want," Lillian said. "This time it's going to happen."

"Really. And why is this time different?" Brent asked.

"Because Mabel's going to direct it, and she gets things done," Lillian said.

I grinned.

Brent looked at me, a flicker of hurt in his expression. "Directing? I thought you were going to carve. Now that your shoulder's better you can go back to the agents."

"I know, but I don't think carving is what I want to do. Not as a career. Or, not yet, anyway. I have so many options right now. I want to explore all of them." I considered writing to Dr. Thaddeus to tell him how much his book helped me. Maybe he would use me as one of his case studies in a follow-up book. "You're not upset, are you?"

Brent shrugged. "Not really. I mean, I was looking forward to making some money off of your art, but... No, I understand. I do hope you will go back to it, though, or at least seriously consider it."

"I will." Especially now that we were both out of

Sevrin's organization.

When Jeff, Chris, and Hannah arrived, Lillian pounced. "Hannah. Mabel is going to direct our movie. Would you please, please, please write the script?"

"What a great idea! I am so in. Let's meet a couple of days after Mabel's premiere and we can start planning. This is so exciting. Where should we meet?"

"How about my place?" I offered. I really liked having my friends over.

"Perfect," Lillian said. "The fellows can come too. We'll need Brent's input on sets, anyway. I'm sure we can find something for Chris and Jeff to do."

I broke out of our huddle to see Brent smiling at me. I smiled back. I had put him through so much and he was still my friend. He still cared.

There was another reason I didn't want a career in the art world.

While everyone else was loudly discussing the latest gossip from Studio City, I took a deep breath and leaned toward Brent. My cheeks were burning already. "Would you be willing, you know, if you're free, and want to, um, go to the premiere of my movie, with me? As my date?" I asked, quickly adding, "Or my friend? Either way, really. You don't have to if you don't want to. I just—"

Brent put a hand on mine. "I'd love to be your date, Mabel."

Eeeep! I had a date! And it was so easy.

CHAPTER 22

AFTER TWO days of desperate shopping, Lillian and I finally had outfits for tonight's premiere. Mine was a black trouser-tunic set, with blue sapphires and diamonds around the cuffs and neckline, and a blue cap with sapphires and diamonds to match. I wasn't so sure—I thought maybe it was too sparkly—but Lillian's enthusiasm about it won me over. Especially when she kept saying Brent was going to love me in it.

We were at Mam's getting ready. Mam had insisted we all go to the premiere together. Going with my best friend, a date, and Mam; I couldn't imagine doing it any other way.

Lillian fastened the buttons of her burnt orange

tunic, highlighted with diamonds. "What time did Brent and Sam say they would pick us up?" she asked.

I looked at myself in the mirror. This outfit made me look too thin. I should have kept searching the stores until I found something to give me a bit more girth. "Brent said they'd be here at six."

"Stop pushing your belly out," Lillian scolded. "You don't need stoutness, remember? You're perfect."

"Hardly. Besides, a little bit more width would be nice." I doubted I would ever shake the ingrained Gilliam belief that stoutness equaled desirability.

"Not on you. You're not exactly skinny, you know. So stop thinking you are."

"You should see the females back home. You should see anyone back home. I am absolutely tiny compared to them."

"Really? And yet none of them are in movies."

"All right. I get your point."

"All joking aside. Are you going to be all right watching the movie tonight? Is it going to be too painful to see your home and friends in it?"

"I did see it already, when I was helping Aramis. But no, I think it will be kind of fun."

"I bet your friends and brothers will all be lined up at the Gilliam theatre to see your movie when it comes out. They are going to wish they'd never let you go."

"That would be nice, but I doubt it." Max might.

He missed me enough to write. The others hadn't even bothered to send a note. Of course, I hadn't written them yet, either. Still, it would have been nice to have received something from someone, asking me to come home.

Lillian clapped her hands. "I almost forgot! I have a little something for you. A present to celebrate the opening of your first movie."

"You didn't have to do that."

"Of course I did. You're my friend, and this is a big night for you. I hope it will be a memorable night, the first of many movie openings, and a sign of the great career you have ahead of you, in whatever capacity you choose." From her bag she handed me a small box wrapped in blue paper with a silver bow tied around it.

"Thank you so much, Lillian." I hugged her and blinked back the tears.

"Hey, you didn't even open it yet. You have to open it before you get all weepy about it, because it's a horrible gift."

I undid the bow, setting the ribbon on my dresser, and carefully opened the box. Inside was a silver chain with a large diamond pendant cut in the shape of an axe. Tiny sapphires lined the handle. "Lillian," I gasped, taking it out of the box, holding it up and letting the light reflect off it. "This is incredible. You really, really shouldn't have. I love it."

"That's all that matters. Here, let me put it on you."

I turned around and looked in the mirror as she put it around my neck and fastened the clasp. It was beautiful. It was perfect.

"Stunning. Absolutely stunning," Lillian beamed.

"I'm so sorry I don't have anything to give you. I could give you a carving, but I hardly think you want to drag that around all night. If you do, next time you're at my place, please, take one, any one you want. All of them." Lillian laughed. "That's not how this works, Mabel. This is your special night, so you get the gift. If it were my movie opening, I might get a gift, or I might not, that's fine. It isn't my first movie. It's kind of like what you were saying once about first gems: when you find the bed of emeralds, you get the first one plus a share of the others. But it's the first gem that is the special one. This is your first movie, so you get a special gift."

"You both look splendid," Mam said, coming into my room.

"You too, Mam," I said. She wore a spectacular dark blue outfit with diamonds down the sides of the sleeves of her tunic and the trouser legs, and a diamond studded dark blue cap to match.

"Elegant," Lillian said.

"Thank you. I believe I heard Brent and Sam arrive. We should leave shortly."

"We're ready," I said.

The three of us traipsed down stairs. Brent smiled up at me and my stomach flip-flopped.

"You look fantastic," he whispered.

"Thank you. You too."

Mam drove the cart, with me and my friends in the back.

Brent held my hand. It was comfortable, sitting there together, hand in hand. Lillian and Sam, thankfully, talked plenty for all of us.

The closer we got to the theater for the premiere, the more anxious I became. It was a cool evening but sweat was forming on my brow. My chest was constricting. Having Brent beside me went a long way to keeping me calm.

I was concerned about what the reaction of the audience would be to the movie, mostly because I knew how much work Aramis had put into it to make it perfect. It was his first movie as director and star. The reception of it would be so important for his career.

I also hadn't seen Aramis since the day I returned from Radier's. Mam said she didn't know what had happened, or if Aramis had done anything to Aubrey or Radier. All she knew was that Aramis hadn't been seen in Studio City since then either.

I missed him. I'd learned my lesson on acting out of impatience. I was desperate to know if he'd taken his time to think about what he was going to do.

Our arrival at the theater was met with crowds of screaming fans along the road.

The theater was bigger than three of Mam's houses combined. Its outer walls were covered in banners and posters advertising the movie, Aramis, and Mam. Oak leaves lined the sidewalk leading up to the door like a carpet. We stopped the cart and got out, a valet taking the cart from us to park it somewhere out of sight.

We began the walk up the road to the theatre. Aramis arrived a moment later and joined us on the walk. He was nervous, I could tell from his rigid posture, though he hid it well, waving and smiling to the fans cheering, calling his name. I stared, wishing I could ask right then but knowing I'd have to wait. I tried to figure out what had changed, if he had done anything.

Brent squeezed my hand and I smiled, relaxed, and waved. No one knew who I was, but they didn't care, they cheered me anyway. I enjoyed it until a wave of gasps swept through the crowd.

The six of us turned around slowly, as did the other actors and crew on their way in to the theater.

Aubrey and one of his guards strutted up the walk, smiling, relaxed, reveling in the attention.

My heart raced, my mouth went dry; I couldn't breathe.

Aubrey smiled, arms outstretched, "Aramis." He embraced his son. "Congratulations."

"Thank you, father." Aramis winked at me.

"Mabel, are you all right?" Brent asked, tugging on my elbow. "Ready to go in?"

I stood there, frozen. What was going on? Radier was getting out of another cart.

"Mabel?"

"Yes," I whispered. I shuffled alongside Brent, letting him lead me.

Aramis and Frerin joined us. I ended up sitting next to Aramis in the center of the theater, with a nice spacious walkway in front of us. There was a lot of talking. Everyone was here. Not just movie executives, but top business people of all species. Even some of Aubrey and Sevrin's top associates were here.

Aramis walked to the front when everyone was inside. Everyone cheered for him. He smiled his gorgeous smile showing off those beautiful dimples.

"Thank you. Thank you. I want to thank you all for coming to see this little movie I directed."

We cheered again.

"I could not have done this alone, obviously. We had an amazing crew, from wardrobe and casting to set design and recording. Our cast was spectacular. I would like to introduce a newcomer. She came to us as a raw talent. Tonight is her acting debut. Not only does she show promise as an actor, as you will soon see, but as a director as well. Please, everyone, a round of applause for my good friend Mabel Goldenaxe."

I was shocked and embarrassed. Brent nudged me. Mam smiled at me and encouraged me to stand up. I did and waved.

"Casting directors, take note. You will want her for your next project."

As embarrassed as I was, I hoped word of this

would get back to Da in Gilliam.

"Next, before we actually show the movie, I have a little surprise for all of you. So sit back, relax, and enjoy."

Everyone cheered and shook Aramis's hands as he made his way back to his seat.

The candles were blown out. The images from the wizard's crystal projected on the screen in front of me. It was a close-up of my face, then my hand as the crystal went into my pocket. The screen went dark but the muffled sounds were heard and moments later, Radier's voice.

I let out my breath slowly. I was confused, and yet I was sure this wasn't a bad thing.

As the conversation between Radier and myself continued on screen, murmurs started in the audience as they realized what they were hearing.

Aramis had chosen to publicly expose not just Radier, but Aubrey and Sevrin too!

I looked at him. His eyes were on the screen, but he was smiling, beaming.

He put his hand on mine, curling his fingers around my palm.

Outrage among the elves erupted, directed toward Aubrey and Radier. The dwarves weren't far behind. The crowd was ready to lynch them both.

Aramis leaned over and said in my ear. "I cannot thank you enough, Mabel. You saved my life."

CHAPTER 23

I SAT down at a table near the bar, quill in hand and a stack of parchment in front of me. I could finally, comfortably, and without worry, write to Max and tell him everything that had happened. It was difficult to write. I didn't know how much detail I should put in. I wanted to leave most of it out. I told him about my friends, about all the creatures I'd seen, especially Dakkar and Percy.

I told him about Mam and Sevrin, that they'd split for a while, but they were back together. I didn't tell him that Mam had been involved in the Dwarven Mafia, or that she and Sevrin were back together on the condition that she was out of his organization. I didn't want Max to be upset but I suspected that one of these days Mam was going to remove the golden ring Da had given her and when she did, Sevrin was going to propose. I hoped that when it happened, Max would be able to find a way to join us. In the end, I told him about Radier and Aubrey, how they had manipulated everything, that Mam had been a victim as much as the rest of us. I didn't tell him that Radier had held me captive. I asked him to make sure that Phillip and Jimmy were all right though I didn't tell him why.

As I wrote to my brother, I realized I didn't miss my friends and family in Gilliam as much as I thought I would. Leitham had so many more exciting opportunities I was anxious to explore.

I hadn't figured out everything about myself yet, but I was a whole lot closer than I was a year ago. What I had figured out was that for the first time I knew I was where I belonged.

When I finished the letter, I folded it and put it in a box with my onyx carving of Dakkar.

I would send it later. My friends would be over soon to plan out our movie.

Did you enjoy Mabel the Mafioso Dwarf?

Consider leaving a review on Amazon or Goodreads and help spread the word about Mabel to your friends and other readers.

Sign up now for Sherry Peters's newsletter and receive exclusive content, special offers, news on release dates, and more, FREE, just for signing up!

Visit now: http://www.sherrypeters.com

ABOUT THE AUTHOR

Sherry Peters attended the Odyssey Writing Workshop and holds an M.A. in Writing Popular Fiction from Seton Hill University. Her first novel *Mabel the Lovelorn Dwarf* won the 2014 Writer's Digest competition for Self-Published ebooks in the Young Adult category. For more information on Sherry, visit her website at: http://www.sherrypeters.com.

CPSIA information can be obtained at www.ICGtesting.com
Printed in the USA
LVOW10s0250210515

439106LV00006B/267/P

9 780992 053536